FOLLOW
ME
HOME

ALSO BY D.K. HOOD

Don't Tell a Soul
Bring Me Flowers

D.K. HOOD

FOLLOW
ME
HOME

bookouture

Published by Bookouture in 2018

An imprint of StoryFire Ltd.

Carmelite House
50 Victoria Embankment
London EC4Y 0DZ

www.bookouture.com

ISBN: 978-1-78681-513-2
eBook ISBN: 978-1-78681-512-5

To my readers, with thanks and appreciation.

PROLOGUE

Then

Stop. Please stop, you are killing her. Trapped in a filthy cage beneath the bed, she pressed both hands against her ears and curled into a ball. Nothing would muffle their crude comments or the stink of their rancid sweat burning the inside of her nose. As she grasped the thin blanket, her elbows dug into the cold wooden floor. The unpolished planks scraped against her naked flesh, forming sore patches on knees and hips. She trembled in terror as Jodie's screams penetrated through the gaps in her fingers.

She would be next.

The bed above her head squeaked, dropping dust into her eyes and suffocating her. The ritual was the same. The men barked orders then the click, click, click and flashes of a camera. Each time they visited, Bobby-Joe took her from the barred enclosure in the cellar and stuffed her in the cage under the bed. After they tired with Jodie, she would suffer the same humiliation.

The men owned her.

Silence followed an uttering of curses. The next moment, Jodie hit the floor; her head rolled toward her and she stared at her with wide, fixed gray eyes. The chain of the gold locket Jodie treasured had left an ugly red pattern on her neck. She stared at her in horror. The girl she had known no longer existed. Her open mouth was set in a horrific grin and the purple hue of her lips resembled one of the clowns who had brought her to this terrible place. Gripped with fear she pressed a fist to her mouth to muffle the shriek threatening to spill from her lips. Bad things happened to girls who screamed.

"Jeeze, Bobby-Joe, you've gone and killed her."

"Shut your face, Ely. Dammit, now I'll have to find me another blonde."

"Pick her up, Ely."

"I ain't touching no dead girl."

"Amos. Grab her feet. We'll put her over there." Bobby-Joe's sweat-soaked face came into view as he lifted Jodie.

Ely bent and looked at her. "You'd better be a good girl. Shut your mouth and do as I say."

"She will unless she wants me to take my knife and pay her mom a visit." Bobby-Joe chuckled, sank to his knees, and grinned at her. "You've just become our star attraction."

"What you gonna do with the other one?" Chris peered at her friend with a concerned expression then looked away. "We can't leave her here to stink up the place."

"Wrap her in plastic and we'll bury her over at Craig's Rock like the others. I'll get Stu to pick up a replacement as soon as he can find one."

"The critters are getting into them at Craig's Rock." Ely dropped a roll of plastic on the floor with a grunt. "We'll need a new place for the next one. What about Old Corkey's place? It's downhill from here and it will be easier. There's plenty of room under the floorboards for at least six or more."

"That sounds like a plan." Bobby-Joe reached one long arm inside the cage, snagged her around the waist and dragged her out. She did not struggle or try to run. Legs weak, she fell face first on the bed. Panic caught her breath. She wanted to scream but pushed her mouth against the pillow and closed her eyes.

I will survive. Determined to make it through another day, she bit down hard on her lip and chanted in her head. *I am thirteen years old, my mother's name is Daisy and my father's name is Luke. I live in Black Rock Falls, Montana. I have been here 140 days.*

"Forget her. It's getting late." Amos grabbed Bobby-Joe by the shoulder. "We'll need to bury the other one tonight. We can start fresh tomorrow."

"She is all wrapped up and ready to be planted." Ely chuckled. "Anyway, I'm plum tuckered out already and after diggin' I'll need a rest."

"I guess. We'll need tools You carry her and I'll bring the spades." Bobby-Joe yanked her from the bed and stuffed her back into the cage. "Come on then, let's get this over with. Grab your flashlights and one of you bring a rifle. I don't fancy meetin' up with a bear."

As their footsteps and voices faded, the house fell silent and she gaped in astonishment at the cage door. The lock and chain lay on the floor. Terrified of one of them catching her, she pushed on the bars and the entrance opened with a familiar squeak. With her heart in her mouth, she crawled out and peered around the cellar.

The room was empty.

Gasping with panic, she stared at the cellar steps, surprised to see the door slightly ajar and light streaming in from the room above. She froze then moved her head from side to side listening for any noise, any creak of floorboards.

She heard nothing.

Will I have time to escape? A discarded black T-shirt and a pair of socks lay on the floor. She grabbed the shirt and pulled it on then the socks, doubling them over to protect her feet. Trembling with every uncertain step, she inched up the stairs. At the top, she found herself in a pantry and eased inside then peeked out the door. After sucking in a deep breath, she slipped into the kitchen. Beer bottles, water, and candy bars littered the table. She looked nervously around but the small cabin appeared to be empty and a clear path led to a door at the back. *I can make it to the back door.*

With her stomach knotted in fear, she edged toward the door and turned the knob. The handle turned with ease. She shrank back as anxiety trembled her knees. The moment she opened the door, light would stream out into the darkness, alerting them. Frantic, she searched for the switch and turned off the kitchen light. Waiting until her eyes adjusted to the darkness, she listened again. When no noise came from outside, she snatched up some candy and a bottle of water from the table and opened the door.

Heart pounding hard enough to break her ribs, she ducked low then slipped out the door, closing it gently behind her. Two steps down and into darkness, she could see the men's flashlights moving into the forest. The roar of water came from her left, and on the breeze, the familiar smell that only comes from a mountain-fed waterfall. *Black Rock Falls. I know this place.*

She turned away from the forest and ran toward the noise of pounding water. Ignoring the rocks and broken twigs cutting through her socks, she kept moving. Her family had camped close by last summer and the area was familiar to her. If she could reach the narrow track running alongside the falls, she could follow it all the way to the bottom of the mountain. Panic-stricken they would discover her missing at any moment, she gasped at every noise but kept moving. The roar of water guided her and soon the thick pine forest gave way to a narrow path bordered by rocks. The moon offered a ghostly light but rocks littered the trail and a constant spray of water from the falls made it slippery underfoot.

Throwing caution to the wind, she ran. *I have to get away.* Throat dry and chest heaving, she lost her footing and fell, sliding down the steep incline. She dropped the water and grabbed a large prickly bush. Thank God it stopped her toppling over the edge of the falls. She lay panting, one hand still gripping the candy, and sighed with relief as the bottle of water rolled to her side. It seemed like she had been running for ages and she desperately needed a few moments to catch her breath. Flat on her back, she stared up into the star-filled sky then a sound came over the noise of the falls. She listened and every hair on her flesh stood up at the sound of loud voices and someone crashing through the undergrowth. She scrambled to her feet and tiny rocks rolled down from above her peppering her back. She turned and her heart leaped in her chest. Bobbing flashlights lit up the mountain behind her. *They're coming.*

Terrified, she dived under the bush and curled around the woody trunk. So close to the edge of the falls ice-cold water splashed over her legs. Footsteps and heavy breathing heralded the arrival of two men so close she could reach out and touch them. With her pulse throbbing in her ears, she held her breath, too frightened to breathe, and tucked in her head. A light skimmed the top of the bush.

"If she ran this way, I figure she'd fall over the edge." Bobby-Joe kicked at the loose rocks. "It's steep and dangerous."

"Yeah, and we passed a pile of fresh bear scat. I doubt she got this far and if she did, she'll be his dinner before morning." Chris turned his flashlight back up the mountain. "We'll look around your cabin some more. You should send Ely and Amos home in case she drops by their cabins for help."

"Good thinkin'."

The footsteps faded and she waited until the lights moved out of sight, then crawled out of her hiding place and moved down the mountainside. As dawn came, she reached a cabin set close to the falls. Frightened one of the men would be inside, she grabbed women's clothes from the washing line and slid into the hen house to steal some eggs. After changing in the bushes, she headed back to the falls. Too scared to risk the monsters catching her, she kept away from the trail and hid during the day to rest.

Days later, sick and starving, she reached the highway. She waved down a school bus and told the elderly driver she was lost. On the trip back to Black Rock Falls, she chewed on her nails. Bobby-Joe knew where she lived and if she told, he would kill her mother. She would lie and say she ran away, then no one would ever know. As she glanced out of the window at the mountain, she smiled for the first time in a very long while. *I'm free.*

CHAPTER ONE

Now

Tuesday, week one

Amos Price opened the paper sack and checked the items he'd purchased on Monday afternoon. The fourteen-year-old girl he met online insisted he bring a bottle of bourbon and a few other items to their meeting this afternoon. Tuesday had seemed to take a year to arrive but he could not believe his luck and grinned. Excitement rippled through him. Her parents worked and she had played hooky from school to be alone with him. It had taken weeks to convince her to meet him and they had spent hours online in a games chat room. She thought he was eighteen and was so keen to meet him. Last night, after he'd given her the number of his burner phone, she had called. How sweet her voice sounded, so young and innocent.

He pulled his vehicle up some distance from the address she had given him and grabbed the bag. Seeing the street empty and no other houses for some distance, he strolled to the front door. Finding it open just as she had said, he slipped inside. "It's me, Pete."

"I'm here." A glimpse of the back of a girl with pigtails tied in pink ribbons rounded the top of the stairs. "I'll be down in a moment."

Desperate to have her, he headed for the steps. "I'll come to you."

"No, I want my outfit to be a surprise. Go into the kitchen, I've made you a drink – cola and ice. You did bring the liquor, I hope?"

He nodded and smiled at her. "Yeah, I have everything you asked me to bring."

"Great. Have a drink. I'll be right down."

Amos strolled reluctantly into the huge kitchen and dropped his bag onto the counter. Nervous and excited at the same time, he took out the bottle of bourbon, added a splash to the drink, and gulped down half the glass.

The sound of footsteps came on the stairs and she walked into the kitchen carrying a cellphone and wearing sunglasses. She paused in the doorway, and with the afternoon sun streaming through the window behind her he could not make out her face. "Come closer so I can see you properly."

"I want a photo of you first. You're not eighteen. Why did you lie to me?" She held up her cellphone and took a shot but remained in the doorway, hesitant.

"You wouldn't have come if I'd told you my real age but I wanted to meet you so bad. You're special and we get along so well." Amos needed another sip of his drink but smiled. "Look at me, I'm harmless. I've had tons of girlfriends your age."

"I guess."

His hands trembled and his chest felt tight. They often tried to back out but he had ways to subdue them. He could slip some pills into her glass. "Come here and have a drink so we can get to know each other."

"Finish your drink first." She moved closer and with the sunlight streaming behind her, it was as if she wore a halo. "Is it good?"

His heart pounded and he pushed on the counter to stand but his twitching legs failed to respond and he sat back down. "What's your name?"

"Oh, I'm no one." She moved closer and allowed the light to stream onto her face.

She was no more than five two and had the slim body of a girl but close up he could see she was at least twenty. He pushed into his foggy mind to find a memory. "Do I know you?"

"I'm the Grim Reaper and it's your time to die. The drink was poisoned. It will be a slow and painful death."

Fear clutched his pounding heart. He tried to speak but his tongue had swollen, filling his mouth. His throat constricted and he struggled to breathe.

"Having trouble breathing? Is every inch of you screaming in pain? Good. I wish I could make it last for weeks but you're not worth any more of my time." She scooped up the glass then headed for the front door. "Goodbye. I'll see you in hell."

Agony spread through his shaking limbs and he slid from the chair, falling hard on the floor. An ant scurried across the polished wood toward him, leading a few of its friends. He tried to move, to brush them aside, but a dark fog was surrounding him. *Oh, shit.*

CHAPTER TWO

Wednesday

It was late afternoon and Sheriff Jenna Alton stepped from her vehicle and took in the intense colors of fall. Shades of green through to golden brown bathed the entire landscape and the air carried the sweet smell of wildflowers. She loved this time of year, but plans to take a few days of her long overdue vacation to spend away from town had been shattered. *It's like I'm cursed.* She stared into the blue sky and sighed. The moment life returned to normal in Black Rock Falls, something else happened to spoil her plans. Although, in truth, nothing in her life would ever be normal again. Under threat of death, she had left her life as DEA Agent Avril Parker and assumed a new identity as the sheriff of Black Rock Falls. Her experience in the Drug Enforcement Administration was of little use in the spate of murders she had encountered in her time here, and at first, she had coped with two inexperienced rookies and her old deputy Duke Walters. She had to admit after losing Daniels, Deputy Rowley had become an asset but the sun had certainly been shining the day two ex-marines joined the team.

After a harrowing start, she discovered her second in command, Dave Kane, was a slightly damaged, off the grid DC's Special Forces Investigation Command agent with incredible profiling skills, and a sharpshooter. The next bonus came in the guise of Shane Wolfe, a widower with three daughters and not only the town's ME but a man with incredible computer skills. Wolfe had settled well into life in Black Rock Falls and become a crucial part of her team. These new deputies had her back and sure made life easier.

Jenna entered the ranch-style house set amidst the shade of maple and pine trees. She covered her nose and peered through the kitchen door at the bloated body of a middle-aged man sprawled on the polished wooden floor. His eyes bulged from a blue-tinged face. She turned to Deputy Kane and raised one eyebrow. "He's been here for a while."

"By the smell, I would say so." Kane's eyes narrowed. "The real estate agent says he isn't the owner and the house is listed for sale."

"Why is it so hot in here?" She turned to Deputy Wolfe, her in-house medical examiner. "What do you think happened to him? There's no sign of a struggle as far as I can see. If the house wasn't unoccupied, I would have figured he was unpacking his groceries and dropped dead. I'll leave this one to you, Wolfe. We'll check the rest of the house."

"The thermostat has been set to eighty-five degrees." Wolfe tapped one gloved finger on the wall control. "Do you want me to turn it down, ma'am?"

"Yeah, and get the windows open." She turned to Kane. "We'll do a sweep of the house."

She picked up her bag of equipment and followed Kane through the meticulously furnished ground floor. They checked the cellar and finding nothing of interest headed upstairs. Three bedrooms, all seemingly undisturbed. The faucet dripped in the main bathroom, leaving small splashes of water inside the basin.

"That's unusual, seeing as everything else in here is perfect. I'll dust the vanity for fingerprints." She pulled the kit from her bag and tossed Kane a sample container. "Remove the trap under the sink and collect the contents." She waited for him to complete the task.

"It looks clean." Kane held up a plastic container and frowned. "I don't think anyone has been here."

Jenna dusted the vanity and faucet for fingerprints. "Nothing but a few smudged prints. If cleaners had been here, it's likely they left their prints, but someone left the tap dripping as if the sink was used in a hurry."

"It could have been an oversight."

"Maybe." She led the way downstairs and reported their findings to Wolfe. "I want to know how that man got into the house and what he was doing here. Check his pockets for a key." She turned away. "With me, Kane. Who found the body?"

"Alison Saunders. She is the realtor working at Mr. Davis's agency and also the woman Deputy Rowley's apparently dating."

Jenna followed Kane outside. "I wondered why she was blubbering all over him."

"I guess finding a dead body in a house she was planning to sell to a young couple this evening was a little traumatic." Kane gave a nonchalant shrug. "Maybe she can shed some light on how he got into the house."

"Maybe he was a potential buyer?" Jenna strolled toward Deputy Rowley and a young woman with dark hair dressed in a neat skirt and blouse under a jacket. "Miss Saunders? I'm Sheriff Alton. Are you up to answering some questions?"

"Okay, but please call me Alison." She dabbed at her red eyes and gave Rowley a mournful look.

"What time did you find the body?"

"About twenty minutes ago. I called Jake straight away."

Not 911? Jenna pulled out her notepad and pen. "Do you know the deceased?"

"No, and he wasn't here on Monday when Mr. Davis did the house inspection. I don't know how he got inside. The door was locked when I arrived." Alison blinked her long, wet lashes. "I came to make sure the carpets had been cleaned before I showed the clients."

"How many people have keys to the house?"

"Let me think." Alison tapped her bottom lip with a red fingernail. "This house used to be a rental. We have master keys for the houses and we have two extras at the office, and the owner has a set. I have one with me. I gave one to the carpenter, Adam Stickler, and one to the cleaning service. That is the Clean as a Wink housekeeping service, here in Black Rock Falls. We use those people all the time and they are very reliable."

Jenna made notes. "Did the cleaning service return the key?"

"They keep a master key for their own use but they finished here before Mr. Davis's inspection on Monday; I think they came after the carpenter left on Friday. He did mention some yard work needing doing." Alison's brown eyes fixed on Jenna's face. "How did the man die? Was it a heart attack?"

"I don't know and we won't have a cause of death until the ME has examined the body." Jenna replaced her notebook and pen. "You'll need to cancel the viewing for this evening. We'll be here most of the day and tomorrow, and when we clear the scene, you'll need to get the cleaners in again to get rid of the smell."

"Oh, Lord, nobody will buy the place now. We have to tell buyers about any deaths occurring in the houses."

"Who owns the property?" Kane's gaze moved over the house then back to Alison.

"Three Maple Lane is one of the seven properties Mr. Rockford has on our books. I met him recently and so I know the man in the house is not him. Mr. Rockford moved to Texas after his son went to jail. Mr. Davis is acting as his agent for all the sales." Alison looked as if she carried the world on her shoulders. "That's why I moved back to Black Rock Falls to work. There are so many properties on the market since those teenagers were murdered last summer."

Jenna let out a long sigh. She remembered the Rockford case well. " Did you have any tradesmen in to repair anything after the last inspection?"

"As far as I am aware, all the repairs were finished." Alison's dainty fingers trembled on the folder in her hands. "I'll have to ask Mr. Davis if he sent anyone out."

"Call me when you find out." Kane handed her a card with a compassionate smile. "My cellphone number is on the back. You can call anytime."

Jenna stared at him then turned her gaze back to Alison. "Okay. That's all I need for now. You had better get back to work."

"I'm not sure if I can drive." Alison looked forlorn. "I'm still shaking."

"You've had a nasty shock." Jenna turned away from her and spoke to Rowley. "Drive her car into town and give me your keys. I'll drop your car back to the office. While you're there, find out if Davis sent any tradesmen out to the house."

"Yes, ma'am." Rowley's mouth twitched into a smile as he handed her the keys. "Thank you." He led Alison to her vehicle.

"Sheriff. I need a word." Deputy Wolfe came out the house carrying a large evidence bag. "The victim is Amos Price, forty-nine years old, and according to his driver's license he has a cabin in the mountains on Sunset Ridge. From what I found in his bag, I believe he was here for a romantic interlude, although he was also carrying tranquilizers in his pocket."

Jenna listened to the list of items found with the body. "I see. Time of death? Cause?"

"Hard to determine the time of death from the body temperature. I'd say approximately forty-eight hours but someone turned up the heat, so I could be off by days. From the artificially heightened body temperature it would be a few hours ago but from the decomposition, it could be Tuesday afternoon. I'll have to say undetermined. He is bloated so the cause will have to wait for the autopsy. Maybe a heart attack, but right now I'm not sure." Wolfe pulled down his face mask and scratched his blond stubble. "I can't rule out homicide at this time, so I'll dust the entire house for prints and do a complete search. I'll need the real estate agents' prints as well as they both had access to the house."

"Okay." Jenna stared after the departing car. "I'll call Rowley and get him to scan Stickler, Saunders and Davis."

"I wonder if the battered truck parked down the road belongs to the victim." Kane rolled his shoulders and strolled toward the vehicle. He pulled out his cellphone and ran the plate then turned to look at her. "Yeah, it's his."

Jenna turned to Wolfe. "Any keys on the body?"

"Yeah." Wolfe dug into the evidence bag then held out the keys between two gloved fingers. "I tried these in the front door lock. They don't belong to the house. Do you have gloves?"

Jenna pulled two pairs out of her pocket and tossed one pair to Kane. "We'd better check the vehicle." She strolled to the truck.

"Roger that." As he kept pace beside her, Kane's attention moved over her face. "I need to ask you something."

"Sure."

"You know, I was talking to Rowley about how hard it is to get to some of the more remote places around town. He suggested it would make sense for us to get a horse. You don't use the stables at your place and the grass in the corral is a foot high."

She nodded. "Sounds like a plan but the stables are a bit run-down."

"It won't take me long to fix them—a couple of new hinges and they'll be fine. Do you ride?"

Jenna gave him a sideways glance. "I can ride; well, I did the horse-riding thing when I was a kid."

She liked having Kane living in the cottage on her ranch and spent a lot of downtime with him. He was reliable and smart and always had her back. Often after viewing a nasty crime scene he would change the subject to lighten the mood and his diversions somehow kept her human. "It will be an added expense though, and I guess we could rent horses if we need them."

"Then we'll have the availability issue." Kane shrugged. "I'll pay for any upkeep because with the expanse of forest and mountains we have in our county, we might need them in a hurry. The last time we investigated a murder, we trekked for miles up trails looking for evidence. A horse would have made life easier. We know Amos Price lived up in the hills, and if he doesn't have a family, we'll have to check his property. Some of the ranches are in remote areas, and neighbors are few and far between." Kane's lips thinned. "His property could be miles up a trail."

She considered his words then shrugged. "I doubt it. He has a truck and looks a little overweight to be walking miles, but if you want to buy a couple of horses, that's fine by me."

"I'll go and see Gloria on Sunday and I'll fix up the stables." Kane's mouth twitched at the corners as he opened the victim's truck.

"Gloria?"

"Yeah, Rowley insisted Gloria Smithers is the best person in town to go to if you want to buy a horse. I've been in touch with her and she has a few mounts available at the moment." Kane allowed a pile of garbage to fall out the door then pulled on a mask and slid his large body inside the old truck. "Man, this guy was a pig; there's mold half an inch thick on the garbage in here."

Jenna covered her nose. "How do people live like that?"

"What do we have here? Grab this, I'm going in again." Kane peered over the mask at her as he tossed her a rifle then bent inside again. Moments later, he stood and peered into a paper sack. "Diazepam. Hmm, these must be what Wolfe found in his pocket. I wonder why he'd take tranquilizers on a date."

Jenna stared at him in disbelief. "Ah… maybe to drug her. It seems feasible considering he was inside someone else's house."

"Yeah?" Kane's brow furrowed. "If you discovered a guy trying to drug you, would you just leave or call the cops?"

"I wouldn't get myself into that position with a total stranger in the first place." Jenna rested one hand on the handle of her weapon and sighed. "Maybe she didn't show and he died of boredom waiting for her." She shrugged. "There was a bottle of bourbon on the counter—maybe it wasn't a date after all. He could have committed suicide. Diazepam and booze would do it."

"I've never heard of anyone taking condoms, lube and a box of chocolates to a suicide." Kane's eyes danced with mirth. "Have you?"

Jenna snorted back a laugh. "I guess there's always a first time." Embarrassed, she glanced around. "Oh Lord, that's not a professional thing to say. The poor man is dead. Probably murdered and we're fooling around."

"Nah, just stating facts." Kane glanced at her over one shoulder. "Did you know it's not unusual for people to laugh at murder scenes?"

She met his gaze. "No, I didn't, but I'm sure you're going to tell me the reason."

"It's not because they think death is funny, it's an emotional release to guard against overwhelming anxiety." He disappeared inside the truck. "In our line of work, I guess it's better to laugh once in a while than suffer from PTSD." He backed out and examined something in his palm.

"What have you got there?"

"I found a thumb drive in the glove compartment. It might shed some light on his life, apart from the fact he liked takeout and bourbon." Kane threw the junk back inside the vehicle and locked the door. "He has been here for a couple of days and lives on the mountain. Those places are pretty isolated and he might have livestock on his property that needs tending."

"Yeah, most do up there. We'll head back to the office see if Walters knows him or his relatives. He might have a family and they can handle any animals. I'll see who lives close by as well and ask them."

"Roger that." Kane ripped off his mask and his lips curled into a smile. "If we don't have any luck, I figure I'd enjoy a drive into the mountains, spectacular views, and all the peace and quiet you could wish for. We'll be able to find the location of the victim's house using the GPS."

Jenna's vacation plans would have to wait, but she had to admit the idea of getting away for a morning to enjoy the fresh mountain air sounded like bliss. "Sure, now can we stop daydreaming and get back to work?"

CHAPTER THREE

Thursday

Early the following morning, Kane leaned back in his office chair, gaping at the contents of the thumb drive he had found in Amos Price's truck. He glanced away, sickened by the images in front of him. Almost a year earlier, Jenna had found similar images on the cellphone belonging to the ex-mayor's son, but his father had destroyed his laptop, removing any clues to a potential child pornography ring working in the area. The FBI had become involved but even with their extensive resources they had uncovered zip. He figured Josh Rockford had acted alone, and with him in jail, they had solved the problem. *Obviously not.*

The find opened up a can of worms: If Price had been involved, then there could be others and yet nothing had come to light since his arrival in Black Rock Falls. He pushed to his feet and marched into Jenna's office. "Excuse me, ma'am. I think you need to be aware of this information in the Amos Price case."

"Come in and take a seat." Jenna tossed a lock of glossy hair from her face and smiled at him. "What did you find?"

Kane winced. "Images of children. They all came from the camera on his cellphone, so he was involved. It looks like the same child."

"Hmm, did he send them to anyone?"

"Nope." Kane dropped into a chair opposite her desk. "Like the Josh Rockford case, he was too clever to use his cellphone to send the images. My guess is everything we need will be on a laptop somewhere. If news of his death leaks, we might have the same problem as we had with Rockford—one of his friends will take the hard drive and nuke it."

Jenna tapped her pen on the desk. "Predators pop up all over the place but before we start checking out chat rooms for likely suspects, I'll contact the FBI again and see if they have an ongoing investigation in the area."

"Yeah, they wouldn't be too happy if we ruined a sting operation."

"Not only that, I want them involved. They have the resources and know where to look online." She sighed.

A knock on the door heralded the arrival of Deputy Wolfe.

"Ah, Wolfe, you couldn't have arrived at a better time." Jenna's smile was genuine; she obviously appreciated having him on the team. "What did the autopsy tell us?"

"Not much, I'm afraid." Wolfe removed his hat and scratched his thick blond hair. "The cause of death is undetermined pending a toxicology report. Problem is the report takes about two to three weeks. We might hit pay dirt with the stomach contents. He had taken a drink just prior to his death. Apart from the bourbon and cola, it had a very strong smell of cigarettes but his lungs appeared clean. I don't think he smoked."

Kane frowned. "I didn't find any cigarettes in his truck either."

"Or an empty can of cola inside the house." Jenna's white teeth closed on her bottom lip. "If he had a drink just before he died, what happened to the glass he used or the cola can?"

"Exactly. Everything I found points to poison as the cause of death, and from the contortions of his limbs, it was a very painful death. His body literally shut down in painful spasms. There are quite a few poisons that act immediately, for instance, arsenic, strychnine, and of course things like snakebite, but apart from them being difficult to obtain, they leave clues. Bite marks, for instance, and bleeding eyes or coughing blood. This was subtle. As I detected the high smell of tobacco, I asked the laboratory to check for nicotine sulfate. It's a pesticide and extremely poisonous. It would produce the symptoms I detected in the victim. It is colorless and the taste could be disguised with bourbon."

Kane rubbed the back of his neck. "So, this could be a homicide?"

"I'm not ruling that out."

"If it is, then we have a motive." Jenna's dark eyebrows met in the middle in a frown. "He has images of children on his cellphone and it seems he took them himself. I can find no one within a few miles of Mr. Price's cabin and none of the people I called are prepared to venture onto his land. I think we have three main objectives. The first is to hightail it up to his cabin and get his laptop to discover if anyone else is involved. If we find any clues, we'll turn them over to the FBI to investigate. We need to concentrate on the murders and identify the child in the images. For all we know, Price's death could be the parents taking the law into their own hands."

"Yeah." Wolfe's pale eyes narrowed. "If I found someone messing with one of my girls, I might be tempted to pay him a visit too."

"We do things straight down the line here, Deputy Wolfe." Jenna's expression hardened. "No matter who is involved, understand?"

"Yes, ma'am." Wolfe rubbed the back of his neck. "By the way, I would consider poison to be usually a woman's choice of weapon."

"He had an open bottle of bourbon but I tested it and it came up clean. There were glasses in a kitchen cupboard but they all appeared untouched. I will have them collected and test for residue but I doubt I will find anything. The trap under the kitchen sink came up clean. Whoever did this planned it well."

"Suggestions?" Jenna shifted her attention to Kane. "How he got inside the house without a key, for instance?"

"I'm working on it, ma'am. I would like to know his incentive for going there in the first place." Kane met Jenna's intense expression and shrugged. "To meet a girl?"

"It's a possibility." Jenna scratched her cheek. "Say we go with that assumption. What do you know about grooming kids?"

"Pedophiles tend to go for a lonely kid. I figure they profile them to find a vulnerable subject to groom. They spend hours talking to them online." Kane sighed. "The FBI has operatives masquerading as kids to sit online in chat rooms in an attempt to lure them. The predators use games rooms and other social media groups, impersonating teenage boys. They have usernames and post an image of a good-looking guy then start up a conversation. Once the FBI has them admitting to wanting sex with an underage girl or boy, they set up a meet and arrest them."

"Which makes me doubt the FBI has been working our area or Price wouldn't have ended up dead. I guess if a killer wanted to lure a pedophile to his death, that scheme would work just as well. That's something to consider." Jenna's mouth turned down at the corners. "Looking at what Price had with him, he was expecting to have sex and intended to subdue his victim if necessary."

"It makes me wonder how many times he has done the same thing." Kane leaned back in his seat, making it creak in protest. "Like I said, it would take time to groom a kid online and he would need access to a house. We're back to wondering how Price knew when the house was empty and how did he get in?"

"You need to find out." Alton's gaze narrowed. "It's obvious. He had a key. Investigate."

Kane cleared his throat. "Yes, ma'am. The moment we get back from his cabin."

"We know a number of people who could have a key. Alison mentioned tradespeople had worked on the house—any one of them could have made a copy." Jenna's intent gaze moved over the deputies. "Before we leave, Wolfe, I need you and Rowley to pull up any files we have on victims of child abuse in the area. You'll need to check the archives. We found no complaints at all during the Rockford case, so you'll have to search the national database. Check the girl in the photographs against missing persons. Go back some years."

Kane rubbed his chin. "You are talking about hundreds of thousands of missing kids. It is an impossible task. I suggest start in the neighboring towns and work out."

"Yeah, we don't know for sure he intended to meet a kid or in fact if he met anyone at all." Wolfe looked chagrined.

"Well, further speculation will have to wait until we look at Price's computer." Alton picked up the phone. "Deputy Walters, did you locate Mr. Price's family?" She listened for some time then shook her head. "Give me the coordinates to his home. Thanks." She made notes, disconnected, then pushed the pad toward Kane. "Price has no living relatives. Walters believes the unsealed road up to Price's cabin should be passable this time of the year. Check if we can access the area by SUV. Apparently, another road leads way up on the north side to a few cabins locals hire out when fishing at Black Rock Falls, but a rock fall blocked the road. The water from there feeds Black Rock Lake, a huge area on the other side of the mountain. Apparently the rock fall doesn't show up on the GPS." She stood. "I'm sure your SUV is powerful enough to climb the hill."

"Oh yeah, that baby will do it with ease." Kane could not help the smile. "I'll check the road conditions and get the gear together. Will you or Wolfe be coming with me?"

"Oh, I'm coming." Jenna's eyes flashed. "Wolfe, I want you to coordinate the search for the victim in the photographs and cases of child abuse here or in neighboring towns. Notify the FBI, we have a potential pedophile ring operating in the area. They'll know all the usual haunts of these people and will be able to handle that part of the investigation. Make sure you insist we are kept in the loop." She glanced at Wolfe. "Before you start, send Rowley to collect the glasses from the murder scene. I've trained him in the correct collection of forensic evidence. "

"Yes, ma'am." Wolfe gave her a curt nod, picked up his hat, and headed for the door.

"I want you both ready to go in ten minutes." Jenna's voice followed them.

Kane followed Wolfe from the room and noticed Rowley deep in conversation with Alison Saunders, the young woman who had found the body.

He strolled toward Rowley's cubicle and cleared his throat. "Problem?"

"No, not exactly." Rowley's cheeks pinked. "Alison wanted to know how long it will be before she can get a cleaning crew inside the house."

"I didn't mean to get Jake into trouble." Alison's big brown eyes moved over his face. "I just needed to know when I could get back into the house and if the man was murdered."

Kane shot a glance at Rowley. The deputy was usually discreet and professional. "And what did Deputy Rowley tell you?"

"He told me the sheriff would let Mr. Davis know when she had finished the investigation."

Kane heaved a sigh of relief. "Well then, you have your answer. At the moment, we have no idea how the man died. It could take weeks, so if Mr. Davis is pressuring you to obtain information from Rowley, tell him to contact Sheriff Alton."

"Oh, sure."

"If that is all, Miss Saunders, Deputy Rowley is needed elsewhere."

"I'll see you later." Alison smiled brightly at Rowley and headed for the door.

Kane watched her go. "I'm sure I don't have to remind you not to give out information, even to your girlfriend. We could have a possible homicide and we don't want any leaks."

"No, sir. I wouldn't tell her a thing." Rowley swallowed hard, making his Adam's apple bob up and down. "What did Deputy Wolfe discover in the autopsy?"

"Nothing positive yet." Kane lowered his voice to just above a whisper. "We believe the deceased was involved in some kind of child porn ring. Wolfe will be coordinating a search for the kids in the images and bringing in the FBI. Hunt up any reported cases of child abuse and do a complete rundown of Price's employment history. Find out if he worked with kids in the last couple of years. We'll need to find out if he procured kids from another town, so search the other counties' data banks for missing kids or reports of anything suspicious."

"Okay. I'll get on to it as soon as I get back from collecting the evidence Wolfe needs from Maple Street."

"Okay. I'm heading up the mountain with Sheriff Alton to search Price's cabin."

"Oh, make sure you take a rifle with you." Rowley's face broke into a grin. "Folks up that way tend to shoot first then ask questions later."

"Wonderful."

CHAPTER FOUR

The adrenaline rush of killing slipped away, leaving a wave of contentment. She glanced around her neat home, everything in its place, all surfaces polished to a high shine. She liked clean. In fact, one thing out of place, one speck of dust annoyed her, and right now she had some cleaning to do.

She opened the cupboard door in the spare bedroom and stared at photographs of the monsters. To enforce her determination to rid the Earth of predators, she had stuck the images to the inside of one door, and on the other, the missing girls she had found in the newspapers. She touched each young face. *I will get justice for you, I promise.*

She scowled at the men's images and rage sent bile rushing up the back of her throat. Oh yes, she had discovered the monsters' names and where they lived. Now she would stop them from hurting girls. She had tracked down Amos Price after overhearing about the strange behavior of a clown at a kid's party. She wondered how many times parents ignored inappropriate touches and kids' complaints because they were too ashamed to admit such a thing had happened to their child. She had stopped him. The monster hiding behind a painted smile.

With satisfaction, she tore Amos Price's image from the wooden door and ripped it into shreds then strolled into the bathroom and flushed it down the toilet. The sight of him writhing in agony and the fear in his eyes as his life slipped away had ignited the dark side again. She enjoyed his suffering, could almost taste it, and wished it had lasted longer. The craving to lure the next man into her web had become an obsession.

An absolute need to hunt down and kill.

Who will be next? She let her gaze drift over the photographs then dragged her nails down the image of a monster. "Are you ready to die?"

CHAPTER FIVE

As Kane's powerful SUV climbed up the winding mountain roads, eating up the miles, Jenna let out a sigh. A vista of intense beauty stretched out forever, pine forests climbed up magnificent mountains, swirling rivers and dancing waterfalls threw a myriad of rainbows, making the view magical. "Oh, this is magnificent. I wish I had ventured up here earlier. I can't believe I've missed seeing this before."

"It is amazing but not somewhere you should venture alone." Kane's large hands gripped the wheel as he negotiated a tight bend in the road. "Rowley mentioned that the mountain men, wherever they are hiding, tend to shoot first and ask questions later." He grinned at her. "Then there are the black bears and the bobcats. I guess you'd look like dinner to them."

"You wouldn't." She returned his grin. "You're all gristle."

"Thanks." Kane's eyes sparkled. "I'll take that as a compliment."

Jenna stared at the GPS. "Price's cabin should be down a track on the right about a hundred yards ahead."

The car bumped over the dirt road, tipping from one side to the other. The trees came close to the road, sending zebra shadows flashing past as they moved in and out of the sunshine. "There on the right. See the 'private property' sign?"

"Got it." Kane spun the wheel and expertly negotiated a bend then a dip in the road. "No wonder his truck was so beat up. This place would be murder during the winter." He indicated ahead with his chin. "There's the house."

Jenna stared at the log cabin. It was larger than she expected with a woodshed and a small barn. An old hunting dog ambled out to greet them. It was pitifully thin with its bones showing. "You were right about the livestock. I wonder what he has in his barn."

"I guess we'd better check there first." Kane slipped from the car and raised both eyebrows. "I can't smell livestock." He trudged off toward the barn.

Jenna patted the old dog on the head. "Don't worry, we'll find you something to eat."

"His water bucket is empty." Anger radiated from Kane. "A hunting dog doesn't get that thin in a couple of days. Up here, he could have caught his food." He bent and filled a bucket from a faucet attached to a rainwater tank. "Come here, boy, there you go." He turned and pulled open the barn door. "Nothing in here."

"Okay, let's check the house." Jenna pulled on a pair of latex gloves then took a set of keys from her pocket. She strolled onto the porch, opened the door, then took a step backward. "Man, this place stinks."

"Not death; that's the smell of the unwashed." Kane's mouth curled into a grin. "It seems Amos Price wasn't one for personal hygiene." He moved inside the door. "Wait there. I'll open some windows."

"I'll check the bedrooms." Jenna strolled into what looked like the master bedroom and her attention settled on an array of wigs on the nightstand.

She threw open the cupboard doors and gaped at the rack of brightly colored clown costumes. A shudder of revulsion went through her. When Kane walked into the room, she turned and grimaced at him. "He was a clown. I hate clowns."

"He's a dead clown now." Kane's blue gaze moved over her face. "It's a real phobia, isn't it? Clowns, I mean."

"Yeah, and John Wayne Gacy didn't do much to help their cause either." She shuddered. "In case you forgot he was a mass murderer of little boys."

"I'm not likely to forget him but I wish I could." Kane squeezed her arm and the heat of his hand felt comforting against her skin. "You okay?"

"I'm fine." She turned away and walked down the passage into a family room with a fireplace, a couple of old sofas, and little else. Through an open door, she found a kitchen with a sink piled high with dishes. "I'll see if there's anything to feed the dog."

She had not taken three paces when she heard a noise. "Did you hear that?"

"What?"

A tiny sound froze Jenna on the spot. She tilted her head from side to side. An eerie feeling crept over her as if a ghost was reaching out of a grave to speak to her. "I thought I heard a voice—a really creepy sound like a whine maybe. Listen."

"Maybe it's the wind or it may be a cat. I had a Siamese who sounded like a baby crying."

She strained her ears and the sound came again, sending goosebumps running up her arms. "It sounds like a child."

From behind, Kane dashed back down the hallway, pushing open bedroom doors, then he turned his large frame slowly and stared at a door sealed with a wooden slat. "Oh no, not the cellar again. I am so over going into dark cellars." His biceps bulged as he lifted the substantial piece of wood barring the door. "This is strong enough to keep out a bear." He glanced at Jenna over one shoulder. "You don't think he has a pet panther, do you?" His brow wrinkled. "A very hungry pet panther?"

The whine came again, throwing every horror movie to the front of Jenna's mind. Real she could deal with; spooks not so much. She forced her mind to think rationally. "It can't be a ghost, they move through things."

"I didn't think it was a ghost but some people do believe spirits get trapped in places." Kane shrugged. "It's more likely a big cat."

"I think I'd prefer a ghost." Jenna moved to the door, keeping her back to the wall. "Open the door a crack and be ready to slam it shut if it is a damn panther. I've heard they have a strange call."

"Yeah, they sound like a yell or a cry. I'll wedge my foot behind the door."

She moved closer. "This is Sheriff Jenna Alton, is anyone down there?"

A small, quivering voice echoed from the darkness. So ghostlike, cold chills slid down Jenna's back.

"Yes, I'm down here."

Every hair on the back of her neck stood to attention. "Are you alone?"

"Are you really a sheriff?"

Jenna nodded at Kane to open the door a few more inches. "Yes, I'm here with Deputy Kane."

Jenna gagged at the stink of sewage wafting up from the dark beyond and turned to Kane. No way was she entering the cellar in the dark. "Can you see a light switch anywhere?"

"Yeah, here by the door." His voice lowered to a whisper. "Be careful, Jenna, she could be his crazy old mother and is an unknown quantity."

Jenna slid her Glock 22 from the holster. "Open the door."

Pressing one hand over her nose, she moved onto a small landing and surveyed the cellar. It held a large double bed and a cage. Inside the cage sat a young ten- or twelve-year-old girl wearing filthy rags. *Oh my God!*

CHAPTER SIX

Holstering her gun, Jenna ran down the steps toward the cage. "It's okay, you're safe now. What's your name?"

"Zoe. Zoe Channing."

Jenna went to the girl. "You're going to be okay." She turned to Kane. "She's the one in the photograph."

"So I see."

She shook the sturdy metal door and turned to him. "Get something to bust her out of here and bring some water."

As Kane took off, thundering through the house, Jenna smiled at Zoe. "I'm going to get you out of here. Where do you live?"

"I live in Helena."

"That's a lovely place to live." Jenna squatted by the door. "How long have you been here?"

"A long time, lots of weekends. I can't remember how many." Zoe wrapped filthy arms around her knees, flinching away.

Why does she measure time by the weekends? Jenna turned and did a visual search of the room. She noticed a pile of blankets on a shelf and pulled one down then passed it through the bars. "Here, wrap this around you. Deputy Kane is going to break the door and get you out."

"Can I have a shower?" Zoe's sunken eyes pleaded with her. "Amos didn't let me wash. They never let me wash until they're ready to leave."

"They?" Jenna stared at her.

"Yes, Amos brought three of his friends here every weekend." Her small body shuddered. "When he went out, he said he was bringing a friend home for me. He said her name was Fresh Meat."

The girl's measure of time slammed into Jenna like a steel pole. She stopped the overwhelming wave of disgust from reaching her expression. "Amos won't be bothering you anymore, he's dead."

Kane's footsteps sounded on the stairs and Zoe cringed, her eyes filled with terror. Jenna reached through the bars and took her hand. "It's okay, Kane is my deputy and he's here to help you, just like I am. We will catch the men who did this to you." She took the bottle of water Kane handed her and gave it to the girl.

"My dad is a lawyer. He says bad men go to jail." Keeping her brown eyes firmly on Kane, she opened the bottle and drank thirstily.

"Oh, don't worry, they'll go to jail. Move away from the door and I'll get you out." Kane's expression turned to one of determination as he slid a crowbar between the door hinges.

The metal creaked and groaned but moments later the door clattered to the floor. Jenna offered her hand. "Come with me."

The young girl shrank back, her eyes filled with fear. Jenna held up a hand to keep Kane away. "I think she has had her fill of men. Leave her to me. We'll take her to the hospital. Call ahead and arrange for a female doctor, will you?" She frowned. "The dog will have to come with us too. We can drop it at the animal shelter."

"Yes, ma'am." Kane's brow creased into a frown. "I noticed a laptop in one of the bedrooms. I'll bag it then do a quick search while you're getting her ready."

"Sure, grab what you can but Zoe is our priority." She waited for Kane to leave then helped the girl to her feet. "I'm taking you to the hospital. The doctors will check you then you can take a shower."

"I'm hungry. I haven't had lunch."

Jenna placed one arm under the girl's arm and helped her climb the stairs. "I have energy bars in my car and orange juice. I'd rather not touch anything here."

"I like energy bars." Zoe seemed to brighten. "I'm glad you found me."

"So am I." Jenna led her into the kitchen. "Sit down for a minute and sip the water. We'll have you out of here soon."

"Can you feed the dog?" Zoe's lip quivered. "Amos was watching him starve to death. He thought it was funny. I'm glad he's dead."

Right now, so am I. "He wasn't a nice man, was he? We'll feed the dog, don't worry." She glanced down the hallway as Kane came out of a room with a laptop, a couple of external hard drives, and a number of DVDs in a large evidence bag. "Did you find any dog food?"

"Not yet."

Jenna frowned. "He must have something we can give the poor thing. Check the freezer."

"Yes, ma'am." Kane stood beside Jenna, despair etched his face. "Zoe, I promise we'll catch the men who did this to you." He pulled open a freezer, grabbed a couple of steaks, and threw them into the microwave to defrost.

Zoe leaned into Jenna and her big eyes moved over Kane's face as if assessing a threat. "Maybe you should just shoot them dead."

CHAPTER SEVEN

With difficulty, Kane tried to force down the rage bubbling inside him. He needed to portray a calm, professional persona in front of the girl. Any show of aggression would make her even more terrified of him. He ground his back teeth so hard his jaw ached. The sight of the girl's bruised face made his blood boil. Amos Price might be dead but three lowlife animals walked the Earth, and right now, he wanted to tear them apart with his bare hands. *What kind of a man does this to a child?*

He waited for the old dog to finish eating and loaded him into the back of his SUV. Jenna had Zoe wrapped up and sitting inside the vehicle munching on energy bars. He slid into the driver's seat and noticed the way Zoe flinched at his closeness. No one ever recovered from what she had endured, and she would suffer repercussions for years. After reading so many case histories of psychopathic killers, abuse as a child was a trigger no psychologist should ignore. He glanced at Zoe. She appeared to be communicating reasonably well, which was unusual after continuous trauma. He had seen kids shut down completely and not speak for years. The ones who blocked out trauma usually crashed and burned.

"Before we leave, get Wolfe and Rowley up here to go over the place. We need to find out who else is involved and tell them we have identified the girl in the photograph."

"Okay."

He contacted Wolfe, brought him up to date with the investigation and arranged for him to lead up a forensics team to sweep the cabin. As Zoe had implicated other men in her ordeal, they needed evidence. If the men had left a trace of DNA, Wolfe would find it. He would work hand in hand with the doctors at the hospital and confirm the findings by using his own lab to process the results.

"I'll contact her parents." Jenna flicked him a worried glance then turned in her seat. "Zoe, do you remember your phone number?"

"I know my dad's number." Zoe rubbed a dirty finger over her nose as if thinking then gave the number. "I think that's right. My head feels strange."

"That's just fine. I'll keep trying until I contact him." Jenna lifted both eyebrows at Kane in a meaningful stare and called the number. "Let's get out of here."

He drove down the mountainside, bumping along the pitted, uneven roads, relieved when they finally reached the highway. Then, lights flashing, he sped down the blacktop in the direction of Black Rock Falls General Hospital.

Jenna had said little to Mr. Channing other than his daughter was alive and she was taking her to the hospital. When she disconnected, Kane turned to her. "It will take him some time to get here from Helena."

"He is going to arrange a ride in a helicopter. He is heading home now to collect his wife." Jenna leaned back in the seat, her face pale. "When we arrive, I'll inform the hospital he will be landing on their helipad." Her brow wrinkled into a frown. "She has been missing for six months."

Jesus. Kane cleared his throat. "As she is talking to you, maybe you should ask about the other people she mentioned. The hospital will sedate her the moment we arrive."

"Yeah, okay." Jenna's mouth turned down. She pulled out her notepad and pen then turned in her seat. "Zoe, what's the dog's name?"

"Stupid but I don't think it is his real name." Zoe chewed on her bottom lip and shrugged.

"Oh, I see. Was he here when you arrived?"

"No, Amos said he came from the animal shelter 'bout three weeks ago." Zoe sipped the orange juice and sighed. "He isn't stupid. I like him. When Amos locked him in the cellar, he would sit with me and listen to me talking. I think he knows what I told him because he didn't like Amos and growled at him." She rubbed the tip of her pink nose. "You won't take him back to the animal shelter, will you? I don't think he likes it there."

A pang of pity wrenched at Kane's heart. "Nope." He glanced at Jenna and shrugged. "I'm going to look after him. We'll find out his real name. The animal shelter will have a record of him."

"Dogs and horses?" Jenna shot him a worried glance. "What next, cattle?"

Kane shrugged. "I'm not sure. I'll have to ask my landlady but I think she'll be a pushover when I tell her about the dog."

Stanton Forest bordered the highway; tall and dappled green, the pines stood like sentries guarding the way to the falls. He looked behind him at the incredible mountainside bathed in sunshine, saddened the majestic beauty had hidden such atrocities. "Not long now."

Jenna gave him a knowing look. "Zoe, do you remember the names of the others who came to visit you?"

"No." Zoe stuffed another energy bar into her mouth and chewed.

"Okay." Jenna's tone was light and conversational. "How many men did you see? Was it always the same amount?"

"Yes. Three and Amos, like I said before."

Unable to keep quiet a moment longer, Kane took a deep breath. "Do you remember what they looked like?"

Zoe's brown gaze narrowed. "I don't want to talk to you."

"Okay, he won't say another word." Jenna gave him a look good enough to freeze Black Rock Falls Lake then smiled at Zoe. "What color hair did they have?"

"I don't know what they looked like. They wore masks." She scratched her dirty, tear-tracked cheek. "One came by yesterday morning real early. He kept asking me where Amos had gone. He didn't let me out but he did leave me a pile of food."

Interesting. Kane glanced at Jenna. "He might live close by. Well, let's say in a five-mile radius, I guess, looking at how the cabins are spread out up here."

"Yeah, it will be a huge undertaking to search the mountain." Jenna's attention moved back to the girl and she smiled at her. "Is there anything else you remember about them? Scars or tattoos?"

"One had a spider with a red back on his hand. He was mean." Zoe's bottom lip trembled. "One had a scar on his belly, low on the right side. I don't want to talk about them anymore."

Jenna gave the girl a bright smile. "I am so proud of you, telling me all those things. Just rest now, we'll be at the hospital soon and your parents are on their way."

"Will they be mad at me for running away?"

"No." Jenna handed her another bottle of water. "I spoke to your dad and he is very happy you are okay."

"That's good and if you speak to him again tell him I was silly to run away because he flushed my dead fish down the toilet. I guess burying them in the garden was a stupid idea."

Jenna gave Kane a tragic stare and he could see her eyes filling with tears. She cleared her throat and her voice cracked a little. "I'll tell him."

CHAPTER EIGHT

Ely Dorsey's day could not get any worse. His friend was missing and had been for three days. After visiting his house and seeing his truck gone, he had let himself in using the key under the flowerpot by the door. The girl told him he had not been there since Tuesday. Concerned about his friend's absence, he fed the girl and left. After calling Amos's cellphone from a public phone and getting no response, he went home, not sure what to do.

He waited until late afternoon then decided to drive past the house where Amos planned to meet the new girl. He discovered his truck parked some ways from the house, and to his horror, crime scene tape barred the front door.

Immediately, he headed back to his friend's house to grab the girl. He took the alternative route, parking his vehicle along an old logging road and hiking the half-mile down the mountain to Amos's cabin, glad he had taken the extra precautions when he found it infested with deputies. Amos wasn't the smartest so he might have guessed his friend would mess up.

He rested his binoculars on the edge of the rock and peered down at the cabin. The deputies' vehicles had been outside the house for hours but there was no sight of Amos or the girl. An anxious gripping rolled his stomach. If the new girl's parents had come home early and caught Amos in the house, the cops would have arrested him, and searching his house would have been normal procedure.

He rubbed his chin and rolled back on his heels to think. The deputies moved in and out of the house carrying plastic bags and it did not take a genius to know they were collecting DNA and fingerprints. He sighed in relief. *They'll find nothing.* He and his friends had been very careful and not one of them entered Amos's house without wearing gloves. They laundered the sheets on the bed after each session and washed the plastic sheeting covering the bed with bleach. After the last scare, they took no chances. Amos might live like a pig but every weekend when he and the boys left the love nest, the cellar was spotless. They even incinerated the paper bag from the vacuum cleaner; they left nothing to chance.

The girl locked in Amos's cellar would not be able to identify them either. Living in fear after one of Bobby-Joe's girls had escaped they had been extra careful, worn gloves and clown masks. The deputies would get nothing out of her. She was as scared as a rabbit, and frightened they would kill her family if she ever told.

It was getting late and he made his way back along the trail to the road leading to his secluded cabin, tucked under an overhang and hidden by trees. He climbed into his SUV and arrived home in time for dinner. Missy clanked around the kitchen, dishing up his meal. At eighteen, she was getting too old for him now but she served her purpose. She cooked and cleaned without complaint. In fact, she told him she enjoyed caring for him, but he kept the chain attached to a well-padded metal cuff around her leg just in case she decided to escape.

He stared at her thin face and sighed. His heart sank. All week he had expected to find a new girl waiting for him at Amos's house. Now it looked like he would have to go to the trouble of finding one. He pushed down the urge to call Bobby-Joe or Chris—they'd all agreed to only communicate face to face or via a public phone. At any time, the cops might arrest one of them just like Amos, and they made sure they did not leave a trail for the cops to follow.

After eating his dinner, he headed into his man cave and opened his laptop. The new wireless tower on the top of the mountain gave him high-speed access to the internet. Confident he could find a suitable replacement in one of the online teens social groups or the many games chat rooms, he signed into one of the sites. After scrolling through the requests, he found an interesting post. A young girl was complaining her date had failed to arrive and left her disappointed. At fourteen years old, she sounded perfect. He responded and to his delight, she replied.

From the conversation, he realized with a jolt this had to be the girl Amos had been grooming for weeks. Knowing what she wanted to hear, he told her lies. One of the many things he had perfected over the years was persuasion. He offered her the world then told her she would be safe with him because he was such a nice kid. He gave her the number of his burner phone and waited with anticipation for her to call.

The ringtone pealed out and he took a deep breath. "Hello."

"This is Needy Girl. As you are going to be my first boyfriend, I would really like to know your real name. Just your first name will do."

Struck by her soft girly voice, he did not think of the consequences and blurted out, "Ely."

"Oh, that's a nice name." She giggled. "See you soon."

CHAPTER NINE

Friday

Depressed, Jenna stared out her office window in an effort to lift her spirits. The town came alive during the carnivals with the townsfolk throwing themselves into events with gusto. The Fall Festival was underway and being Friday there would be an art show in the community hall, a parade down the main street and the usual displays of arts and crafts, home baking, and the like filling tables along the sidewalk.

Wishing she could be anywhere but inside, and facing the terrible fact a group of child molesters had moved into her town or, worse, had been operating under her nose for years, Jenna dragged both hands down her face and moaned.

Her life as sheriff had been complicated and difficult. It was not the cozy neighborhood disputes and parking tickets she expected when she agreed to move to this backwoods town. After leaving her life as an undercover DEA agent and living in witness protection with a new face and name, life should have been sweet; instead, the sleepy town of Black Rock Falls hid more secrets than the Labyrinth of Egypt. It would seem that lowlifes, murderers, and criminals regularly haunted the picturesque streets.

The current horrific crimes made her appreciate her senior deputies' efficiency, although at first it had been a fight of wills. Both highly qualified men, she had utilized their skills and now they worked seamlessly as a team. New deputies would be arriving soon, and although the lightening of her workload would be a relief, she really did not want the hassle.

Voices outside her door reminded her the staff meeting was due to start and she would have to put on a good front to hide her anxiety from Kane. They had become close friends over the last year and his incredible profiling skills worked on every level including reading her like a book. She straightened at the knock on her door. "Yes, come in."

The deputies filed in and took seats, with the exception of Walters; she had him on duty all day at the nurses' station at the local hospital. Although Zoe was on a special floor reserved by the sheriff's department for injured victims or prisoners, she wanted the added security. Worried the other men in the pedophile ring would realize Zoe was missing by now, she wasn't sure what they would do to stop her from identifying them.

Jenna flicked a gaze over her deputies and folded her hands on the desk. "I called the sheriff in Helena about Zoe's case. He told me he had called in the FBI Child Abduction Rapid Deployment Team when she was reported missing. They found no trace of her and he said it was as if she had vanished. He is sending the files and notifying them, so they will be contacting me soon for our case files. As Zoe will be returning to Helena as soon as she is cleared by the hospital, I suggested the agents on her case speak to her then rather than coming here and distressing her further."

"I don't think they'll have any relevant information regarding Price's murder." Kane shrugged.

She nodded in agreement.

"Deputy Wolfe, do you have anything to report?"

"Well, yes and no." Wolfe's eyes brightened. "I've mentioned the strong smell of tobacco coming from Mr. Price's stomach contents and I had a hunch, so I ran a test specifically for nicotine sulfate and it came back positive."

Interested, Jenna leaned forward and scribbled a note in her book. "Can you explain its significance?"

"It's a clear liquid and used as a pesticide amongst other things. It is a highly toxic substance and results in a nasty death. It is not something anyone would ingest on purpose. Due to this finding, I am ruling his death as a homicide." Wolfe sighed. "How he drank the substance is a mystery. It was not present in the bottle of bourbon he had with him. We found no glass or empty can of cola to indicate he drank the poison at the house, but if he had taken the poison earlier, he wouldn't have made it to the location."

"Apart from being a great receptionist, Maggie is great for doing research. I'll ask her to find out if it is available anywhere in town. If it's unusual, the storekeeper might recall selling a bottle to someone local." She cleared her throat. "Do we have a time of death?"

"Not conclusive. The heat inside the house increases the speed of decomposition so using the usual body temperature of the victim as a guide was redundant. It's obvious the killer turned up the thermostat to confuse the time of death. We can only go on the time frame between Mr. Davis' inspection and Miss Saunders' visits to the house."

"What about fingerprints? Who else was in the house?"

"We found Amos Price's fingerprints on the front door, the bottom of the handrail to the stairs, and on the kitchen counter. Miss Saunders' fingerprints were on the front door and on the kitchen doorframe. The others all corresponded to the cleaners and a tradesman. The two cleaners who visited the place two days prior have a GPS in their van. It is a mother and daughter team, Rosemarie and Lizzy Harper. We can place them in the immediate area over the two-day period."

"The tradesman is a carpenter." Kane scanned her face. "Adam Stickler moved into town two months ago. He lived in Blackwater and eight years ago his sister Jane went missing on her way home from school. She vanished without a trace, so kidnapping is a possible motive. The Blackwater sheriff conducted a full investigation; again, the FBI was involved but after a few false leads from people who saw her on the day she went missing, the trail ran dry. He has a motive and was in the area."

"What motive? You'll need more than that to convince me, Kane."

"I have a motive." Kane took a document out of a file and pushed it across the table. "It came to nothing but his mother put in a complaint against Price for inappropriately touching kids at a birthday party. Jane Stickler was at a party the weekend before she went missing. When Jane disappeared, Price was the FBI's prime suspect." Kane placed a photocopy of a newspaper on the desk. "His name is mentioned as a person of interest in the *Blackwater News*."

Jenna sighed. "If Jane was at a party, then everyone there would have been investigated. Was Price even at the party?"

"Yeah, and he was questioned and came up clean. The sheriff searched his place and found nothing but we have vital information the investigation didn't have at the time: More than one man is involved. He could have stashed Jane somewhere else."

"Okay, we'll need to talk to Stickler. He would have been about fourteen at the time and could have waited until he was older to strike." Jenna stared at her notes. "I've been looking into Lizzy Harper, one of the cleaners. She has a key to the house and has a motive too. She served a three-year sentence in juvie for stabbing her abusive father to death, almost six years ago. She has a seven-year-old son fathered by him. At the time, the newspaper reports believed others were involved. The court sealed her case files so all we have to go on is the casebook from the initial investigation and reports in the local newspapers. If her father was part of the pedophile ring, she might want to take revenge on predators. Both Harper and Stickler would know the property was vacant." She lifted her gaze. "The thing is, how did they lure him to the house?"

"If he was actively looking for a kid, say online, they might have played him at his own game." Kane cleared his throat. "The FBI has been active in chat rooms for years to catch pedophiles. It's on TV and it wouldn't take a genius to act as a kid to lure him there."

"Yes, you have a point." Jenna raised one eyebrow. "But it would be difficult to act as a young teenager; they have their own language." She sighed. "They don't get all of their kids online though, do they? I've read about cases involving family members or close friends."

"You have to remember, predators are cunning." Kane gripped the arm of the chair with one large hand. "They often work or become involved in pastimes that involve children. Price worked as a clown to access kids. Pedophiles gain parents' trust then move in to groom the kids. One of the most prevalent is the man who befriends a widow or single mom—he pretends to care for the mom and behind her back, abuses the kids. He becomes the dad they never had and the kids trust him. Most victims keep quiet because they don't want to be without a dad again or he threatens to kill their mom. The problem is pedophiles act both alone and in groups, which makes them difficult to catch."

"I am aware of that, Kane." She tapped her pen on the table. "All this leads to the question: Why attack Price now? It's been years. What would make Lizzy Harper suddenly be out for Price's blood?"

"Harper works as a housekeeper, so I gather she does the cleanup after kids' parties as well." Wolfe's gaze hardened. "Maybe being molested as a kid then seeing a man acting inappropriately with kids at a birthday party might get her angry enough to kill him. She did kill her father. This would be extreme; usually people don't want to get involved, or think they are being a little too sensitive, or are ashamed to report this type of behavior."

She swallowed the rising bile. "I can't believe people could act so irresponsibly." She glanced back at her notes. "Was he the only clown around town?" Jenna swept her gaze over the men.

"No, I checked." Rowley's brown eyes met her own and narrowed. "There are usually two clowns who put up the bouncy house when we have a festival, which is at least once a month. The kids flock there."

More damn clowns. "Who owns the bouncy house?"

"The town council."

"Contact them and find out the names of the clowns." Jenna pushed both hands through her hair. She hated this case. Acting in a cold and professional manner when dealing with child violation was proving difficult. Especially when Kane and Wolfe seethed with anger every time they discussed the case. Knowing Kane would kill on her command, if warranted, without question was not a responsibility she enjoyed.

"Didn't you say Zoe mentioned other men?" Rowley's pen hovered over his notebook. "Do we have any leads on who they might be?"

Jenna smiled at him. "Good question." Her attention moved to Wolfe. "Did you collect any evidence at the cabin we can use?"

"No. From what I can ascertain, only Price and the girl lived at the cabin." Wolfe's pale lashes dropped over his eyes as he flicked through his notes. "All the fingerprints are either his or Zoe's. If anyone else went there they were very careful and wore gloves. I can't understand how the cellar was so spotless. I know it was disgusting in the cage where he kept the child but it appeared he cleaned the rest of the room recently. The bed in the cellar had freshly laundered sheets and I could smell bleach on a plastic under-sheet. Considering the rest of the house is a pigsty, why would he clean the cellar yet leave her cage filthy?"

"Only one person would know." Kane leaned back in his chair and stretched out his long legs. "You'll have to speak to Zoe again, ma'am."

"I will as soon as I have permission from her parents and clearance from the doctor, but she isn't going to recognize anyone if they wore masks." Jenna tapped her bottom lip with the top of her pen. "Perhaps he, I mean Price, didn't clean the room. If he had friends over at the weekends like Zoe told us, perhaps they had concerns about leaving trace evidence."

"Yeah." Kane's eyes flashed. "They wouldn't risk leaving DNA behind, would they?"

"Yet, Amos hadn't allowed her to take a shower since his friends left." Jenna made a few notes. "Wouldn't you think if he was worried about DNA, he would have made her wash?"

"We'll have to wait for the results from the rape kit samples." Wolfe's mouth turned down. "The verbal report I received from the doctor at the hospital said Price had abused her over a long period. We know she had been missing for six months and that would be consistent." He sighed. "The only way you'll find out what happened to her is to ask her and see if she'll talk."

"I find it impossible to believe that Price would only be interested in her on the weekends when his friends were there." Jenna's cheeks grew hot. "Really, he had his disgusting fetish there for the taking. We know he only gave her a shower before the others arrived. If they cleaned up the place as you suggested, they would have made sure she was clean too. My guess is, the rape kit will implicate Amos Price alone and I bet his bed will carry the signs as well."

"I did find seminal fluid in his bed. It will take some time before the DNA tests come back, though." Wolfe's gray eyes met Jenna's. "I'll let you know the moment they arrive."

She pushed to her feet and stared down at him then moved her attention slowly to Kane. "When we find these animals, I expect you to both act in a professional manner. Bring them in so we can interrogate them and see how far this pedophile ring has spread. I don't want to find out they broke their necks resisting arrest. Do you understand?"

"Sure do." Kane's lips formed a thin line. "How do you want to proceed?"

"Hit the streets. Someone must recognize a man with a tattoo resembling a black widow spider on his hand. Look at people who run summer camps, scout leaders, preachers, anything that involves kids."

"Are we looking into the homicide of Amos Price as well?" Rowley gave her a concerned look. "Or concentrating on the pedophile ring?"

"We'll be running with both cases." She chewed on her bottom lip, thinking. "I want to know everything about Lizzy Harper and her mother but go easy. Kane, contact her mother by phone first and find out what you can. As Wolfe mentioned, poison is often a woman's preferred method of killing. We need to know if Lizzy and her mother are involved."

"And follow up with an interview?" Kane was making copious notes in his book.

"Yes, as soon as possible." Jenna sat back down in her chair. "I'm going to see if I can obtain details of Lizzy Harper's case but it will take a court order and right now we have nothing on her. I want every piece of information regarding her you can discover. I want to know if anyone else was involved in her abuse apart from her father."

She turned her attention to Rowley. "Get me a list of tradesmen that the real estate agents used for that house and go and see Mr. Stickler. Ask him to come in for questioning and watch his reaction; if he looks like he has something to hide, contact Kane for backup."

"Have you assigned anything for Walters to do to pass time at the hospital? He has a laptop with him." Kane met her gaze with raised eyebrows. "Rather than playing solitaire all day."

Jenna thought for a moment then nodded. "Yeah, give him a call, would you? I would like him to check the Montana database for any similar cases over the last ten years."

"Yes, ma'am."

When the deputies left, Maggie the receptionist knocked on her door and her huge brown eyes held concern.

"Can I get you anything, Sheriff? You look plum worn out."

Jenna forced her lips into a smile. "I'm fine, thank you, just overworked. Was there anything else?"

"The new deputies are all settled. They'll drop by later this afternoon."

And I thought the day could not get any worse. Jenna slumped into her chair and rubbed her temples. "Thanks."

CHAPTER TEN

Kane strolled out of Jenna's office and grimaced at Wolfe. "If the guy with the tattoo is a local, then he would come into town for supplies, or at least eat at Aunt Betty's Café. I think we should start with the stores in town."

"Yeah and we'll work faster if we split up." Wolfe scratched his blond stubble. "Although if you plan to drive out to the Triple Z asking questions, I think I should tag along."

The Triple Z was a biker roadhouse some miles out of town toward the mountains and not a place to walk into without backup. He grinned at Wolfe. "Yeah, maybe we should try there first. Nothing brightens my day more than seeing grown men run for cover at the sight of a badge."

"You saying we intimidate people?" Wolfe's suntanned face creased into a grin. "Sometimes looking mean gets results, and over at the Triple Z we are an unknown quantity."

Kane snorted with laughter and headed for the door. "We'll take my car. I'll drop you here on the way back. If you take north of town, I'll take south. We'll be able to cover most of the stores and meet at Aunt Betty's for lunch at noon." He reached for his cellphone. "I'll call Walters and give him something to do then we can be on our way."

"That sounds like a plan." Wolfe peered at his cellphone. "During the drive, I'll see what I can find on Lizzy Harper and her mother."

"If you find her number, I'll pull over and speak to her."

As Kane negotiated his SUV through the traffic, he wondered why the Black Rock Falls townsfolk celebrated every festival on the calendar. Although, he imagined visitors from neighboring towns boosted the economy. He rubbed his stomach, glad to find his six-pack not suffering from his overindulgence of homemade cookies and candies he purchased in vast quantities from the stalls lining the streets. The intense morning workouts he performed with Jenna kept him in shape, and her skills had become formidable. After a couple of psychopaths had kidnapped her last winter, she had changed significantly and had worked hard to overcome the flashbacks. Allowing him to train her in mixed martial arts had made them firm friends. They had formed a comfortable relationship and banned talk of work during their downtime together.

As he drove, he scanned the area. The local park was a mass of color with candy-striped marquees and a bounce house. At the sight of two clowns leading kids on ponies, the hair on the back of his neck stood to attention. He pulled into a parking space. "Clowns." He slid his gaze to Wolfe. "I wonder if they have a union or something."

"They require a permit and insurance to run pony rides in Black Rock Falls." Wolfe's gaze lifted from his phone. "We should check the past and present clown permit registrations. We might find if Price had any close friends."

I'll have to brush up on city council laws. "Yeah, great idea. Keep searching, I'll check them out."

He slipped out of the car and strolled toward the line of kids waiting for a ride, tickets in hand. When the clown returned to the starting position, he slapped him on the shoulder. "May I have a word?"

"I have kids waiting." The flash of annoyance in the man's amber eyes did not reflect the oversized smile on his white face.

Kane led him out of earshot of the kids. "It won't take long." He pulled out his notepad and pen. "What's your name?"

"Why? I haven't done anything wrong." The clown had a French accent and narrowed his gaze at him.

"I didn't say you had, but you're working with kids and in this town you need a permit and insurance to run a pony ride. Plus, you need to be able to show the permit on request." Kane straightened. "Now answer the question. You wouldn't want me to cuff you and drag you down to the sheriff's office in front of the kids, would you?"

"I have a permit." He pulled off a white glove, unzipped his costume, and reached inside. "My name is Claude Booval and my associate is my brother Pierre. Both names are on the permit."

Kane made notes, taking down the names and address of the brothers. "Where were you this week?"

"It's the Fall Festival. We are here in the park every day from nine until six. We stay at the Black Rock Falls Motel and before you ask, no, we didn't leave the motel at any time. We used room service for meals."

So, they are in the clear for Price's murder but still might be in the pedophile ring. "Would you please remove your other glove?"

"Why?" Claude's eyes opened wide with surprise.

"I'm investigating an incident involving a clown with a spider tattoo on his hand." Kane narrowed his gaze on the man. "Know anyone fitting that description in town?"

"No." Claude removed his other glove. "See? No tattoos."

Kane glanced up to see the other clown walking toward him. "Pierre Booval?"

"Is something wrong?"

"Show him your hands." Claude gave an exaggerated sigh. "He is looking for a clown with a tattoo."

"Sure." Pierre removed his gloves.

No tattoo.

Disappointed, Kane tried another angle. "Do you know a clown by the name of Amos Price or the names of clowns who frequent the festivals or who live close by?"

"We don't associate with the other entertainers. You see, they are our competition for work." Claude shrugged. "Many of them are clowns one day, elves the next. For us it is a profession, not a chance to put on a costume. Although the rodeo clowns are different."

"I'm not talking about the rodeo clowns but those who work with children."

"Ah, I gather one of our profession has acted unprofessionally?" Pierre's bright red mouth turned down in an almost comical way. "We are aware of child molesters. They ruin our reputation but it is not always clowns. A magician lured our sister, Angelique, away from a birthday party. She was missing for three days but managed to get out of the house when the monster was sleeping. He got seven years in jail."

Bells and whistles went off in Kane's brain. "When did this happen?"

"Eight years ago, in Blackwater. She was only twelve." Pierre's eyes filled with sorrow. "She has never been the same and after years of therapy she still sleeps with a knife beside her bed."

"This is why I need to find this man." Kane stared at the men. "What was the magician's name?"

"Stewart James Macgregor."

"Thanks." He scribbled in his notebook. "Anyone else involved?"

"We don't know. Angelique has never spoken to us about her ordeal. When she escaped, a woman walking her dog outside Macgregor's house helped her. She took her to the police and was able to identify the house."

"You live in Blackwater?" He did not recognize the address on the permit. "Do you live there now?"

"No. We have a place in the low county. Ten miles east of here. We moved there three months ago. We purchased a small ranch from the retired Mayor Rockford. Angelique still lives with our parents in Blackwater." He sighed. "Before you ask, we stay in town because our vehicle is being repaired at Miller's Garage if you need to check."

"Okay, thanks." Kane pulled out his cards and handed them to the men. "If you notice a man with a black widow spider tattoo on his hand, call me. If you hear a whisper about anyone working with children acting inappropriately, call me. I'll keep your names out of any inquiry. I just want to catch this guy."

When both men took the cards and nodded, Kane strolled back to his vehicle. He slid behind the wheel and turned the key, looking at Wolfe. "We have another woman who was molested as a child. Her name is Angelique Booval. The incident happened eight years ago in Blackwater. There would have been a trial—the man charged was Stewart James Macgregor. See what you can find out."

"Do we add her to our suspect list?"

Kane backed the car onto the busy road then spun the wheel and headed out of town. "I think anyone with a motive should be considered. Angelique Booval became unstable after Macgregor kidnapped her, and if she noticed Price acting inappropriately with kids, she could be out for revenge."

"Well, this is interesting." Wolfe's blond eyebrows rose above the screen of his cellphone. "I discovered where Macgregor last worked before his arrest and googled the company. It seems a company by the name of Party Time employs Macgregor and Price. The company's main business is supplying acts, clowns, magicians, Santa Claus, and all kinds of characters for kids' parties and for festivals in at least three local towns including here and Blackwater. I've checked out the list of employees on their website against the sexual offenders register and they all come up clean apart from Macgregor." He held up the screen of his cellphone. "See, Stu Macgregor is still listed as available in a limited capacity street license entertainment, only no kids' parties. He is a low-risk sexual offender. I doubt he gets much work."

"That's interesting."

"Yeah, and I have Rosemarie Harper's number." Wolfe glanced at him. "Want to speak to her now?"

"Yeah." He pulled the car to the side of the road and took Wolfe's phone.

A woman answered after a couple of rings.

"Am I speaking to Rosemarie Harper? Good, this is Deputy Kane from the Black Rock Falls Sheriff's Department. I need to ask you a few things in the strictest of confidence."

He asked her a few questions then disconnected and handed back the cellphone. "That is too crazy to explain right now. I'll fill you in after I've run it past the sheriff." He turned the SUV back onto the highway and accelerated.

"Sure." Wolfe took the phone and smiled at him. "I do understand the term 'confidential.'"

About five miles out of town, Kane turned the SUV into the parking lot of the Triple Z bar and pulled into a space. He turned in his seat and stared at the cellphone. "I wonder how many of the men working at Party Time have priors."

"I'll check them out the moment we get back to the office."

"From what we know about Price, he didn't work alone. It's more than likely he has been doing this for a long time and could have also been involved in the Angelique Booval kidnapping, but she only mentioned one man— Stu Macgregor. It is something we have to consider as they worked together and were both pedophiles." Kane opened the car door. "He would have worked the festivals here and in Blackwater.

Miss Booval might have caught sight of him in costume and it triggered a memory. Although his type of murder takes a lot of planning."

"She could have identified him years ago and she's had years to plan his murder." Wolfe snorted. "It's not something a person gets over easy."

Kane led the way into the Triple Z and strolled up to the bar. In his peripheral vision, he noticed men slipping out the back door and smiled to himself. He had bigger fish to fry.

"What can I get you?" The man behind the counter rubbed a filthy rag over the bar, avoiding his gaze.

"Information." Kane straightened. "Do you have a customer with a black widow tattoo on his hand?"

"If I did, I wouldn't tell you." The barman snorted in disgust. "We don't rat on our friends."

"Okay, I'll take a look for myself." Kane turned and glanced over the room. He moved closer to Wolfe. "Split up and take a look. I doubt we'll find anything."

After moving through the eight men in the bar, they returned to the vehicle and found a woman wearing tight cutoff jeans, a shirt that left nothing to the imagination, and red stilettos leaning against the door. Kane touched his hat. "Do you want to speak to me, ma'am?"

"You asked about a black widow tattoo?"

"Yeah, do you know the name of the man who has one?"

"Nothing's free." She pushed out her chest and winked at him. "Fifty bucks."

Kane barked out a laugh. "Twenty." He slid a bill from his wallet and dangled it in the air "Take it or leave it."

"Okay. Some years ago, maybe as long as six, a biker gang called the Black Widows used to come here from Blackwater. They all had those tattoos on their hands." She pointed one red-tipped fingernail between her thumb and first finger. "Right here but I haven't seen any of them for years." She plucked the twenty out of Kane's fingers then turned and sashayed away.

Kane rubbed his chin and stared after her. "It seems every clue we have leads to Blackwater."

CHAPTER ELEVEN

She strolled in the park, and to all around her, she would appear to be one of the crowd eating cotton candy and enjoying the festivities. The smell of hotdogs and horse manure filled the air as she lingered at the pony rides. She had seen Deputy Kane chatting to the clowns earlier. He had given them his card and smiled then scurried away. She had stared after him and a shiver of hate ran through her. He could be one of the monsters. A man in a position of power was someone no one would ever expect. He had no wife and never dated. That made him a prime candidate. Maybe she would follow him for a while and see what he was doing in town today. *I can see you, Deputy Kane, and I'm watching you.*

She needed an excuse to move into the pony circle to keep Kane in sight and sidled closer to a clown lifting a child onto a small bay pony. Touching the horse's mane, she feigned interest. "How long will you be here? I would love to bring my little sister for a pony ride. She just adores clowns."

"For the entire festival." The clown had a French accent.

"Oh, thank you." She smiled warmly. "We always had clowns for my sister's birthday parties. Do you do kids' parties?"

"Sometimes, but we prefer the festivals." He indicated to the line of kids waiting for rides. "I gotta go."

"Oh yes, of course." She smiled but inside her skin crawled.

Her attention fixed on Kane, she walked slowly back through the crowd and took a seat on the far side of the pony rides beside a frazzled mother with three demanding children. From here, she could keep a close eye on Kane's movements. When he headed for his car, she got to her feet, intent on following him. She needed to know what he was doing and who he had on his list of suspects. As she walked to her vehicle, she glanced at her watch. Goosebumps rose on her arms with the thrill of anticipation. Soon she would meet the next monster on her list. He had been such an easy man to catch. She had played him at his own game, fed his ego, and the jerk had agreed to meet her.

By the morning, another monster would be dead.

CHAPTER TWELVE

Jenna lifted her attention to the two new deputies. Cole Webber, twenty-eight, with brown hair and brown eyes, introduced himself with a soft New England accent. He had transferred to Black Rock Falls from Boston, and having another experienced deputy would be useful.

Standing, she took in the man before her, noting his confidence. She offered her hand. "Welcome to Black Rock Falls. Do take a seat."

"I'm glad to be here, ma'am."

She turned her attention to Paula Bradford, five seven with blonde hair and green eyes. This rookie had started her career in law enforcement only six months previously in Helena. "It's a big step for you to leave your family and come here." She shook the woman's hand.

"I come from a large family and solitude in a small town will be heaven, ma'am." Paula smiled then sat down. "Thank you for arranging the accommodation. My apartment is very nice."

"Yes, thank you." Webber gave her a strange look. "Although, I gather from the neighbor, the house once belonged to a deputy killed in the line of duty."

Jenna cleared her throat. "Yes, Pete Daniels was a valued member of our team but he wasn't killed in the house and his family donated the property to the department."

"Are his killers in jail?"

"They're dead." Jenna's mind flashed back to the crunch of bone as her heel killed her attacker. A knife held at her throat, the discharge of a weapon, and blood on her face. Her hands trembled at the disturbing memory and she bunched them into fists.

"Jenna?" Kane's worried voice broke through the terrifying visions playing in a loop in her mind.

She blinked and, seeing him filling the doorway, noticed the confused expressions on her new deputies' faces. *Oh, God, how long have I been out this time?* Forcing the horrific memories back into their box, she forced her lips into a smile. "Deputy Kane, I'd like you to meet Cole Webber and Paula Bradford. They will be starting tomorrow. I'll need everyone pulling overtime this weekend. Can you ask Wolfe to bring them up to speed? I'd like an update from you as soon as you're finished."

"Yes, ma'am. I've spoken to Rosemarie Harper." Kane's concerned gaze moved over her face as he placed a takeout cup of coffee and a paper sack from Aunt Betty's Café on her desk. "I picked up your lunch."

She glanced at the clock; it was past two. "Thanks, I've been busy." She glanced at her two new deputies. "See you in the morning."

When the door closed, Jenna covered her face with both hands. The flashbacks of her kidnapping and near death had lessened but obviously sat in the back of her subconscious waiting to pounce at any given moment. She felt such a fool, acting like an idiot in front of her new deputies, but Kane would cover for her—he had been her rock throughout the entire ordeal.

She leaned back in her seat and sipped her coffee then peeked into the bag and smiled. Turkey on rye, her favorite. She took a bite and the door opened. Kane walked back in and dropped into a chair. Swallowing, she smiled at him. "Thank you. I didn't notice the time."

"Are you okay, Jenna?"

She waved his question away. "Fine, we were discussing Pete's death and I had a flashback. I hope it didn't last too long."

"I don't think so." Kane's lips twitched into a half smile. "Webber thought you were grief-stricken discussing Pete's death and feels like a heel for bringing up the subject. I know we are all sorry about what happened to Pete but you really need to see someone about the flashbacks and nightmares. Post-traumatic stress disorder isn't a myth, it needs to be treated."

"You can talk. The other night during the movie you dozed off then woke up and grabbed me by the throat, if you remember."

"That was a nightmare, not PTSD." Kane grinned at her. "I wasn't in Afghanistan. I was defending you against a zombie. I shouldn't watch shows with zombies. Next time you want to come over to watch a movie, I'm picking it, okay?"

"Sure." She sucked the mayonnaise from her fingers and looked at him. "Forget movies for a minute. What else did you find out today?"

Kane gave her the details of the clown's sister, the Party Time connection between Macgregor and Price, and his visit to the Triple Z Bar. "We checked about half of the local businesses and asked the waitresses at Aunt Betty's Café. Susie Hartwig came up with someone with the tattoo. She danced with a blond man at the rodeo dance last summer with a similar tattoo but she can't recall anything else; she thinks she has seen him in town. She said he was rough and smelly. He had strange eyes. I tried to push her to give me a more detailed description but she only said he was around fifty and had a beer belly."

"Okay, that's a start." Jenna heaved a sigh. "I couldn't get into the sealed files of Lizzy Harper's court case, so I have zip."

"I have another bit of information." Kane's eyebrows furrowed. "I called Rosemarie Harper and told her we were investigating a case similar to her daughter's and needed her help. She backed away at first but when I mentioned more than one man appeared to be involved, she opened up. She recently discovered her husband was *not* the father of Lizzy's son. The kid became ill a year ago and has a genetic disease. The doctor performed a DNA test and the kid has a different father. As Lizzy refuses to tell anything about her ordeal apart from a few sketchy details, her mother believes this is proof she was subject to more than one man's abuse."

"That's frightening." She nibbled at her sandwich. "Anything else?"

"Since killing her father, Lizzy is under treatment and on medication for behavioral problems. I can place her in the area during the time we have for Price's death. The Harpers live one block away from the crime scene."

Jenna sighed. "All circumstantial. I need proof."

"I don't have proof but a theory. Many people in town use the Harpers' cleaning service for kids' parties and it is reasonable to assume they would run into the entertainment. It's possible, and as Price's contact details are online, maybe Lizzy pretended to be a kid he'd met as a clown and asked him to meet her at the house."

Jenna nodded. "It's feasible. She did have a master key to the house but how did she lure him there? Would she know about those online chat rooms you mentioned?"

"Yeah, if she watched TV, I'm sure she would be aware of the danger of chat rooms for kids." His brow creased. "It's common knowledge predators pretend to be kids online. There are so many groups on Facebook alone and the FBI can't monitor them all. She would just use a 'come get me' username and they would flock to her."

Jenna sipped her coffee and observed him over the rim. "The problem is widespread. I researched the frequency of cases today and there are literally thousands ongoing in the state. It's like an epidemic."

As a shadow darkened her doorway, she glanced up to see Rowley. "Yes?"

"I have Mr. Stickler in the interview room." Rowley's eyebrows rose. "He came in without a problem but seems a little confused about why you want to speak to him." He walked toward the desk and placed a sheet of paper in front of her. "Here is the list of tradespeople the real estate agency uses for the properties they manage. The ones highlighted are those who worked at the crime scene." He met her gaze. "Another thing I found interesting: The properties owned by Rockford were all rentals and managed by the agency. The same master key accesses them all. The cleaning service has one of the keys, and so does Stickler."

"Okay, thanks." She glanced at Kane and stood. "I'll add that info to the whiteboard now and add it to the case file later. We need to speak to Mr. Stickler without delay." She scribbled on the whiteboard then hurried from the room.

In the interview room, Stickler sat hands clasped on the table and looking nervous. The smell of sweat drifted toward Jenna as she entered the room. Stickler, in his early twenties, was lean and muscular. Jenna sat down and smiled at him. "Thank you for coming in. This is Deputy Kane." She waved a hand toward him. "Do you mind if we record the interview?"

"What's this all about?" Stickler's expression was grim. "I haven't done anything wrong." He brushed at the beading sweat on his upper lip with trembling fingers. "Okay, record the interview but I want it known you haven't read me my rights."

You sure look like you have something to hide. She turned on the recorder. "I haven't arrested you, Mr. Stickler. This is just a friendly chat. If I did arrest you then I would read you your rights. What you tell us today would not be admissible in court." She smiled. "For the record, it is two thirty and in the room with Mr. Adam Stickler is Sheriff Jenna Alton and Deputy David Kane. Mr. Stickler has volunteered to speak to us today." She glanced at her notes then lifted her gaze to Stickler. "Miss Alison Saunders, from the real estate office, discovered the body of a man in the house at 3 Maple Lane. I gather you did some work there recently?"

"A body? Anyone I know?" The color drained from his face.

"Just answer the question." Kane crossed his arms across his wide chest and glared at him.

"Yeah, I had to attach new handles to the kitchen cabinets. I finished last week on Friday morning."

Jenna leaned forward. "Were you there before the cleaners? I mean, did the place look as if it had been cleaned prior to an inspection?"

"Nope, I was there before the cleaners. Miss Saunders told me to be out of there by noon. I left around eleven."

"Can you account for your movements between Friday last week and Wednesday of this week?"

"Yeah, I worked Saturday over at Blindman's Peak on old Mr. Starkey's roof. I was there all day. Spent Sunday with my folks. Monday through Thursday I went back to finish Mr. Starkey's roof." Stickler eyed her with suspicion, took out his cellphone, and scrolled through the screen. "I can give you their numbers and you can check."

Jenna took down the numbers. "Do you know a man by the name of Amos Price?"

"Nope." Stickler stared at her and a small shadow of doubt crossed his eyes. "Just a minute, yeah, I *do* know that name. I'm pretty sure he is the clown my parents hired for my sisters' birthday parties when we lived in Blackwater." He narrowed his gaze. "I'm the eldest of seven, six girls and me."

"Yeah, that's him. He was found dead in the house on Maple." Kane rubbed the dark stubble on his chin. "Are you aware Amos Price was a pedophile?"

"No!" A look of anguish crossed Stickler's face. "Sweet Jesus, do you think he was involved with my sister's disappearance?"

Jenna filled a glass with water and pushed it toward him. "I'm not sure. Did you know your mother filed a complaint against him for inappropriate behavior?"

"No, I only remember the cops coming when Jane went missing. I guess they investigated him. I have no idea—I was just a kid."

"Okay." Jenna leaned back in her chair, acting nonchalant; he was getting way too upset, was it genuine or an act to cover his guilt? "How long ago did your sister vanish?"

"Eight years." Stickler lifted his red-rimmed eyes and sniffed. "If he's dead, we'll never find her now, will we?" He took the glass and gulped the water.

"Our job is to find her and we'll do our very best but we need your help. What we want to know is if Price had any friends." Kane's expression hardened. "Do you remember if he worked with another clown or did you see him with anyone?"

"Yeah, I do remember a magician, called himself the Great Dungini, and another clown." Stickler stared into space then moved his gaze back to Kane. "I don't remember any other names." He straightened. "I could ask my parents. They probably have photographs; they took tons and have videos of the parties, although it would be hard to identify them with the clown makeup."

"Okay thanks, you've been very helpful, and any images or videos would be a great help. Interview terminated at two-fifty." Jenna switched off the recorder. "Deputy Kane will give you his card. If you can think of anything at all to help us, please call him."

"I will." Stickler pocketed the card. "Can I go now?"

"Yes." Jenna flicked her ID over the scanner on the door and it clicked open. She indicated toward Rowley. "My deputy will show you out."

After shutting the door behind him, she turned to Kane. "What do you think?"

"From his reaction at finding out Price is dead, he isn't the killer." Kane shrugged. "Problem is, he is angry and believes his sister is still alive, which after so many years the chances are remote. He has confirmed there was another clown. Stu Macgregor, the Great Dungini and Price worked together at one time and we know they worked at Party Time. As Price was clean at the time of the FBI investigation, I figure the media would have gotten hold of Macgregor's case and if Stickler knew the two men worked together, he might have suspected Price had taken his sister. I hope Stickler doesn't think Macgregor is involved as well and seek vengeance."

"Oh, I hope not." Jenna frowned. "We have enough to worry about at the moment."

CHAPTER THIRTEEN

It could not have been easier to turn the tables on the next predator. With a few concerned words about having to slip away from home once her parents were asleep, she convinced him to take a room at the Black Rock Falls Motel. A perfect place, the motel had a variety of clientele depending on the seasons, from randy rodeo cowboys having one-night stands to hockey fans supporting their favorite team. In other words, the room rate started at two hours and the owner accepted every client who walked through the door. Men like him loved motel rooms because they carried so much DNA, proving anything would be difficult.

She persuaded him to leave the room key buried under the big tree beside the school gate and she made plans to meet him inside the room at seven that evening. After watching him drop the key and kick dirt over it, she waited for his SUV to turn the corner before attempting to collect it. As she walked past the school, she allowed oranges to spill from a paper sack in her arms. Retrieving the key and popping it into the sack with the oranges had been easy.

After arriving home that evening, she checked her messages, made a few necessary calls, then turned into a young teenager. She glanced in the mirror: At a slim five foot two, with fried eggs for breasts, she could pass as a much younger girl from a distance. During the day, the heels on her shoes and the clever way she styled her hair made her appear at least five seven. Her padded bra gave her a more voluptuous look, and when she added makeup, she looked all of her twenty-one years.

After slipping on surgical gloves, she pulled on a hoodie and moved through her kitchen and into the garage. She had chosen a mid-range white Ford; with so many in town, no one would notice her parking on the tree-lined lane beside the motel. The Black Rock Falls Motel was in a perfect location. No CCTV cameras to intrude on clients' privacy, and the owners left them alone. Spectacular burnished copper maple trees surrounding the courtyard bathed the area in mottled shadows, which would allow her to enter the room unnoticed.

She arrived at six thirty and slid from the car, leaving the car keys hidden on top of one of the wheels then, keeping to the shadows, entered the motel parking lot. The monster had followed her instructions, taking a room at the back of the building, the last one closest to the trees. Glancing around, she jogged across the courtyard and used the key to gain entrance.

She heaved a sigh of relief, finding the room unoccupied. If he was a pack animal, she would be in trouble if he arrived with a couple of his friends. She removed her coat then took the long metal meat skewer out of her bag and slid it within easy reach beneath the pillow. No poison this time.

This one deserved special treatment.

Glancing at the clock, she turned out the lights and watched out the window for him to arrive. At five minutes to seven, an SUV pulled up outside and she caught sight of the light glistening on his bald head as he walked to the door. Her heart pounded. He was big and could snap her neck like a twig. Virtually defenseless, she would be at his mercy if her plan failed.

When he pushed open the door, she backed into the bathroom, standing silhouetted by the streetlight coming through the bathroom window. To make him believe his date was a young girl, she must keep her face in shadow. A wave of anticipation at the thought of destroying this monster empowered her. She would play the role and make him pay.

"You in here?" His voice sounded excited and shrill for his size.

She sucked in a deep breath to calm herself then giggled. They always liked it when she giggled. "Yes, I'm here. Did you bring the things I asked you to buy?"

"Yeah." He held up a paper sack. "Why the stockings and blind-fold? I don't want you wearing stockings, I like my girls natural. Can I turn the light on so I can see you a bit better? You sure look pretty."

"Not yet, I'm shy." She twirled fingers in her hair, acting coy, and kept out of his way. "You look older than your picture. I thought you were eighteen."

"I shave my head to look older." He gave her a sad look. "I did lie a bit but I so wanted to meet you."

"That's okay." She giggled again. "You like to play games, right?"

"Oh, yeah, I like to play games. What do you have in mind?"

"I watched my sister with her boyfriend – she's eighteen – when they were babysitting and thought I was asleep. I asked you to bring those things because I want to do what they were doing."

"That sounds like fun. What were they doing?"

"Well, my sister tied his hands and feet to the bed with stockings then she blindfolded him." She giggled again at his moan of pleasure. "Then she climbed on top of him. It looked like fun."

"Yeah, yeah, I can do that." His voice trembled as he shed his clothes then dragged the items out of the bag. He ripped open a condom packet and smiled at her. "Why don't you get undressed then come here and tie me up."

Sickened by his lustful gaze, she shook her head. "Blindfold first. I'm shy. We can play your game next time, okay?"

"Sure, I have lots of games we can play." He pulled the blindfold in place and laid back on the bed. "This is going to be so much fun."

"I can't wait." She bent, retrieved his balled-up smelly socks, and dropped them on the bed then turned on the radio nice and loud. "I don't want anyone listening."

"Good idea."

She moved swiftly, tying his ankles then straddling his fat belly to secure his wrists to the slats in the headboard. His heavy breathing and moans of encouragement made her skin crawl. She slid the metal skewer from under the pillow. Satisfied he was restrained, she leaned over to switch on the bedside lamp then lifted up his blindfold. "Look at me."

An expression of terror crossed his face and he trembled.

"Who the hell are you?" He bucked, frantically trying to dislodge her. "Are you a cop?"

"I don't think so. I'm here to kill you." She pressed down hard on his chest, feeling his heart thumping against her palms, and stared into his horrified eyes. "How does it feel knowing you're going to die?"

"Not if I kill you first, bitch."

"Good luck." Her fear slipped away as she looked at the pathetic excuse for a man shaking beneath her. She could not pity him. She hated men like him. "I'm going to kill you in the most painful way possible. Just like I killed your friend."

"Why?" His face had turned a deep shade of red.

Suddenly struck dumb, she stared at him. "Why? For all the young girls you molested. Payback is a bitch, isn't it?"

She enjoyed his struggle beneath her and the way his eyes bulged. She had frightened him, the same way as he terrified his victims. "Your friend died slowly, but unfortunately for you, it will be quicker but so much more painful."

"You don't need to kill me. I'll give you money, anything." Tears welled in his eyes. "What do you want?"

"Justice." She picked up the socks. "Open your mouth."

To her surprise, he complied and she jammed the socks halfway down his throat then pressed down hard. She sucked in a deep breath then plunged the skewer into his ear. As his muffled screams filled the room, she felt *nothing*. No remorse, no pity for inflicting incredible agony on the writhing man. Her mind was a void. He was vermin and she was the exterminator. She leaned down and stared into his eyes as the life faded away. "Suck it up."

When he shuddered and his eyes rolled up displaying the whites, she removed the skewer then wiped it on the pillow. After dropping it into a plastic bag, she pulled out a roll of tape and dabbed a strip meticulously over the bed, lifting a myriad of hairs from the sheet. Satisfied nothing of her remained, she emptied his wallet to make it look like a robbery then collected her things and slipped out the door. *Rot in hell.*

CHAPTER FOURTEEN

Saturday

Early the next morning, after their usual workout, Kane sat in Jenna's kitchen drinking coffee. The hound dog sat at his feet. One call to the animal shelter had revealed his name as Duke, and the dog he thought to be old turned out to be five and listed as a great tracker. After rehydrating, a couple of decent meals, and a bath, he was looking good.

He smiled at Jenna. "I hope I can find time to purchase the horses tomorrow. They might come in useful in this investigation." He leaned back in his seat. "I repaired the corral last night, and the horse boxes in the barn are perfect. All I need to do is order feed and straw." He frowned. "There are a couple of horse trailers for sale in town as well."

"Isn't this going to cost you a lot of money?" She peered at him over the coffee cup. "I mean, you have spent a fortune on meat for Duke. More than you spend on yourself, and his vet bill must be horrendous."

He grinned at her and patted Duke on the head. "Nah, it's all good, and I have money. There was no way I was sending Duke back to the shelter, especially as he is a tracker. He will be a great asset once I get him fit. I like his company and I'm sure you'll grow to love him."

"He has such a sad face, of course I love him. I just hope his name won't offend Deputy Duke Walters."

He chuckled and called the dog to his side. "Nah, I told him and he said he was used it. Apparently Duke is a popular name for hound dogs."

Her cellphone vibrated on the table. "Sheriff Alton. Yes, Mr. Ricker, what is your emergency?" She glanced at him, disbelief etched in her expression. "Don't touch anything, shut the door to the room, and keep Rosa in your office until we arrive. I'll have someone there as soon as possible." She disconnected and the next moment was speaking to Rowley. "Can you get over to the Black Rock Falls Motel? Hold the fort until we get there. The cleaner found a body tied to one of the beds. Secure the scene until we arrive. I'm contacting Wolfe now."

Kane pushed to his feet. "I'll contact Wolfe, you get ready for work."

"Okay then go to the motel straight away; don't wait for me." She gave him a wistful look. "Why do people seem to die on my day off?"

"Dumb luck." He headed for the door then stopped and glanced back at her. "Would you like me to handle this case?"

"The second death in one week? No way, I need to be at ground zero." Jenna shook her head, sending her raven hair spilling in all directions. "I hope it's not another homicide. I'm worried Black Rock Falls is becoming murder central."

Within half an hour, Kane pulled his black SUV into the motel parking lot beside Wolfe's vehicle with the Black Rock Falls' Coroner insignia on the side. When Rowley walked out of the office to meet him, his face pale and expression grim, Kane took him to one side. "What do we have?"

"Homicide." Rowley's brown eyes narrowed. "There is a guy in one of the rooms around back tied to the bed with stockings and with blood running out of his ear. Wolfe is there now. He said to send you down when you arrive." He glanced over Kane's shoulder. "Ah, there's Sheriff Alton now."

"Have you taken statements from Mr. Ricker and Rosa? I assume she found the body when she went to clean the room?"

"Yeah, the room was booked yesterday. Ricker thought it was for a romantic evening. Most people take this side of the motel if they don't want to be seen. The SUV parked outside belongs to Ely Dorsey."

Kane made a note in his book. "I see. Any other customers staying on this side of the motel?"

"Nope, and Ricker said apart from Dorsey's vehicle, he hadn't seen any other vehicles parked here but Rosa was on her way home and noticed a white late-model sedan parked on the road some ways back. She said it was unusual to see a car there because the trees drop berries all over the paintwork." Rowley lifted his chin. "She said the car was gone this morning when she arrived to clean the rooms."

"Did she say what time she noticed the car?"

"Around seven last night." Rowley cleared his throat. "She works two shifts: early morning and six until nine at night."

Kane scratched his cheek, thinking. "Do you know what time the victim arrived?"

"He picked up the key before lunch and paid for the night. I used the mapping app on my phone and located his cabin in the mountains. It is about a mile away from the last victim's residence. It's possible they knew each other but folks up in the mountains keep to themselves." Rowley removed his hat and scraped a hand through his unruly hair. "Ricker said Dorsey did say he was in town for the Fall Festival."

"I wonder if the two dead men knew each other." Kane rubbed his chin. "Hang on a minute, *Ely* Dorsey. Holy shit, I'm sure I saw that name on the list of employees at Party Time. He might have worked with our last victim." He glanced at Jenna as she joined them.

"What have we got?" Jenna moved to his side.

"Another homicide, ma'am. He booked in here under the name of Ely Dorsey. I'm wondering if he is the same man who works for Party Time."

"That's pretty simple to find out. I'll check online." The sheriff gave them both an exasperated look, pulled out her cellphone, and located the webpage for Party Time. "Yeah, there is a clown here of the same name. That's him alright; his photo matches his driver's license." She snorted. "Maybe someone is doing us a favor."

Kane regarded her closely. She appeared agitated to the max. "What do you mean?"

"Oh, come on, Kane." She glared at him. "Zoe said four men visited her. If Ely Dorsey was one of them, then someone is doing our job for us." Her eyes flashed with anger. "Trust me, angry people take the law into their own hands. Someone who suffered abuse could have discovered these men hurting children and they would not want to put a kid through a trial. Ask any brutalized woman—she would rather see the perpetrator dead so they never harm anyone again. When the men who attacked me died I felt nothing, absolutely nothing—*nothing* but relief."

"I'm sure most women would agree with you; most men too." Kane huffed out a long sigh.

Jenna pressed long fingers to both temples. "If someone knows the names of the molesters, they could be taking revenge against them. It would be impossible for Zoe to identify Ely because the men wore masks. I suggest we target his associates anyway and find out if they are involved."

"*If* we can find them before they're murdered." Rowley's brown gaze dropped to the ground. "The mountain men are a pretty tight bunch. They won't rat on each other."

"Maybe things will change when they discover Ely was murdered as well. They'll be running scared." Jenna lifted her chin and a determined look crossed her face. "Pedophiles like them young, but the killer probably isn't a kid, so we could be chasing down a close relative hell-bent on vengeance. If a pedophile ring is operating in our town, we need to close it down. It looks like I'll need to make another call to the FBI."

"They had nothing on Price." Kane shrugged. "I've checked and he wasn't on any sex offenders list or had any priors statewide."

"Now he is dead they have no case to pursue but I'll keep them informed." Jenna gave an exasperated sigh. "They do have ongoing investigations statewide at the moment, and with any luck the other men in the pedophile ring will drop into their net."

Kane shook his head. "With the internet, it could be operating anywhere in the country. Finding who is involved will take a heck of a long time."

"Then we walk all over their friends until one of them talks; someone must know something about these men. People gossip, although I gather predators often keep their predilections secret." Jenna shot him an angry look. "They worked together. There has to be another link… someone knows both of them. Find them."

Kane wanted to sooth her agitation and lowered his voice. "We are all working around the clock on this, Jenna."

"I know but I want results." Jenna pushed a hand through her hair and glared at Rowley. "Which room?"

"The victim is this way, ma'am." Rowley's face paled as he led the way. "This homicide is different from the last one."

"Right." Jenna's shoulders slumped as she glanced at Kane. "Have you been on scene yet?"

"Nope. I just arrived." Kane grabbed his crime scene bag from the back seat of his SUV and headed toward the room. "Wolfe is working it now."

The motel room door was open when they arrived. Kane dropped his bag outside and they suited up in crime scene gear. He surveyed the area. "If I planned to murder someone, this place is perfect. No CCTV cameras, trees to give cover. No one has a chance of seeing anyone coming and going."

"Murder or a place for illicit sex with a minor?" Jenna's forehead creased into a frown. "As the killer didn't book the room or pick up the key, Ely must have snuck his murderer into the parking lot in his car, or the killer came in that white sedan."

Kane peered into the door and nodded to Wolfe. Tied to the bed, the naked victim was wearing a condom and had a gag of some sort pushed into his mouth. A blindfold covered his forehead. The man's face had turned a deep shade of blue. "Sex play gone wrong?"

"No, I don't think so. This is a homicide and we can add robbery as well; his wallet is empty." Wolfe's eyes peered at him over his face mask.

"Okay, let me take a look." Jenna shot him an inquisitive look and peered inside the door. "Oh, I see. What have you found in his personal effects? Is there anything to tie him to the Price case?"

"Yes and no." Wolfe strolled to the door with a grocery sack and held it open for her. "Chocolates and wine, condoms. His wallet and clothes are here. No cash. It could have been a hooker but if so, she wore gloves. I found no prints other than the victim's on his wallet. There are hundreds of others, far too many to consider."

"Hookers don't generally murder their clients; it's bad for business. They don't wear gloves either." Jenna sighed. "Any initial findings?"

"He has a scar on his right side that fits the description Zoe gave you of one of her attackers, but appendix operation scars are quite common. I'm not 100 percent sure but I think the killer stabbed him in his ear with something like a knitting needle. I'll give you a definite cause of death after the autopsy." He sighed. "Doing something like that would be taking BDSM a little too far but as our victim was obviously expecting sex and his wallet is empty, I suggest we look at the local hookers."

"I don't think so." Jenna cleared her throat. "I'm not aware of any who do call-outs, they all work discreetly at the Cattleman's Hotel. In my time here, we have not been able to find cause to charge one of them. I've never been able to prove they accept money for sex." She chewed on the end of her pen. "This murder is far more complex. We know this man was a clown and worked at Party Time with Amos Price. We have no indication to suggest he was involved in the pedophile ring unless Zoe can identify him. If she does then we could have a vigilante situation. Suggestions?" She lifted her concerned blue gaze to Kane. "Two murders in a week. I'm not ruling out the possibility just yet."

Kane cleared his throat. "If he is an associate of Price then I would agree. The killer could have staged the murder to keep us guessing."

"And it may not be related to Price's murder at all. I'll be interested in what Wolfe discovers during the autopsy." Jenna gave Kane an agitated look. "Suspects?"

"That depends." Kane flipped through his notes. "If we take the vigilante killer angle for now and include women molested as kids, Lizzy Harper and Angelique Booval fit the profile. Eighteen to say twenty-five, unstable due to kidnapping or other traumatic event involving a man. We have to take into account these men traveled around and could have molested kids in other towns. It's not unreasonable to believe one of the suspects traveled here to kill them."

"You mean the killer was molested by them as a kid and is seeking revenge as an adult?" Jenna tapped her bottom lip thinking. "Yeah, that makes sense."

Kane glanced at Rowley. "We need information from as long as ten years ago. Do you remember anything similar happening in town when you were a kid?"

"Yeah, I do. There is someone else in Black Rock Falls we should consider." Rowley's head bobbed. "Yeah, I remember a couple of years back hearing about one of the teachers at the elementary school having a breakdown, caused by some trauma as a kid. I'm not sure what happened. She still works here but it's common knowledge she hates men."

Kane took out his notepad. "You got a name?"

"Yeah, Miss McCarthy. I think her name is Patricia or Pattie. I'm not sure where she lives but I figure she will have a house near Stanton Forest by the college. All the teachers seem to live in that area. I hear she rarely leaves the house unless it is to teach the young kids."

"Okay. Good work." Jenna's expression brightened. "Rowley, I want you to head back to the office. Open a case file for this victim and log the interviews of the motel owner and the woman who found the body – that's a priority. After that, continue to search for cases involving child molestation or disappearance here and in other counties. Go back eight to fifteen years. Get Bradford and Walters involved in the search; split up the counties, it will be quicker. Any cats peeing on cars or domestics that come in today send out Webber. He is experienced enough to handle the smaller cases without supervision." She took a breath then blew it out, making her bangs fly off her forehead. "I'll drop my car at the office then I'm heading up the mountain again with Kane to check out the victim's residence. We might find some evidence to link him to the pedophile ring."

"Yes, ma'am." Rowley touched his hat and jogged to his cruiser.

Kane rubbed the back of his neck. "With potentially two more pedophiles on the list, if Zoe's account is correct, we'll need to find out who else is involved before the killer strikes again."

"Yeah." Jenna raised one black eyebrow. "I guess we'd better bring in the clowns."

CHAPTER FIFTEEN

Jenna chewed her fingertips in frustration. Her long-awaited day to relax had slipped into oblivion. She sipped takeout coffee and watched the countryside dash by as Kane's SUV burned up the miles. The beauty of Montana was inspirational. So many different vistas from lush pine forests to dazzling mountain views that went on forever. She liked the people, and overall, life was perfect, until a killer wandered into her town and shattered the peace.

The road ahead narrowed and rocks tumbled down the mountain-side, pinging against the doors as they drove past. Although Kane had slowed the car, a rush of fear rolled over her. The narrow dirt trail fell away to a deep ravine on one side, and the impenetrable pine trees on the other gave no space to get off the road if another car approached. As the back wheels of the SUV slid trying to gain traction and peppered the trees with rocks, Kane's concerned gaze moved over her.

"You're as white as a sheet. You okay?"

She gripped the seat. "Keep your eyes on the road. I'm fine."

"Don't worry. I'm used to driving in these conditions. My vehicle won't slide down the mountain, I promise." He flashed her a white smile. "Well, not on the way up anyway. The way down we might slip a bit." He chuckled and tapped the GPS screen. "The cabin is just around the next bend."

She gave him her best sarcastic look. "I'm so thrilled."

They turned down a wider road that had not seen a grader for a long time. Someone had placed planks of wood over the deep ruts and the dry wood creaked and groaned as they edged forward. The cabin, a small roughly built log structure with a front porch, had a rusty water tank attached to one side. A pile of firewood, complete with ax sticking out of a cutting log, appeared to have been there since settlement. Jenna gaped in amazement. "People actually live in that hovel?"

"Seems so." Kane pulled the SUV to a halt. "People like to drop off the grid and live up here, so it's not fancy."

She pointed to the roof. "Good Lord, is that a satellite dish? All the perks with none of the comfort."

"Yeah and now the communications tower is perched on top of the mountain, their phone and Wi-Fi would be better than most are getting in town." He glanced at her. "Shall I take the lead, ma'am?"

She liked the way he deferred to her seniority on the job. It had taken him some time to adjust to not being in charge. Although he gave her the utmost respect, sometimes she could almost see him chomping at the bit to take the lead. She handed him a pair of gloves then pulled on her own. "Yes, go ahead."

Standing back to allow Kane to lead the way, she waited for him to hammer on the door and announce their arrival. When no response came, she used the key Wolfe had found with the body and pushed open the door. "Sheriff's department, is anyone there?"

Jenna heard a sound like the clanking of chains and ducked away from the door, pressing her back to the rough log wall. "What was that?"

"He might have left his dog chained up in there." Kane did a turkey peek into a window, looked at her, and shook his head. "Is anyone there?"

A slight shuffling sound came from within then silence. The wind howled through the trees making the hair on the back of Jenna's neck stand on end. She moved closer to Kane. "Be careful, a shotgun blast would go straight through these walls."

"Roger that." Kane dropped down low to the ground and eased his way to the door.

The trees creaked and the breeze sent leaves spiraling around their feet. Jenna dropped her voice to a whisper. "I'm sure someone is inside. I can hear floorboards creaking."

"Unless you want me to open fire, I suggest you call out." Kane edged closer to the front stoop. "You have three seconds and I'm coming in."

"Don't shoot."

Jenna bit her lip at the sound of a terrified female voice. "It's okay. We won't hurt you. Come out with your hands up."

"I can't." A sob followed. "I'm chained to the wall."

"Holy mother of God." Kane's astonished glance met hers. "Let me take this, Jenna."

Her first instinct was to protest but Kane could shoot the feelers off an ant. She nodded. "Okay."

"Watch my back." He moved through the door, Glock in hand. "Are you alone?"

"Yes."

Jenna kept her back to the wall and Kane's footsteps thundered through the small cabin as he checked every room.

"Clear." His voice repeated the word as he moved through each room in the house.

Jenna stepped inside and gaped at the skinny teenage girl, face pale and with black circles under her eyes. The girl wore nothing but a long, tattered T-shirt bearing the name of a local beer manufacturer. In her periphery, she noticed Kane dragging a blanket out of a cupboard and heading her way. She took the blanket from him and walked toward the girl. "I'm Sheriff Jenna Alton from Black Rock Falls and this is Deputy Kane. You're safe now. What's your name?" She draped the blanket over the girl's shoulders.

"Jane Stickler." She glanced fearfully at the open door. "He'll be back soon and he don't like strangers. He won't be happy you came inside uninvited."

Adam Stickler's missing sister. "He won't be coming back today." Jenna led the girl to a chair at a scrubbed wooden table. "What's *his* name?"

Jane's shoulders slumped and she shook her head. "I don't know for sure, he made me call him 'Daddy' but he ain't my father." She swallowed hard. "I don't even know if my family is still alive."

Jenna smiled at her. "Yes, as far as I'm aware they're fine. And your brother, Adam. He lives in Black Rock Falls. Deputy Kane spoke to him recently."

"Can you take me home to see my mom? I live in Blackwater." Jane blinked. "He took me to town to see a doctor and said we could visit my mom but he didn't get the time."

Jenna opened her mouth to ask why she had not told the doctor Dorsey was holding her prisoner when Kane cleared his throat. She turned and walked with him to the other side of the room. "What is it? I need to speak with her."

"She has Stockholm syndrome." Kane's eyes flicked to the girl and back. "She has been held captive for so long she figures she belongs here, that is normal. The brain shuts down and protects them from what is really happening. She isn't afraid of me. That was the clue: Seeing strange men is normal to her. She likely has feelings for Ely as well. Some kids cry for their captors when rescued even after suffering abuse. You'll have to tread easy."

She gave him a nod and returned to Jane. "He sent us to have you see a doctor at the hospital but I promise to speak to your mom and see if she'll meet us there. Do you know where he kept the key to your manacles?"

"With the keys to his car." Jane pushed matted hair from her face.

"We have his keys." Jenna glanced at the lifeless eyes of the various elk heads hanging on the walls. The house appeared to be surprisingly clean, unlike the girl standing before her. She was pitifully thin. The skin on her bony arms had bruises, some clear indication of fingermarks, her feet and legs appeared scratched, and she had a festering sore on one ankle. Jenna had seen similar marks to the bruising on her neck on strangulation victims.

"Can I get you out of those chains?" Kane's gaze slid over the girl, his face etched with concern.

Jane leaned into Jenna and looked up at him. Jenna patted her hand. "Kane is a very gentle man; all he wants to do is set you free."

When Jane nodded, Kane moved closer and Jenna could feel her trembling against her. "Take it slow, Kane."

"Okay." Kane dropped his voice to almost a whisper and avoided eye contact with her. "I spoke to Adam recently about you. He has never stopped looking for you. I'll call him straight away and he can meet us at the hospital." Kane went through the keys then he unfastened the cuff. "There you go."

As Kane pulled the cabin apart collecting boxes of thumb drives and a computer, Jenna used her cellphone to access the driver's license image of Ely Dorsey. She held it up for the girl to see. "Is this the man who chained you up?"

Jane nodded then turned her face away. "Is he in trouble?"

"No. Can you tell me anything about him or his friends?"

The girl shook her head, sending dirty hair falling over her face. Jenna sat beside her. "How did you come to be here?"

She lifted her troubled gaze. "His friends will kill my family if I tell."

In an effort to hide her distress, Jenna took a deep breath. "No, we'll protect your family. His name is Ely Dorsey." She glanced at the girl. "We are looking for his friends." She gripped the girl's hands. "We need your help. Will you at least tell me how you met him?"

"That was a long time ago." Jane stared into the distance. "I don't remember."

"When he left, did he tell you where he was going?"

"No." Jane gave her a wary stare. "He had a new girlfriend, didn't he? That's why the others stopped coming here."

Jenna sighed. "I'm not sure. Do you remember anything else at all about the other men? Scars, tattoos?"

"One had a spider tattoo on his hand between his thumb and index finger."

"I'm done here." Kane came back into the room and Jenna noticed a flash of anger in his eyes. "There are a few chickens out back running loose. They'll survive on their own, there's a stream running through the property." He held out an evidence bag filled with pills. "I found a massive supply of contraceptive pills in the bathroom. I gather that's why he took her to the doctors. You might need to mention them to the doctor at the hospital."

"Okay. Let's go." Jenna looked at the girl. "Is there anything you want to take from the house before you leave?"

"I'm not coming back?" Jane appeared agitated. "Maybe we should leave him a note."

Jenna shot a glance at Kane. "Don't worry, we'll tell him."

CHAPTER SIXTEEN

After delivering Jane to the hospital and leaving Walters to watch over her, Kane waited for Jenna to speak briefly to Jane's brother and the doctor before returning to the office. The girl would remain in the hospital for a few days to complete tests and a mental health evaluation then return to her family. Any further interviews with her would have to wait until the doctor had cleared her later that day.

Kane glanced at Jenna on the way back to the office. "What next?"

"We are in a wait-and-see situation right now." Jenna's head bent over her notes. "I've requested another interview with Zoe and the doctor will speak to the parents shortly." She glanced at him. "While we wait for the autopsy on Dorsey, it means some grunt work. We have no other men who might be implicated in the sex ring, so we'll have to shake the murder suspects and see what falls out. One of them must be withholding information on the men involved or is the vigilante killer."

Kane drummed his fingers on the steering wheel and considered her plan. "I gather you want to find the two remaining men in the pedophile ring but how will this lead us to the killer? They could have kidnapped a dozen girls over the last ten years."

"If we find just one of them, we could use them as bait." Jenna smiled. "If the vigilante is coming for them, we'll catch her in the act."

"Okay, I guess we have no choice. Right now the vigilante is all smoke and mirrors but I suggest we keep a close eye on, Harper,

Booval and McCarthy as our three prime suspects. Where do you want to start looking for these men?" He sighed. "We can't set up a sting operation by pretending to be a young girl in one of a thousand possible chat rooms. We'll be stepping all over a possible FBI investigation and it would take too long. Predators are cautious—they would have groomed the girls for months. They might kidnap a girl but they are unlikely to risk meeting a girl they've just met online. They are aware of the traps. By the time we lure one, the vigilante will have killed the other two in the ring. Plus, we might end up with a man from another county. These men travel miles to meet up with kids."

"One of the FBI agents mentioned much the same to me on the phone the other day. We do have one lead to follow up, though. Zoe and Jane mentioned a spider tattoo; we'll start there." Jenna snapped her book shut. "I'll make some calls and get permission to re-interview Zoe. I'll talk to the parents of both girls and see if they have alibis for the time of death of both victims so we can rule them out." She flicked him a glance. "Take your lunch break now and I'll go when you get back."

Kane smiled at her. "I'll call you if I find out anything interesting." He pulled up outside the sheriff's office.

"See that you do." Jenna slipped from the seat and strolled to the office without a backward glance.

Kane headed down to Aunt Betty's Café for lunch but food was the last thing on his mind. In the space of three days, they had found two kidnapped girls and the same number of dead men. They had no suspects to arrest for the kidnapping crimes, as according to the girls, the dead men had acted alone, but they needed to find at least two other men involved in molesting the girls. *It will be like finding a needle in a haystack.*

He walked into the café, took his favorite seat by the window, then ordered his lunch from Susie Hartwig. Sipping his coffee, he mulled over the suspects and possible scenarios. The killer or killers knew the molesters' identities, which meant at one time the men involved had not been as careful as they were now. His mind wandered to his meeting with the Booval brothers. Although as mad as rabid dogs about their sister's ordeal, her kidnapper, Macgregor, had spent time in jail for the crime. They had no apparent motive to hunt down the other men unless they had reason to believe they had been involved in taking their sister. *Had she told anyone?*

A child going through the ordeal of kidnapping would be in shock and might not remember details. Angelique could well have identified Macgregor as her kidnapper and years later recognized two of the clowns working with her brothers as the other men involved. Maybe she did not want to go through another trial or believed that too much time had passed since her kidnapping to bring the other men to justice. If she had informed her brothers, it was feasible for them to take the law into their own hands to save their sister from reliving the events.

Who else on his list of suspects had a motive? Could Lizzy Harper's father tie in with this case? From what her mother told him, at least one other man was involved and the timeline fit. He would need to look deeper to find the answers.

He understood how predators worked on kids' minds. The lies they told went way past telling the child their parents had died. The kidnapper often threatened to kill the kid's family if they escaped, and if the molester held the kid for months or years, that type of programming would be difficult to break. *What would happen if one of these kids came face to face with their captor as an adult? Would they suffer a flashback then plot revenge?*

He pulled out his cellphone and accessed the case files. He meticulously read everything on the kidnapping and murder cases. Nothing seemed to overlap although he needed to locate Stewart

James Macgregor, the man who had kidnapped Angelique Booval. As the court had sealed Angelique's file, he would like to speak to her as well in case she had overheard the mention of other men. If he presented the facts to her as an adult, she might cooperate. Then again, she could have been the first girl the men had kidnapped and might have escaped before the other victims became involved.

He turned his attention to the dwindling list of suspects and wondered if Rowley had discovered similar cases in any of the other towns. Adam Stickler's alibi had checked out, so he deleted him from his list of suspects then considered the women living in town who had suffered abuse as kids. Lizzy Harper and her mother went to the top of his list. A mother and daughter seeking revenge was a distinct possibility, especially as they moved around the area frequently. He would need to speak to the schoolteacher, Pattie McCarthy, and with Jenna busy, he would have to take the rookie, Paula Bradford, with him. If Miss McCarthy had a problem with men, having a female deputy along might be of assistance.

He dropped some bills on the table then strolled back to the office. Glad to see Rowley fully in control, he sat down in his cubicle and planned his afternoon. If Angelique Booval was living with her parents in Blackwater, he would speak to Jenna later and maybe they could arrange to visit Angelique. His mind went to Jenna. With another murder, he worried about her PTSD flashbacks. If he could take her mind off the case for an hour or so, it would help, and he wondered if she would accept an invitation to dinner. Perhaps if he tied up as many loose ends as possible this afternoon, he could try to convince her to put work aside for an hour. Yes, dinner would be a good idea for a start. She had to eat. *I will take her to the Cattleman's Hotel. I'll need to book a table.*

He put that on his to-do list and, flipping open his notepad, found the number of the Clean as a Wink cleaning service and called them. When he identified himself, the person on the end of the line informed him where to find the Harpers that afternoon. He jotted down the details then went online to look up Pattie McCarthy's address. As Rowley suspected, she lived on School Road close to Stanton Forest. He took down the details then pushed to his feet and scanned the office for Bradford. He strolled to her desk and cleared his throat. "I'm going to interview a suspect." He stared into her big startled eyes and wondered how she would cope in a crisis if he scared her by speaking to her. He offered her a comforting smile. "I want you to ride shotgun."

"Yes, sir." Bradford gave him a curt nod, collected her things, and followed him to his SUV. "May I ask what case?"

Kane slid behind the wheel, waited for her to buckle up then took off down the road, lights flashing to disperse the crowd. People strolling around as if jaywalking was legal leaped back onto the sidewalk and glared at him. Once off the main street he flicked her a glance. "The murders. We have a theory that a vigilante is murdering a group of pedophiles. The killer could be taking revenge on the men who abused her as a child or it could be a family member of an abused child."

"What do we have on the pedophile ring?"

"Not much. We believe there was a group of at least four men involved, and going on the fact they kept one of the girls for eight years, we must assume the group has been active for some time. Nothing came to light from an FBI investigation into child exploitation last year after we arrested a man for child pornography. I believe these men are very smart or not hanging around chat rooms or other online forums long enough for the FBI to notice them. I think considering the time between the cases, they slipped through the net."

"How could that be possible with an ongoing FBI investigation?"

"Lack of boots on the ground." Kane grimaced. "Last count there were 346 listed sex offenders in Montana alone, which are their main priority. They have a grading system as to how dangerous they are considered. There are probably thousands of predators they haven't detected yet." He sighed. "I wondered how many kids went missing over the last ten years so contacted the National Center for Missing and Exploited Children and they told me approximately 800,000 children are reported missing each year. That's about 2,000 per week." He looked at her startled expression. "Yeah, horrific but true."

"That's terrible. What about Zoe?" Bradford looked shocked. "Didn't anyone look for her?"

Kane shook his head. "Not here, she went missing from Helena. The Blackwater records listed Jane Stickler as a runaway. I did find one local case involving Angelique Booval and investigated by the Blackwater sheriff. It led to the arrest of Stu Macgregor; he is on the register as a low-risk pedophile. The other one involved Lizzy Harper, who killed her father for molesting her."

"Okay. What do I need to know about the suspects we are interviewing?"

"They are women who suffered abuse in the last fifteen years. The first is Pattie McCarthy, a schoolteacher." Kane flicked her a glance. "I found a note on her case. It seemed the sheriff at the time was convinced she was making up a story to get attention. He failed to follow up with a medical examination. It was a botched investigation from the start. I want to know if anything really happened."

"So you need me along as a woman not as your deputy." Bradford gave him a disappointed look and dropped her gaze to her hands.

"As the women involved have issues with men, I want Miss McCarthy to feel comfortable during the interview." Slightly annoyed, he cleared his throat. "As my deputy, it will be your responsibility to ask her the questions. It is unlikely she will speak to me about such a sensitive issue."

"What do you want me to ask her?"

"First of all, ask her whereabouts between Monday through to last night. Then lead into questions about her complaint, when it occurred, how many men were involved. Does she remember any names at all?" He glanced over to see her writing in her notebook. "Tell her we found two kidnapped girls this week and we're investigating similar cases to see if they're linked. Ease into the questions. I want you to wear your earbud and mic, so I can hear you. Then if I think of anything else to ask her, I'll contact you."

"So you're not coming to the door with me?" Bradford searched his face as she attached her earbud and switched on the receiver.

He turned the car onto School Road, found the house, and pulled up outside. "I'll be close by but I don't want to frighten her." He pulled out his communication device and waved her from the car.

When Deputy Bradford knocked on the door, Kane caught sight of an athletic woman in her mid-twenties. He listened with interest as Bradford explained the reason for her visit.

"As you can imagine, we are following any possible leads to prevent this from happening to other children." Bradford's voice dropped to a confidential whisper. "Any information you could offer might save another girl from being taken."

"Really? Why come to me now?" Pattie McCarthy's voice was shrill. "No one offered to help me at the time, did they? My parents thought I was lying and so did the sheriff."

"I don't think you lied or I wouldn't be here." Bradford straightened. "Do you mind telling me about your whereabouts this week?"

"I was home most of the time. I don't go out much." Pattie sneered. "Oh, this isn't about the girls you found, is it? I watch the news. You think I had something to do with the men's bodies showing up all over town." She snorted as if in disgust. "Well, let me see, I went out on Wednesday into town to buy groceries and walked around the festival. I did see a few people I know. Let me see, Susie Hartwig at Aunt Betty's Café, will that do?"

"I'll speak to her." Bradford made a few notes. "Anyone else?"

"Not that I recall but I'm sure many people saw me in town."

"What about Saturday night?" Bradford cleared her throat. "Did you go out at all?"

"I was home alone. I don't go out on dates."

"What make of car do you drive?" Bradford looked down at her notebook.

"A Jeep." Pattie stared past her at Kane. "Do you need the earbud communication device so Deputy Kane can listen? Does he get off on hearing the lurid details?" she snorted and her lip curled. "Yes, I know your name, Deputy Kane. I don't see you taking women out on dates. Prefer little girls, do you?"

Kane turned his head, disturbed by her disgusting insinuation. He spoke into his mic. "I can't believe she teaches children with that kind of attitude. Keep asking the questions."

"Miss McCarthy, if you have a valid reason for that comment, I'm sure Sheriff Alton will be more than happy to take your complaint, but right now we need information." Bradford tossed her blonde head in an agitated manner. "You told the sheriff someone kidnapped you as a child. Can you remember how many people were involved?"

"Okay, fine, but you need to watch men like Deputy Kane."

"I'll make sure to." Bradford hunched her shoulders. "Please, Miss McCarthy, any details you can offer would be of great help."

"I remember the kidnapping like it was yesterday. A man grabbed me from my bed, dragged me out the window, and bundled me into his car." Pattie grunted in anger. "Four men abused me then one of them dropped me back inside my window. When I told my dad, he said I was having a bad dream." Her eyes blazed. "They didn't even call a doctor to examine me. My father hit me and told me he was ashamed of me." She bit down hard on her lip, leaving marks. "He took me to the sheriff's office as a punishment; he wanted him to lock me up for the night to scare me straight. No one would believe me, no one."

"I believe you. Where did the assault occur—in a house?"

"No, not a house." Pattie shook her head. "It was the Fall Festival, like now. I'm pretty sure he took me to a tent in the park. I could hear the canvas flapping."

The hair on the back of Kane's neck stood on end. "Ask her if they wore masks."

Bradford relayed the question and he waited for Pattie to reply. "They put a bag over my head and gagged me but I remember things about them. The smell of them, for instance, but it is too late to do anything now. It would be my word against theirs, wouldn't it?"

"Maybe not. Can you remember anything significant at all? Any small thing might help us to find these men."

"Enough questions. I am not going to rake this up again. It gives me nightmares. I've been in therapy for years." Pattie shook her head and backed away. "That's all I'm going to say. I have to go. I have an appointment in town."

"Just one more thing. How long ago did this happen?"

"Fourteen years ago this week." Pattie's gaze moved back to Kane in the car, and if looks could kill, he would be toast.

He barked out a question. "Ask her if one had a spider tattoo on his hand and tell her two of them have been murdered. Watch for her reaction."

When Bradford relayed the question, from Kane's viewpoint he could see the color drain from Pattie's face.

She snarled her reply. "I don't remember but I'm glad they are dead. They got what they deserved."

CHAPTER SEVENTEEN

Meddling cops. She strolled down the main street in an effort to cool her anger. The sheriff was obviously arrowing in on victims and not concentrating on catching the monsters. She hated crowds, hated men, but had to act "normal" to rid the world of pedophiles. She strolled past the Community Hall and forced her lips to smile at the old women selling their wares on the white-linen-covered stalls, then wove her way through the hordes of kids trailing balloons. Kids she liked just fine, but men she could not trust.

With the Black Rock Falls County Sheriff's Department crawling all over the mountains, the next monster would have to wait. She needed to take her time with him, and would have to distract the sheriff away from the area. Killing a monster took time. As they liked to play games with the little girls they violated, she would return the favor. The previous day in a chat room with him, he told her he wanted to play a special game with her and she willingly agreed. She smiled into the sunshine. *I guess a dying man deserves a final wish.*

Sipping her takeout coffee, she stared at the young girls moving through the crowds enjoying the festival, oblivious to the threat close by. Little did they know, like an eagle spotting a rabbit, a destroyer of innocence could swoop down and steal them away in seconds.

Predators believed they were invincible, untraceable, and safe, but she would find them and she would kill them.

She would kill them all.

CHAPTER EIGHTEEN

Jenna's cellphone chimed. She stared at the unidentified caller ID and leaned back in her office chair. "Sheriff Alton."

"This is Doctor Allan. You'll be pleased to know Zoe is well enough to speak to you this afternoon. Zoe's parents are more than happy for you to speak to their daughter but I must insist you keep the question time to a limit. You should be aware shock can creep up on a person."

She sighed with relief. "Thank you. I can assure you, I will be most careful. I am coming alone."

"I'll let them know."

"How long before I can talk to Jane?"

"It is early days, Sheriff. Her parents have just arrived. I'll be in touch when she is available."

"Sure, thank you. I'm on my way now." After disconnecting, she called Kane and relayed the news. "Did you get anything out of Pattie McCarthy?"

"Not much. She can't identify the men who took her."

"Okay, I have to go, we'll talk later. Have a chat with the Booval brothers again and find out if their sister is willing to speak to us."

"I was heading that way. Good luck with the interview."

Jenna smiled. "Thanks."

Twenty minutes later, she parked her car in the police and emergency services parking lot at the hospital and made her way inside. She rode the elevator up to the restricted ward. The hospital smell brought back a wave of bad memories from her near-death experience the previous winter and she fought the need to turn around and leave. *I have to stop acting like an idiot and help the kids.*

She found Zoe scrubbed clean and with her hair tied in a ponytail, sitting up in bed looking quite bewildered as her siblings dashed around the room playing with latex glove balloons. A woman stood when she entered, and as she approached, Jenna could see she had been crying. "Mrs. Channing? I'm Sheriff Alton. I've come to have a few words with Zoe if that's okay?"

"Yes, yes of course. I can't thank you enough for bringing Zoe home to us." Mrs. Channing waved hopelessly at the other children. "My husband went to buy coffee. He'll be back soon and will take the children outside."

"Mom." Zoe's small hands gripped the sheets. "I want to speak to Sheriff Alton alone."

"I really should be here." Mrs. Channing patted Zoe's arm. "You need your mother's support."

"I don't want to speak to you about what happened and I don't want Dad listening either." Zoe's eyes filled with tears. "*Please*, Mom. I need to do this on my own."

Jenna smiled at the anxious woman. "I'll be five minutes or so. I won't upset her, it's just routine questions."

"Okay, I'll be right outside the door." Mrs. Channing ushered the noisy kids into the hallway, shutting the door behind her.

"I need to know something." Zoe's frightened gaze raked her face. "When you catch the men, my dad said I would have to be brave and tell the judge everything that happened. I'm not sure I can do that in front of everyone." A tear welled up in her eye and ran down one cheek.

Jenna pulled up a chair and sat down. "No, you won't be in front of everyone if it gets to court." She took a deep breath. "It will be what we call a closed court, and if you need to testify, it will be just you in a room on your own with a camera. No one outside the court will even see your face or hear your name." She sighed. "Didn't your dad tell you we close the court to protect you?"

"He did say something but I don't want to talk to him right now. Why are you here?"

Jenna took out a notepad and her cellphone from her purse then turned on the voice recorder. "You mentioned the men on the weekends. During the week, did you sleep in the cellar or with Amos?"

"Amos." Zoe's cheeks pinked and she stared at her hands.

She needed to move away from the subject and smiled to reassure her. "Who cleaned the cellar after the men left?"

"They did before they left."

"That's really helpful." Jenna made a few notes. "Did Amos let you shower at all?"

"Yes, he wouldn't let me to waste the hot water during the week but at the weekends he let me to shower and wash my hair with nice soap." She sniffed. "He locked me in the cage all day."

Jenna tried to keep her voice from showing her anger. "If I show you pictures of three men, can you tell me if you recognize any of them?"

"Okay." Zoe straightened as if steeling herself.

Opening her phone, Jenna showed her a compilation of three men: Amos Price, Ely Dorsey, and a picture of a stranger taken at random from the files. "Do you recognize the man that kidnapped you?"

"Yes, that is Amos. I'm not sure but that one—" Zoe pointed to Ely "—has a brown mark on his neck the same as one of the others."

Goosebumps rose on Jenna's flesh. "Good girl. You have been very helpful." She noticed the girl brighten. "You don't have to be scared of Amos or the man with the mark on his neck any longer. They are both dead."

"I hope Deputy Kane shot them dead with his gun." Zoe smiled.

Deciding not to explain, Jenna turned off the recorder and stood. "That's all for now, Zoe. You have been very helpful." She patted her arm and headed for the door. "I'll send in your parents."

Outside in the hallway, she approached the parents. "We know the man responsible for kidnapping Zoe."

"Give me his name, I'll tear him apart." Mr. Channing's hands balled into fists.

"His name was Amos Price." Jenna cleared her throat. "We found him deceased. It was when we checked his cabin we discovered Zoe. She gave me a positive ID. He was the man responsible." She swallowed the bile in her throat. "Although Zoe refuses to discuss her abduction, you should be aware we know four men were involved. We found a second man murdered this morning and she identified a distinctive birthmark on his neck." She looked at Mr. Channing. "May I ask where you and your wife have been since we found Zoe?"

"Here." Mr. Channing blanched. "The hospital gave us the room next door. Apart from visiting the café for meals, we haven't left her side."

She eyed him critically. "You do realize I have a deputy on duty."

"Well then he will prove we have not left the building. He checked us out before we were allowed to come near her." Mr. Channing shook his head. "Haven't we been through enough without you accusing us of murder?"

Jenna lifted her chin and met his gaze head on. "I am just doing my job, Mr. Channing. I doubt the hospital will keep Zoe for long. Do you have adequate security to protect her?"

"I fully intend to take my family back to Helena the second she is released, which I'm told will be later today." Mr. Channing bristled. "You don't think for one second I would leave her or any of my other children anywhere near Black Rock Falls, do you?"

"Well, I have your cellphone number and I will contact you personally and update you when necessary. Thank you for your cooperation." She turned and headed toward the elevator.

She got out her cellphone and called Kane. "Zoe gave me a positive ID for Price as her abductor. She confirmed Price cleaned her up for his friends on weekends and they scrubbed the place down before they left."

"Did she ID Ely Dorsey?"

"Not exactly but she did recognize the birthmark on his neck. The chances of two men having the same mark would be remote. That's good enough for me. I hope we find their associates soon. I'd like to close this case." She sighed. "I'm heading home. I'll work from there, you keep interviewing suspects."

"Roger that."

She disconnected. *I will catch you soon, you bastards.*

CHAPTER NINETEEN

Kane swung the SUV around and headed back to town to speak to the Booval brothers again, wondering how cooperative they would be about asking their sister to speak about her ordeal. With his mind locked on the case, he had not said more than a couple of words to the new deputy. Her references from the Helena Sheriff's Department had been outstanding but he had yet to see if she would be an asset to the team.

He glanced at Bradford, who had not stopped gawking at him since she got in the car. "You did a great job questioning Miss McCarthy. She isn't the most pleasant person. I'm keeping her on the list of suspects. Nothing she said convinced me she is innocent. What vibe did you get from her?"

"Not much. She was pretty aggressive and the attack on you was unexpected."

"Many abused kids see men as a threat, and her response is quite common." Kane shrugged. "Once the crime was reported, she would have told her story many times. It would have been hard on a young kid."

"I guess so." Bradford bent her head over her notes. "It was great having you in my ear prompting the questions."

But you won't make a profiler if you fail to notice body language. He sighed. Making small talk was the last thing on his mind but not wanting to appear rude or aloof, he smiled at her. "What made you ask for a transfer to Black Rock Falls?"

"I think the chances of promotion are better in a smaller office, plus working with a superior team is a good way to learn." Bradford returned his smile with a flash of straight white teeth. "I'm not trying to brown-nose you but I heard what happened last summer and wanted to be part of the team. Webber told me about your profiling skills, and working alongside a deputy who is also the ME can only improve my skills." She cleared her throat. "I was hoping to be partnered with you to gain experience."

He kept his gaze on the road. Moving into town, the traffic slowed to a crawl. "Well, technically you're partnered with Deputy Rowley. You will ride with the sheriff or me as needed. Most times, I'm on call-outs with the sheriff." He glanced over to see her face drop. "We prefer to ease our rookies into the way of things here but I'll take you to the practice range once a week and I'm sure Rowley will introduce you to his dojo. The more hand-to-hand combat you can practice, the better. We have to deal with some rough types."

"Okay." She brightened. "I would appreciate some extra training. I heard you shot a man holding a knife to the sheriff's throat last winter. Wasn't that a risky thing to do?" She gave him an accusing glare. "You could have killed her."

"Not likely." Kane pulled the vehicle to the curb. "I never miss."

He found the Booval brothers in the same area of the park giving pony rides to a line of kids. Parents stood patiently ignoring the *eau de* horse and swarming flies as they waited for their child's turn. Glancing at Bradford, he indicated with his chin toward the clowns. "Wait here and log the interview in your notebook while it's fresh in your mind. I need a word with the Booval brothers." He strolled in their direction and walked beside Claude Booval. Smiling at the little girl perched on top of the pony he lowered his voice. "May I have a quick word?"

"What is it now?" Claude Booval's red-and-white spotted shoulders slumped.

Kane ignored his hostility and kept in step with him, moving carefully around the piles of horse dung lining the circular path around the park. "Do you think Angelique will speak to the sheriff? We have a few leads and she might remember something significant."

"I doubt it. She doesn't like to speak about it at all but I know something of interest. Our family has been clowns for generations, so she has no need to fear clowns, but since it happened, she will not have a clown costume in the house. This is why my brother and I left Blackwater and moved to Black Rock Falls to prevent her distress. She is here today visiting a friend but she won't come near us in costume. We will meet her later without the paint."

Kane pushed a little harder, but aware of the child on the pony, he kept his words ambiguous. "Her information might save the same thing happening again."

"Okay, I will ask her and if she agrees, I will call you." He let out a long sigh. "I have your card."

Kane smiled. "Thanks. Monday would be good if that suits?" He patted the pony then strolled back to Bradford. "Next stop, I'm dropping into the real estate office. I want to speak to Mr. Davis or Alison Saunders, his assistant. We can walk from here, it will be quicker."

People on the street stepped aside to give him access to the real estate office. He took in the clean windows and new listings posted in neat containers and smiled. Old Mr. Davis did not have the attention to detail Alison offered. He pushed open the door, surprised to find the usual heavy odor of cigar smoke replaced with a citrus bouquet. One thing remained the same: Mr. Davis sat behind the main desk staring at his computer, but he could see Alison Saunders speaking to a client in the back room.

"Ah, Deputy Kane, anyone been murdered today?" Davis's mouth twitched into a grimace. "It's not good for business, you know?"

Kane straightened. "I'm sure it's not too good for the victims either." He cleared his throat. "Just one question. Are all your master keys accounted for, and where in town do you normally have them cut?"

"Every key is signed in and out." Davis took a book out of his drawer and opened it on the desk. "Here." He prodded the page with the tip of a pudgy finger. "The keys are cut at the hardware store but we haven't lost one in over five years."

"How does it work? I mean, different houses can't have the same type of lock, can they?" Bradford's brow creased.

"All the locks are changed for any houses we sell or agree to lease." Davis smiled at her, displaying yellowing teeth. "Then we have a master key for all the properties. When a new owner takes residence, they receive their own unique set of keys. Once they use their key, the master key no longer works. Amazing but true."

Kane pulled out his cellphone. "Do you mind if I take some pictures of the book? I'd like to know the people who had keys over the last couple of months."

"Be my guest."

Kane used his cellphone camera to record the pages then straightened and smiled. "How is Alison working out?"

"She is an asset to the business." Davis gave him a knowing smile. "Pretty, isn't she? I think Deputy Rowley likes her too. He drops by all the time to speak to her. He's like a lost puppy."

Kane raised a brow. "Really? I'll have to speak to him about wasting time."

"I see you have a new assistant as well." Davis flicked a glance over Bradford.

Annoyed at the man's chauvinist regard for women, he narrowed his gaze. "Yes, this is Deputy Bradford, she has joined the team."

He glanced at her and, seeing her discomfort, decided to remove her from the situation. "If you would prefer to wait outside for me. I won't be long."

"Yes, sir." Bradford gave him a relieved look as she pulled open the door and strolled into the sunshine.

He cleared his throat. "Does Alison manage all of Rockford's houses?"

"Yes, and more. She is a good worker and sold two properties last week."

Kane placed one hand on the door handle. "She does seem efficient. That's all I need, thank you for your time." He swung open the door and walked to Bradford's side. "What a disrespectful jerk. You okay?"

"Yeah, I'm fine. Thanks for getting me out of there. I hate men like him."

Kane took in her pale face and pinched expression. "Maybe we need to take a break."

"A coffee would be bliss." She smiled at him. "I'm not hungry."

The hardware store was opposite. "Okay, I'm going to the hardware store." He pulled out his wallet and handed her some bills. "We'll need to find the Harpers and it might take some time. Do you want to slip over to Aunt Betty's Café and grab us a coffee? Flat white with four sugars for me. If you wait outside, I'll go grab the car and pick you up."

"Sure."

He watched her disappear into the crowd and called Jenna. "Hey, it's me."

"What's up?" Jenna yawned. "No more bodies, I hope?"

"No more bodies." Kane smiled. "I thought you might like to have dinner out tonight. I have a reservation for a table tonight at eight at the Cattleman's Hotel." When she said nothing, he drew a deep breath. "We both have to eat and I need to discuss the case with you."

"*Okay. Why not?*"

"Great! I'll pick you up at seven thirty."

"*Sure. I'm heading over to see Wolfe and attend the Dorsey autopsy, then I'm going home. I'll bring you up to speed with the post. Rowley is locking up. Catch you later.*" The line went dead.

Kane caught a break in the traffic and darted across the road. The bell on the top of the hardware store door chimed as he entered. He glanced around at the old-world-style interior with a variety of goods for sale. The place could not have changed since prohibition. The slight odor of paint and chemicals brought back memories of shopping with his father. As he strolled to the counter, an elderly man tottered out from the back. He wore round spectacles and his long black eyebrows curled up, giving him the appearance of an owl.

"Afternoon."

"What can I do for you, Deputy Kane?"

"I wondered if you keep a record of the keys you cut for people."

"Nope, can't say that I do." The old man rubbed his long nose. "Too many to keep a record, three maybe four this week." He lifted cloudy blue eyes to his face. "My son is a locksmith. He does the work now and is cutting keys all the time from his van."

Kane blew out a sigh and tapped the counter with his fingers. "Do you sell pesticides containing nicotine sulfate?"

The old man waved at a shelf crammed with bottles. "There are quite a few brands. What do you need it for?"

"Oh, it's not for me." Kane let his gaze drift over the bottles. "Are you required to keep a list of purchasers?"

"Nope." The storekeeper gave him a concerned look. "I do for rat poison and a few other dangerous chemicals. I have a book and they have to produce a current ID, but that stuff is used in gardens most times and the bottles carry warnings." He sighed. "We sell a fair few bottles—not sure when I sold the last one, maybe a few days ago, or maybe last week? I'm not sure."

So, it's readily available. Kane touched his hat and turned to the door. "Okay, thanks for your help."

He moved down the street and paused to purchase some cakes from one of the stalls. As he waited for his change, he caught sight of a magician making animals out of balloons, surrounded by kids. The crowd parted and a woman emerged. He recognized the pale face of Pattie McCarthy strolling by. He checked the time and made a note in his book. *Hmm, she sure isn't acting like someone scared of crowds.*

CHAPTER TWENTY

Jenna stuffed some cookies into her mouth, jumped in her car and headed to the new ME's office. She entered the building using her swipe card and headed down the cool white passageways until she came to the pathology laboratory, knocking on the door as she entered. Wolfe sat at a computer and his assistant, a young pathology graduate named Steve, was preparing tissue samples. "Am I too late for the post?"

"Just a little but I haven't finished yet, so I can go over my findings with you." Wolfe's gaze slid over her then he brushed a few crumbs from the sleeve of her shirt. "Just eaten? I'm glad you have a strong stomach."

Jenna shrugged. "I'll be fine."

"Okay." Wolfe stood and led the way into the morgue. "I have a cause of death and I've found a few other interesting clues."

The room resembled an operating theater apart from the rows of drawers to store corpses set into two of the walls. The air was chilly and the smell of dead bodies and cleaning chemicals hung in the air. On a long aluminum bench lay what remained of Ely Dorsey after the autopsy.

She moved closer to Wolfe. "What do you have?"

"As I thought, the cause of death was a puncture wound through the left ear and into the brain." He pointed to a specimen. "If you look at the cross-section of the brain, I would say death was instantaneous."

Jenna peered at the slice of human tissue in the petri dish and nodded. "I see. Was it painful? I don't recall anyone complaining of hearing screaming."

"Yeah, it would have been extremely painful." Wolfe pointed one gloved finger to Ely's mouth. "See the marks on his cheek? The tips of fingers caused the bruising. He had a pair of socks stuffed into his mouth, and the killer pressed down with a great deal of force with the left hand then thrust the knitting needle or perhaps a meat skewer into his ear. I'm leaning toward the latter. I would say from the position of the marks, the killer was straddling him at the time. The killer was dressed as well. I found a few obscure filaments of denim stuck to the condom he was wearing at the time of death."

She stared at the body and her mind went into overdrive. Her time spent in the vice squad in her other life had taught her many things, and one of them was that many people enjoyed unusual sexual fetishes. Whatever a person craved there was someone out there willing to accept payment to satisfy the most perverted needs. "I thought this case was connected to a pedophile ring but now I'm not so sure. This man looks as if he had a date for some rough sex, maybe with a dominatrix. From what I saw in the motel, the killer blindfolded him at some time and tied him up. If he paid for rough sex, he would not be alarmed when she covered his mouth."

"Do you have reason to believe this killer is female?" Wolfe looked at her over his face mask. "I admit the fingertips are small, but a number of men have small fingertips as well." He sighed. "Then there is the handprint on the cheek. I believe the killer slapped him, and as his body goes into rigor, the print has become more evident. Can you see it is a small hand? It could be female."

Jenna walked around the body. "I think so. Going on the chocolates and wine, I'm leaning toward a hooker or a kinky sex date."

"It points to that but I'm not convinced." Wolfe met her gaze. "I think your instincts were right the first time. I think the killer is the same person who murdered Price. Both crime scenes stink of a predator. The gifts, for instance; the majority of predators arrested for luring kids to places with the intention of having sex have a bag of gifts with them."

Jenna chewed on her bottom lip, staring at the body. If the men knew each other, her assumption of a vigilante killer was becoming a reality. She glanced up at Wolfe. "Did you remove the blindfold on scene?"

"No, it was on his forehead when I arrived."

"Then I'm going with the vigilante theory, and the removal of the blindfold is crucial evidence. I figure she wanted to see his eyes as she killed him." She stared at Wolfe. "Now all we have to do is figure out who she is."

CHAPTER TWENTY-ONE

Kane moved through the crowd on the way to the park and headed for the magician working the street. The man was not wearing gloves and did not have a spider tattoo but he needed to ID him. He waited for an opportune moment and tapped him on the shoulder.

The man turned slowly and small black eyes moved over his face. "Is there a problem?"

"I'd like your name." Kane pulled out his notebook and pen. "Are you with Party Time?"

A relieved look passed over those black eyes and the magician nodded.

"I am, and I'm licensed. My name is Stu Macgregor."

Kane stared at him in disbelief. He knew Macgregor was classed as a low-risk sex offender in Montana but was surprised the local council had issued him a license to be anywhere near kids. "Really, show it to me?"

"I'm rehabilitated, certified. I haven't offended for seven years. I agreed to chemical castration so I could continue working in a restricted capacity. In any case, how could I do anything wrong with all these people around?" Macgregor glared at him then unzipped his costume, dug into a pocket, and thrust it at him.

Kane examined the documents. Macgregor's license restricted him to public street performances. Attached to it was a notice giving his classification as a low-grade sex offender. He shook his head in disbelief; it seemed every state and town council had a different way of dealing with pedophiles. "Okay." He thrust the paperwork back at him.

"I did my time and you are hassling me for no good reason."

"I'll do more than that if any kids go missing from my town." Kane eyeballed him. "I'm watching you." He turned and strolled toward his vehicle.

As he made his way to pick up Bradford, he wondered if there was a connection between Stewart James Macgregor and Pattie McCarthy. The age seemed to be right but getting information out of Miss McCarthy would be like getting blood out of stone.

He double-parked outside Aunt Betty's Café, much to the annoyance of the cars behind him, and Bradford jumped into the passenger seat, coffees in hand. He took the cardboard carry container from her and deposited the cups in his console. "Thanks."

"I asked Susie Hartwig if she remembers seeing Miss McCarthy in town but she can't be sure with the hundreds of people she has served during the festival. She does remember seeing her on Saturday evening around six; she stopped by for a meal."

Kane scratched his cheek. "So Pattie McCarthy was lying about staying home."

"Looks like it. Now what?" Bradford glanced at him.

"Next on my list is Lizzy Harper."

"I know about her. She stabbed her father to death and served jail time." Bradford's gaze moved over Kane's face. "Why would you suspect her?"

"She was in a juvenile detention center for three years and had her son in there." Kane reached for his coffee and took a sip, keeping his eyes on the road ahead. "I have a gut feeling there were more men involved in her case than she told the court. She claimed to have stabbed her father because he was constantly abusing her. Problem is, the boy she claimed was fathered by him belongs to someone else.

As she was fourteen at the time and her mother helps her raise the kid, I wonder if Lizzy finally told her about the other men. They could be taking out the pedophiles one at a time."

"And if they're not the killers, then you figure they might know the names of the men involved in the pedophile ring."

Kane nodded. "Exactly." He turned the SUV around and headed toward a cluster of small landholdings on the outskirts of town. "They are working on two houses this afternoon. Let's see what we can find out."

He drove to the first address on the list but as their work vehicle was not out front, he started to back out of the driveway, stopping when the front door opened.

"Someone is home after all." Bradford's mouth curled into a smile. "It looks like the mother. Maybe she'll be easier to talk to."

Kane slid from the seat. The woman standing at the door wearing a thin cotton dress, apron, and a pair of kitchen gloves eyed him with suspicion. He strolled toward her with Bradford close behind. "I'm Deputy Kane and this is Deputy Bradford. We're looking for Mrs. Harper and her daughter Lizzy."

"I'm Rosemarie Harper. Lizzy had an appointment in town but she should be back soon. What do you want? I've already told you more than I should have."

"I appreciate your help, ma'am, but I have a few more questions." Kane pulled out his notebook and pen. "I believe you and your daughter cleaned the property at 3 Maple Lane?"

"Yes, but that was a week ago last Friday afternoon."

"So I've been told." He observed how nervous she appeared and stepped back. "So where were you this week?"

"We've been cleaning all of Rockford's houses for the real estate office, so we've been all over the last couple of weeks." She gave a nervous shrug. "They would have a list."

"Okay, what about Friday night? Did you or Lizzy go out for any reason?"

"Lizzy is always in and out, she hates being cooped up in the house." Mrs. Harper sighed. "She went into town for a couple of hours. She wanted to have a look around at the stalls and pick up some takeout. I remember she was gone for quite some time. She said she had a long wait at Aunt Betty's due to the festival. Why?"

Kane made a few notes in his book. "We found a kidnapped child in a cabin in the mountains. The man involved is Amos Price. Have you heard the name? Could he have been involved in the incident involving Lizzy and her father some years back? Did Lizzy ever mention anyone else?"

"No. There wasn't anyone else involved the day Pete died. Lizzy waited for him to come home that night and killed him." She glared at him. "Don't look at me like that. She never said a word. Yes, I should have known, should have seen something, but it happened on their weekends away. My husband used to take her fishing with him." She bit her bottom lip. "Lizzy hated fishing but he insisted she do outdoor activities and would spank her if she refused to go with him."

"Has she ever said why she didn't tell you something was wrong?" Bradford flicked Kane a glance as if asking his permission.

"Not in so many words but the truth came out in the trial." Mrs. Harper's eyes hardened. "A bit too late for me to do anything to help her after she stabbed him to death." She wet her lips. "My husband threatened her. If she mentioned one word of their secret, he would kill me."

Sick to his stomach, Kane pushed on. "Are the names Ely Dorsey or Stewart Macgregor familiar to you? Could they have been friends of your husband?"

"Why?"

Kane observed her face and the way her eyes blinked. "Just answer the question."

"I know all about Stu Macgregor. My husband loved magic tricks and he made friends with a magician by the name of Stu. It was sometime after he died I discovered Stu is the man who went to jail for kidnapping the Booval girl over in Blackwater." Mrs. Harper placed one hand over her mouth. "Oh my God, was he involved with my Lizzy as well? There had to be another man but Lizzy refuses to speak about it." She glanced up as the sound of a car engine came down the road. "There she is now but don't expect her to open up to you. She will only get angry."

Kane rubbed his chin. "Angry, huh?"

The van pulled up beside Kane's SUV and a young woman stared at him open-mouthed. She slid out of the door, collected a number of takeout boxes, and walked toward her mother. Kane moved closer to Bradford and dropped his voice to just above a whisper. "If she is hostile toward men, you might have to question her instead."

"Okay."

"Is something wrong? What are you doing here, Deputy Kane?" Lizzy Harper's eyes flashed with anger. "Mom, what's going on?"

"Nothing to worry about. I'm sure Deputy Kane will explain." Mrs. Harper's agitated demeanor spoke volumes.

"Well?" Lizzy stood, hands balled on her hips, and glared at him.

Kane kept his distance but met her gaze head on. "May I speak to you in private, or would you prefer to speak to Deputy Bradford?"

"Okay. I know you will use any excuse to make me break my parole. I'm not stupid. I'll talk to you over by your car." Lizzy thrust the takeout into her mother's hands then strode away, back straight and head high.

He followed and waited for her to turn around. "Miss Harper, this is not about your parole. We are trying to discover the names of a group of men who kidnapped and abused a twelve-year-old girl."

"How the hell should I know anything about a group of pedophiles? In case you missed the news, I killed my father."

Kane cleared his throat. "I don't think you are telling me the whole story, Miss Harper. I believe our latest victim's situation was much like yours. We know your father took you to his fishing cabin to abuse you."

"That's not a secret." Lizzy glanced toward her mother and grimaced. "I'm sure she knew but she is weak and every time I tried to tell her she'd shut me down." She glared at him. "Don't come over all social worker on me and ask me why I didn't tell a teacher or someone: I was ashamed, that's why. He made me feel like shit, like I was nothing, dirty. No one would listen to me so I had to deal with him myself."

Kane leaned against the car, taking a casual pose in an effort to put her at ease. "Was it just him or did he have a few friends visit while you were there?"

"Why?" Her eyes flashed dangerously and if she had been a rattlesnake, he would be dead.

"The girl we found told us she was held in the mountains and men would visit at the weekends." He noticed the color drain from her face, and her agitation. "We need to stop these animals before they grab another kid off the street."

She shrugged and looked away.

"Miss Harper, I know this is hard for you but did your father place you in the same situation?" He took out his notepad and flipped through the pages. "We found Amos Price murdered then Ely Dorsey both had kidnapped girls at their homes. I know these men are involved in a pedophile ring. Do these names mean anything to you?"

"No. Oh shit, I know what this is about; I take it my mother told you my son isn't my father's child. So now you want all the dirty little details. You men are all the same." Lizzy pushed both hands through her silky hair and lifted her chin. "I don't have to tell you anything. Yeah, I killed my pervert of a father and did my time. Now unless you want to charge me, I have work to do."

"Fine." Kane rubbed his chin. "But the longer we have to look for the rest of these men, the more chance there is of them snatching another child." He inclined his head. "As a matter of interest, as your son had a DNA test, I can obtain a court order to check it against our victims. If we get a match, you do realize I could arrest you on suspicion of murder?"

"Really?" Lizzy lifted her dimpled chin and smiled at him in an unhinged way. "It sounds like he deserved to die. The problem with you, Deputy Kane, is you are no different from any other man who has questioned me. You want me to tell you all the disgusting things they did to me so you can fantasize about it later." She held up a hand to prevent his reply. "Arrest me or leave me the hell alone." She turned and stomped back toward her mother.

The disgusting things "they" did to her. Her Freudian slip gave him all the information he needed.

CHAPTER TWENTY-TWO

That evening Jenna stared at Dave Kane over the table at the Cattle-man's Hotel restaurant. Filled to capacity, she had had to squeeze past people to get to her seat. She could not help but notice the admiring glances Kane received from just about every woman who walked by, and the way he ignored them. She had to admit, he did look suave in a dark blue suit with his hair neatly combed rather than plastered to his head from his cowboy hat. He smelled good too.

"Do I have food in my teeth?" He raised one black eyebrow then smiled. "Or does that look mean something else?"

They had become close friends in the last year and it was good to relax off duty with him and not be the sheriff for a short while. She chuckled at his bemused expression. "Maybe." She sighed. "I like this, what we have. I've never had a close friend quite like you before."

"I'm glad we can be normal after hours as well." Kane winced. "I have to admit, at first, not running things was difficult but I adapt pretty well."

She chuckled. "You certainly do. I haven't had to take you out back of the barn and teach you a lesson once."

"Uh-huh." Kane flashed a white smile at her. "Even my dad wasn't game enough to try that means of punishment with me." He cleared his throat. "I was fully grown at fourteen."

She dropped her voice. "Do you miss them, your parents and family since you moved way out here?"

Kane's face took on a thoughtful look.

"More than you could imagine but I guess I'm preaching to the converted."

At once, she regretted intruding on his privacy and nodded. "I miss friends but I lost my parents before I signed up for my last gig." She sighed. "There's no going back, is there?"

"I would without a second thought if I could do something useful." He narrowed his gaze at her. "I'm sure you understand my reasoning?"

She understood his carefully disguised conversation only too well and cleared the lump in her throat. It didn't take a genius to know Kane would vanish from existence if offered the chance to take down the people who murdered his wife. "Yeah, I do, and if you plan on going to a *reunion*, I'm going with you."

"As my date?" Kane gave her a long, considering stare. "Maybe."

Picking up her glass of wine, she sipped, allowing the rich-bodied flavor to spill over her tongue. She needed to change the conversation before the evening was a total failure. "I know you are dying to talk about the case. Since you arrived on my doorstep this evening, you've had a smug smile on your face."

"Really? Hmm, I must be losing my edge." He sipped his pop and his blue gaze slid over her face. "Bradford rode shotgun with me today to question a few suspects. She did very well for a rookie."

"That's good." Jenna smiled. "So, let's cut to the chase. What did you discover?"

"Not much." Kane shrugged. "Truth is I wanted to discuss the interview with Lizzy Harper with you."

"Then discuss it before you blow a gasket."

"First of all, her mother mentioned she was out for some time on Friday evening, apparently getting takeout. We'll need to check with Davis at the real estate office and find out where the pair of them were working this week."

"Okay, so what did Lizzy Harper say?"

"She didn't say much at all, mainly put all men down as pigs, but she did let it slip that more men were involved." Kane's lips curled into a satisfied smile. "I didn't push for more information but now she has given us a motive to obtain a court order for her son's DNA results. We'll be able to discover if one of our victims is his biological father."

Jenna leaned forward. "Really?"

"Yeah, and her mother identified Stewart Macgregor as a friend of her husband as well, so likely he was involved."

"Great, I'll get the paperwork underway for the court orders. I hope that's all because my brain needs a rest." She sighed. "Dinner with you tonight is a luxury; I hardly get time to eat lately."

"It's good to take an hour to think; we're not machines." Kane huffed out a sigh. "These cases are horrific and you've covered every angle for now. The suspects in the girls' abductions are dead and we have little to go on to find their killers. If the DNA profile from one of the victims matches Lizzy's son, we'll have a motive."

"Okay, I'll delegate. Rowley's on duty with Webber on Monday. They'll keep searching for associates of our murder victims, and providing we get the court order, I'll ask Wolfe to run a check of the boy's DNA against our DNA database as well. There was a rape case before I arrived here and many of the men volunteered their DNA. We might fluke a match."

"Let's hope so." Kane grimaced. "I'm convinced the group of predators is bigger than we thought. We need to catch these assholes."

Disturbed by the implications, Jenna placed her glass on the table. "I've seen terrible things in my life but this beats all." She lifted her chin. "It plays on my mind twenty-four seven. I can't sleep so it makes it difficult to follow the shrink's recommendation and turn off for a while to prevent the flashbacks kicking in again. This information is so disturbing. Have any feel-good movies at your place to lull me to sleep?"

"Yeah, I'll find something to cheer you up." He waved at the waiter for the check. "If you want to get away for an hour, I'm going to see a couple of horses in the morning. I said I'd try and drop by around ten unless we get dragged out to another damn murder."

The one thing she liked about David Kane was his gentle side. When they were alone, his tough persona relaxed and she could laugh with him. It was nice to put the job aside for a few minutes and be herself. She smiled. "We should be on the case but unless Wolfe and Rowley come up with anything new, I guess we could grab an hour. I do need time to clear my head."

"It's harder when kids are involved. Trust me, Wolfe will be working on those laptops all night and you deserve a time out." He handed the waiter his credit card and signed the bill then looked at her. "We'll have fun tomorrow but I guess we'll have sore muscles on Monday. I haven't ridden for years."

She laughed. "Me either. Maybe you should add a hot tub to your list of essentials."

"That's a thought." He took the credit card from the waiter and pushed to his feet. "I'll look into it."

Jenna gaped at him. *Just how rich are you?*

They walked out into the balmy night and made their way to the parking lot. A light breeze carried the scent of roses from the tubs set each side of the entrance to the hotel. When his warm fingers cupped her elbow, the small touch surprised her, as he had not touched her intimately since the night he cuddled her a few months ago. She doubted anyone would see them as they walked between the rows of parked cars, and she leaned into him, enjoying the hard muscular arm pressing against her bare flesh. The comfortable friendship they had established suited her well. He complemented her in so many ways, respected her at work, and understood her demons.

As they reached the car, Kane's cellphone rang. He gave her an exasperated look and reached inside his pocket.

"David Kane." His expression changed to alarm and he held up one finger then put his phone on speaker. "Who is this?"

A distorted voice came through the speakers, sending Jenna's teeth on edge.

"Why do you protect pedophiles? Don't bother making up excuses. I know getting all the dirty little details from their victims turns you on."

"I can assure you—" Kane flicked Jenna a worried glance.

"Sure you can. Men like you 'love' kids, don't they? Love them to death most times. I am ridding the world of the scum and you are protecting them. Stop getting in my way or you'll be next."

The line went dead.

"Oh my God." Jenna stared at his cellphone in disbelief. "How the hell did the killer get your number?"

"I give out my cards all the time and Maggie has a pile at the front desk, along with yours." He ran his fingers though his thick hair and grimaced. "All the suspects I interviewed today have cards as well. As the caller electronically disguised their voice, I don't know if it was a man or woman. Damn it, I haven't activated the record call app on this phone and now we have zip."

Unsettled by the call, Jenna squeezed his arm. "Even if you had a copy it would have been useless."

"Not really. Wolfe has the equipment to decode the voiceprint." Kane moved his blue gaze around the area. "We'd better get out of the open just in case there is a shooter watching us."

Jenna climbed into the car. "I doubt the caller will stop at one call. I think we should all download the app in case something like this happens again."

"Roger that." Kane glanced around. "We need to get out of here."

Jenna fastened her seatbelt. "What do you make of it—the call, the threats? Who would do that?"

"They know I'm interviewing the victims." A nerve in his cheek twitched. "So they are either following me or they are acquainted with one or more of them." He started the car and headed out of the parking lot. "One thing that comes to mind is the caller almost paraphrased what Pattie McCarthy, the schoolteacher, said to me today. She became angry when Bradford interviewed her and accused me of not dating women because she believes I prefer young girls." He cleared his throat. "She is very astute and knew I was communicating with Bradford through the earbud and listening to their conversation."

Jenna chewed on her bottom lip, trying to evaluate everything he had said. She turned in her seat to look at him. "We have not considered the victims might know each other. There is every chance they could be in the same support group, for instance. I don't know of any here but then I haven't been involved with any cases of child abuse in Black Rock Falls. It's something we need to look into."

"Yeah, but so far most of the ones we've discovered occurred in Blackwater." He spun the wheel as they turned into Jenna's driveway. "I completed most of my interviews today, and come to think of it I only spoke to two victims of abuse: Pattie McCarthy and Lizzy Harper." He pulled into his garage and turned to her. "I asked the Booval brothers if they could arrange for us to speak to their sister, Angelique. They mentioned she was in town today." He blinked then scratched his cheek. "Pattie McCarthy said she had an appointment in town and Lizzy Harper was on the way back from town when we arrived at the house they were cleaning today."

The hairs on the back of Jenna's neck rose. "That puts the three suspects in the same place at the same time. They could have easily met somewhere. It's too much of a coincidence to ignore." She stared at him. "They could be working together to confuse us."

"If they are, we'll have one hell of a time catching the killer." Kane's dark eyebrows rose. "There is strength in numbers."

"I can't imagine three women capable of murdering together. Men maybe, but not many women have a pack mentality."

"Oh, yes they do." Kane's gaze hardened. "It depends on how well their leader influences them. Don't forget Manson's girls."

He had a good point and Jenna nodded in agreement. "True. How did Lizzy Harper act toward you during questioning?"

"Hostile." He met her gaze and his narrowed. "In fact, I would say pre-warned would come close." He pulled out his notepad and put on the interior light. "She thought I was asking her questions because it turned me on, so she ties in as well."

Mortified, she gaped at him. "What did she say?"

"Something along the lines of I wanted her to tell me all the dirty little details, and men like me are all the same. Similar phrasing to Pattie McCarthy's." He gave her a dejected look, pocketed his notebook then turned off the light. "Coming inside, or do you just want me to find you a movie to take home? I sure could do with some company and I want to check out the local support groups."

"I'll stay for a while." She squeezed his arm. "It's not you, Dave. After what those women have been through, trusting men would be difficult, and I guess your questions opened up old wounds."

"I know, but if we don't ask the difficult questions, we'll never catch the animals who did this to them." He sighed and scrubbed both hands over his face. "They don't seem to understand we want to bring the men responsible to justice, not protect them." He shook his head slowly. "I can't imagine why they think I would find hurting little girls stimulating. I've seen some terrible crimes but child abuse makes me sick to my stomach."

Jenna looked into his eyes and sighed. "Me too but there is nothing more we can do tonight. Check out the support groups. I'll dash home and change then let's watch a movie."

"I'd like that, thanks." Kane flashed her a grin and headed for the front door.

Jenna dashed to her house and changed. As she walked into Kane's cottage, the old manager's residence on her ranch, she found him staring at his cellphone. "Any luck?"

"I'm still looking." Kane lifted his gaze and smiled at her. "Could you make the coffee?"

Jenna strolled into the kitchen and filled the coffee maker. "I haven't heard of any support groups. We have the breastfeeding mothers' group in town, and a few others, but nothing like abused kids."

"I can't find anything at all." Kane wandered into the room with his dark head bent over the screen. "I'll call a social worker on Monday and see if they can help. It's possible they're not listed for privacy reasons."

"If there's a link between Lizzy Harper and Pattie McCarthy, it would make sense they met in a support group." Jenna leaned against the counter as the coffee pot sent out the tempting aroma of freshly ground beans. "I'd bet they know our murder victims and were abused by them. One of those women could be our killer."

Kane lifted his head from his cellphone and his dark gaze met hers.

"Or both."

CHAPTER TWENTY-THREE

Halfway through the movie, the silent alarm set into the wall flashed violently. An intruder had breached the perimeter of the property. Automatically reaching for his Glock, Kane jerked upright and switched off the TV. He turned to Jenna. "Someone is outside. I'll go and check."

"I'm coming with you." Jenna's whisper came close by. "We'll stick out in our light-colored shirts. Can you grab a couple of your black T-shirts?"

"Roger that." Kane felt around the floor for her shoes and passed them to her then slipped his feet into his boots.

Duke scrambled to his feet and tipped his head from one side to the other as if listening. Kane patted the dog on the head. "Stay."

As Jenna moved silently through the house extinguishing the lights, Kane padded into the bedroom, dragged a couple of black T-shirts from the dresser, and, finding her waiting in the doorway, he tossed one to her. "Put this on. I'll check the cameras."

He moved stealthily down the hallway then slipped into his office, and after closing the blinds, flicked on the flat-screen array. Moments later, Jenna sneaked to his side. He leaned on the table and peered into the screens. "Why didn't your house alarm trigger the floodlights?" He glanced at her. "The sensors I installed mean someone is moving close to the cottage. Too damn close."

"I have no idea." She glanced at him and pushed a hand through her tousled hair. "I set the alarm before I left home."

Intrigued, Kane stared at each monitor for any movement outside. "Where are they?"

"I can't see anything at all. Maybe it's a rabbit or something."

He shook his head. "Nah, the sensors are set for chest height, and we'd see a bear if it walked in—they don't exactly sneak around."

"Do you really believe anyone who knows us would be stupid enough to walk in here?" Jenna glanced up at him with a scowl. "I mean, really?"

He straightened. "After the range of psychopaths we've had drifting into town of late, anything is possible. I'm going to take a look out the windows."

"I'll be right behind you."

Adrenaline pumping, he killed the flat screens to block any light and slipped out into the hall, then moved from window to window, turkey-peeking outside to check the immediate area. The moonless night was as dark as a cave. "I can't see a damn thing and my night-vision goggles are in my SUV. Maybe we should wait and see how this plays out."

"No way." Jenna lifted her chin. "If someone's breaking into my house, I'm going to arrest them."

Concerned for her safety, Kane turned and looked at her shadowed face. "We don't know the threat, and after the phone call earlier, we could be walking into a trap."

"Or they could be walking into ours." She tipped back her head and glared at him. "It could be a simple break and enter or a pervert—who the hell knows, but dammit, Dave, together we're a bigger threat."

A car horn wailed outside and Kane heard Jenna's sharp intake of breath. He touched her arm and her muscles bunched under his palm. He turned to glance at her. "Okay. What do you want to do?"

"Whoever is out there has to be pretty stupid to set off my car alarm. Unless they want to know our position. With my car parked outside the house, they wouldn't know I'm here with you." Jenna grabbed her keys from the table then moved to the window and pointed the fob through the glass at her vehicle, stopping the noise in a blink of lights. "Now they are aware we know they're here. I say we meet them head on. They haven't got our skills, and I sure as hell want to know who is sneaking around my house at night."

He couldn't argue with her logic. "Roger that."

In his periphery, he caught sight of a dark outline against the white wall of Jenna's ranch house. The figure hesitated then moved in their direction. "Unknown bogey is by your living room window and heading this way. If we leave by the back door, we could take the advantage and come round behind them."

"Take the lead. I'll watch your back." Jenna's hand rested firmly on his belt.

He strode swiftly to the back door with Jenna right on his heels, Glock raised. He punched in the code to deactivate the alarm, eased open the door, then turned to her and lowered his voice to a whisper. "Count to three then follow me; keep your back to the wall."

A cold certainty crept over him, and battle-ready he eased out of the door gun in hand. Behind him, Jenna moved without making a sound and they crept down the steps. Silently they dashed along the side of the cottage then crouched at the corner. He sniffed the air but no stink of bear hung on the breeze. After bobbing his head around the corner and seeing no trace of the intruder, he waved her forward. After making a visual search of the immediate area, he led them to the front of the house. The back wall of the garage obscured the view of his front door and he duck-walked along the perimeter, listening.

A sound like a splash came from nearby, too darn close, and followed by a clatter as something hit the ground. He turned and waved Jenna back the way they had come. An unholy stench rose up, burning his nostrils, and behind him, he heard Jenna gag. Inside the house, Duke let out a wail. The smell was very familiar to Kane and he pulled the neck of his T-shirt over his nose.

The overpowering stink surrounding them was death.

A slight crunch of footsteps broke through the silence as a dark figure ran up the driveway. Kane dove around the garage and searched the darkness but the intruder had slipped out of view.

The next moment Jenna was at his side.

"Dammit, they're getting away." She lifted her weapon and shot twice into the air then raised her voice. "Stop or the next one will be in your back."

In the distance, a car engine burst into life, and with a shriek of tires, a dark shape barreled out from behind a shed across the road, skidded onto the blacktop, and sped away without using lights. Kane dropped his gun and turned to Jenna. "Who the hell was that and what is that stink?"

"I don't know but they're long gone. It's pointless giving chase now." Jenna covered her nose. "If we had a flashlight we could at least find out where the stink is coming from." She tugged at his arm. "I don't think it's a good idea to go to the front door."

Kane stared into the darkness; nothing moved. "I have my keys in my pocket. I'll get the flashlight out of my car."

"Don't." Her small hand closed tight, nails digging into his flesh. "You'll have to go inside the garage and we have no idea if anyone is lying in wait." Her voice lowered. "It could be an ambush or a bomb." She looked up at him, her face a pale shape in the darkness. "I'm not risking my house either; we have no choice but to go back the way we came and call for backup."

He rubbed the back of his neck. She did have a valid point and he followed her to the back door of the cottage. "If this is a well-organized trap, they could also be in my cottage by now as well. I'm not sure what Duke would do if strangers tried to get inside. I figure he would welcome them. We should check."

"Okay." Jenna slid back into the shadows.

He followed her, sticking close to the wall. When they reached the back door, he touched her back then signaled for her to be quiet. He listened intently then whispered close to her ear, "My floorboards creak and I can't hear anyone walking around." He edged toward the open door. "Cover me."

He slid into the kitchen and did a reconnaissance of the entire house with Duke on his heels before calling Jenna inside. "All clear." He shut the door behind her. "This is getting stranger by the second."

He moved around the rooms, closing the drapes then switching on lights, and stopped dead at the sight of a red pool of stinking blood oozing under the front door. "Oh shit!"

CHAPTER TWENTY-FOUR

Covering her nose with her arm, Jenna gaped at the spreading crimson pool. "Call for backup." She glanced at Kane. "I hope there's not a dead body hanging on your door."

"I'm more worried about a bomb." He scratched the dark stubble on his chin. "The blood could be a ploy to make us rush outside and take a look, in case someone is injured. They would expect us to follow duty of care protocol." He glanced around. "It's not safe here."

"Unless the bomb has a timer, it isn't going to explode unless we trigger it, but I'm not taking any chances. We'll wait in the barn just in case. You'd better bring Duke." Jenna moved away from the door and followed Kane into the kitchen. "Get Wolfe and Rowley out here. Explain what happened. Tell them to proceed with caution and call me before they enter the property." She headed to the back door.

As they hurried toward the barn, Kane explained the situation to the deputies. She used the keypad on a side entrance to gain entrance to a door set into the side of the barn then turned on the lights. When Kane disconnected the call she led him through the steel door and down a flight of stairs to a fully furnished safe room. "I had hoped never to use this place but it has everything we need to hole up until the cavalry arrives."

"Nice. I thought it was a storage area." He whistled and strolled around, looking in the bedrooms. "This place is almost as big as my cottage. How come you've never told me about it before?"

She shrugged. "It's a safe room, Kane. To keep *me* safe."

"Okay, I understand." He dropped into a chair at the small kitchen table.

Jenna busied herself by pulling out the coffee maker and fixings. It was promising to be a long night. She glanced at him over one shoulder. "I'm trying to figure out why my alarm didn't activate the moment someone came through the gate. If you remember it was working fine when we arrived."

"Yeah, but you deactivated it when you went inside to get changed, didn't you?" He shrugged. "Maybe you forgot to reset it?"

Running her movements through her mind, she shook her head. She had forgotten once after a near-fatal accident and always double-checked since. "No, I clearly remember juggling a bottle of wine and punching in the code."

"Then why didn't the intruder trigger the lights when they came onto the property?"

A cold shiver ran down her spine. "They could have arrived before us. The lights have a delay and could have gone off again before we arrived. They didn't get into the house because I disabled the alarm when I went inside." She lifted her gaze to him. "We know whoever was here parked behind the old shed across the road."

"They could have slipped inside your house while you were changing and deactivated the alarm after you left." Kane frowned.

"How? The door locked behind me."

"There's a hundred ways. You walk in and let the door swing shut behind you and someone could sneak up behind you and catch the door before it closes."

Dread made her heart race. "You're saying they were inside the house watching me to get the code?" She met his gaze with a shudder. "I wonder what's waiting for me when I get home."

"You'll be fine because I'm the target. You haven't received any threats." Kane moved to her side and leaned his large frame against the kitchen counter. "They needed time to carry out their plan, and with your alarm and floodlights deactivated they would have had plenty of time to set things up." His gaze slid over her. "Just as well they didn't know about my silent alarm."

A wave of panic rushed over her and she pushed both hands through her hair. "How the hell did they know about *my* alarm?" She chewed on her bottom lip. "I installed it myself, and although it's possible people might think I have sensor lights in the driveway, whoever came here tonight knew they are wired into the alarm."

"I have no idea." Kane raised one eyebrow then turned away. "It's going to be a long night."

She handed him a cup of coffee. "Really? We could be seconds away from being blown to pieces."

CHAPTER TWENTY-FIVE

Jenna's cellphone rang and she directed Rowley to approach the house. "Aim your spotlights on the front door of the cottage but keep well back."

"*Yes, ma'am.*"

"What can you see?" Jenna put her cellphone on speaker and glanced at Kane, who had not stopped pacing up and down.

"*This is Wolfe, ma'am. I'm looking through binoculars and seeing a patch of red liquid and an upturned black plastic bucket. There seems to be pieces of paper floating in the puddle and a note on the front door. No other foreign objects in the immediate area and nothing I can see anywhere on the porch or any wires at all, but anything could be under the liquid.*"

"Keep your distance and put a few rounds into the ground in front of the step." Kane moved to her side, towing Duke on a leash. "They may have planted a pressure plate; the blood would cover it."

Jenna listened as the SUV door opened and Wolfe used his rifle. *Putt putt putt.* Then silence.

"*All clear, ma'am.*" Rowley's voice came through the speaker.

She heaved a sigh of relief. "Hold your position. We're in the barn and we're coming out."

After handing Kane one of her halogen flashlights, she led the way out of the safe room. They skirted the cottage and sprinted to meet Wolfe and Rowley. Jenna peered at Kane's front door and looked at her deputies. "Suggestions?"

"I'm familiar with explosives and tripwires. I'll do a recon of the area." Kane's expression went deathly serious. "But I suggest we clear your house first, ma'am, as you believe someone has been inside."

Jenna appreciated the fact Kane changed from friend to deputy in front of the others, and nodded. "Yeah, good idea, but I doubt anyone had time to plant a bomb in my house."

"It would only take a few seconds to slip a device into your house, ma'am." Wolfe strolled to the back of the SUV. "I'll grab my kit."

The smell of putrid blood drifted toward her on the breeze. She glanced up at Kane. "Whatever happens here, you can't stay in the cottage tonight. You will have to bunk with me. Unless you want to take a room in town?"

"I'm not leaving you out here alone and I doubt the motel allows dogs." Kane's expression was unreadable in the dark. "I would rather be close by with a lunatic hanging around." He rubbed his nose and grimaced. "Do you know a good cleaning service who works on Sundays?"

Jenna chuckled. "You mean apart from Clean as a Wink?" She took the gloves Wolfe offered her and pulled them on. "Yeah, I know a cleanup crew. I'll call them first thing in the morning."

"No need, ma'am." Wolfe gave her a reassuring smile "Once we've checked out the area, bleach and a hosing-down will fix it. Plus I'm sure you don't want to advertise the fact someone is stalking Kane."

"I'm not being stalked." Kane gave him a reproachful glare. "Vandalized and threatened, maybe, but whoever did this is trying to make a point."

"Really?" Wolfe snorted. "Then why are we checking for bombs? If they wanted *you* to stop the pedophiles, they wouldn't be trying to kill you or Sheriff Alton." He glared at Kane. "This is the killer warning you off."

Jenna cleared her throat. "Stand down, the pair of you. We'll do a sweep of the area just in case there are any explosives. In this situation, we can't be too careful. Whatever the reason, my security was breached." She glared at them. "Stay alert."

She turned to see Rowley looking at her with a wide-eyed, startled expression. Her young deputy was super-efficient but seemed to wilt if she barked at the older men. "Yes, what is it?"

"We'll need more vests, ma'am." Rowley pulled two from the back of the SUV. He handed her one and gave the other to Kane.

"I have two in the back of my car." She tossed Kane the keys. "Don't forget to check underneath for bombs before you open the door."

When he gave her a long, cold stare, she could have swallowed her tongue. How could she have forgotten Kane's wife had died in a car bombing before she opened her big mouth? Her face grew hot. "I'm glad you're an expert on explosive devices."

"So am I." Kane's mouth formed a thin line when he handed her Duke's leash. "Better keep him here. He may trigger a tripwire."

She could sense the bad memories crushing down on him as she took the dog's leash. "Okay."

"I'll help Kane, ma'am." Wolfe scooped the vest from her hands and shrugged into it. "Not that a vest will do much to stop an explosion." He strode toward her SUV, flashlight in hand.

She glanced at Rowley. "Don't ask."

"I wouldn't think of it, ma'am." Rowley's dark gaze narrowed. "Who do you think has it in for Deputy Kane?"

Jenna kept her attention fixed on her deputies. She noticed the careful way both men surrounded her car, peering underneath and moving their flashlights in all directions. "He had a call earlier this evening warning him off. This might be a ploy by the killer to get him to stand down. They obviously don't know him very well."

"The murders were all over the news this evening but nothing was leaked about the links to the girls you found." Rowley tipped back his hat and scratched his head. "Why would they threaten Kane? His reputation is untouchable and the locals know it."

When Kane opened the back of her SUV and pulled out the vests, she heaved a sigh of relief. She shrugged and turned back to Rowley. "Most killers don't think logically. Whoever is killing the pedophiles believes they are doing a community service and figure Kane is getting in their way. He was interviewing suspects today and maybe got close to the killer." She headed toward her house with Duke following close to her side. "Problem is, some people think jail is too good for pedophiles and would turn a blind eye."

"I could see why there would be a split opinion." Rowley walked beside her and gave her an uncomfortable stare. "People who were abused as kids and parents who lost kids to these creeps would be happy someone is killing them." He cleared his throat. "We want to catch them and bring them to justice. I can see both sides of the argument."

Jenna stopped walking; she had to admit she could see both sides too, but her job was to enforce the law. "We follow the letter of the law and personal opinions don't apply. Not ever."

"Yes, ma'am."

After waiting for Kane and Wolfe to clear her house, she headed up the steps in time to see Kane checking the alarm system. "Find anything interesting?"

"You tell me." Kane's mouth twitched as he held up two wires torn from the main box. "The floodlights, I gather? It didn't take a tech-head to work out the wiring. The label you stuck on the control panel is a dead giveaway." He raised one eyebrow and his lips quivered as he attempted to smother a grin. "Give me a few seconds and I'll have these reattached."

"What about prints?" She unhitched the dog's leash then moved to Kane's side.

"Wiped down." Wolfe came up the passageway and pointed to a small scuff on the floor outside the broom closet. "I would say they parked across the road behind the barn then walked here before you arrived. Kane mentioned he drove into his garage. You have a seven-minute turn off delay on the lights, so he had plenty of time to return to the house, is that correct?"

"Yes, I jogged to the house, went inside, and disabled the alarm, got changed, re-set the alarm, and came back here. The lights were working fine then."

"They hid the bucket of blood somewhere close." Wolfe sighed. "They followed you inside and hid in here." He swung open the door of a small cupboard and shone his flashlight inside. "There are a few smudges of soil but no footprints. When you went to Kane's they disabled the floodlights and alarm."

"How did they know you planned to go over to Kane's cottage tonight?" Rowley's questioning gaze moved between them.

"We went to dinner at the Cattleman's Hotel. It was crowded— anyone could have seen us arrive in my vehicle. We chatted about watching a movie over dinner." Kane rubbed his chin. "It's possible someone overheard us. They would have had plenty of time to get here before us and set this up, or they just got lucky."

Jenna chewed on her fingernails, thinking. "We spend a lot of downtime together. If someone has been watching us, they would assume we'd spend some time together after going for a meal. We usually do."

"Just a minute." Wolfe held up a finger then turned back to the front door. "Do you often use a wedge to keep the door open?"

Jenna followed him. "No, never."

"I noticed this when I came up the steps." Wolfe pointed to a small wedge of wood on the porch. "Come outside and close the door." He led the way.

Jenna complied and watched as he slid the wooden wedge near the door hinge and the floor.

"Okay, I want you to go inside as you would normally." Wolfe handed her the bunch of keys she had given him.

She used the keys to open the door, strolled inside, and allowed the door to swing shut behind her. A few moments later, the door swung open and Wolfe smiled at her. "The wedge prevented the door from closing completely but not enough for you to notice."

"Oh my God." Jenna shook her head in disbelief. "I wonder if the killer was seated beside us at dinner?"

"I can't believe you didn't notice if a suspect was close by." Wolfe's astonished expression moved over Kane's face. "Think. Did you notice anyone at all?"

"People were coming and going all the time; nobody in particular registered with me. To be honest, I wasn't looking for a threat. I was concentrating on discussing the case and eating."

Jenna sighed. "Mr. Davis was chatting to George Miller and his wife when we arrived but none of them are on our list of suspects."

"Yeah, I noticed them in the lobby." Kane cleared his throat. "If we're done here, I'd like to check out the cottage now, ma'am. With the floodlights, it should be easy enough to find any tripwires." He patted Duke on the head. "Stay here, boy." He picked up the flashlight and headed out the door.

Jenna turned to the other deputies. "Don't just stand there, let's go." She followed them out the door.

"Ma'am." Wolfe strode beside her. "Leave this to Kane and me. We have specialized training in this area."

They seem to be specialized in everything. She gave him a curt nod. "Okay, we'll keep away from any potential blast zone. Be careful. Don't forget you have kids at home."

"Not for a second." Wolfe flashed her one of his rare smiles then jogged to Kane's side.

Her heart raced as her deputies checked the area. As they moved around, she heard Kane's deep voice call out, "Clear."

When Wolfe crouched at the crimson pool at the front door and Kane bent to take photographs with his cellphone camera, she wanted to run over to them but kept her distance. If it was a crime scene, the fewer people stamping around the better. By the lowered voices, her deputies had found something significant and her heart pounded in anticipation. Moments later Kane waved her forward.

"Clear."

Jenna took the face mask Kane held out to her and pushed it over her nose. The smell was disgusting. "What do we have?"

"Wolfe is doing a test on the blood but he thinks it's animal; it has fur in it, maybe from a cow." Kane indicated to the puddle and his mouth turned down. "In the blood are photocopies of old newspapers. Wolfe will have to clean them up but from what we can see from the headlines, they all feature missing kids."

The sight of blood dripping from the innocent smiling faces depicted in the newspapers made Jenna's stomach clench. She moved closer, trying to read the headlines. "Some of them look old, yellowed."

"Yeah, they're all cut from old newspapers." Kane moved his flashlight to a few Wolfe had laid in a line on the grass. "Some of the articles are more than ten years old. Wolfe will be able to get all the pertinent information and the names of the journalists."

"How many kids?"

"Six, and all missing girls." Kane's eyes searched her face then he moved his flashlight onto his front door. "Then there's this."

Scrawled over the images of Amos Price and Ely Dorsey were the words: "Monsters kill kids". Jenna turned to Kane and waved a hand at the newspaper articles. "Oh my God, do you think they mean Price and Dorsey killed these children?"

"It sure looks that way." Kane removed his gloves with a snap, and his troubled gaze moved to her face. "With both of them dead, we have no idea where they buried the bodies. We only have one option."

Jenna frowned at him. "Yeah, I know. We have to find the vigilante before they finish their killing spree."

CHAPTER TWENTY-SIX

Parked in the bushes opposite the junction leading to Sheriff Alton's ranch, she sat in her car tingling with excitement from her close encounter with the law and watched the road. Sweat soaked her shirt and her heart still raced from sprinting from the sheriff's ranch. It had been a stroke of luck to be standing at the reception counter of the Cattleman's Hotel when Deputy Kane called to make a reservation. It had given her plenty of time to work out a plan.

Outwitting the sheriff would not be easy, and she actually admired her grit. Jenna Alton was one tough cookie and not easily swayed by emotion. She wondered how the sheriff would react when she called Kane to give him the next clue.

She could never explain to Kane how she knew where to find the missing girls. She would send him to the isolated Craig's Rock then down the mountain to Old Corkey's place—a deserted cabin a short distance from where one of the monsters lived. That would keep the sheriff and her team occupied for at least one day.

A wave of anticipation of what was to come thrummed through her as she stared into the darkness at the sheriff's ranch. Some time had passed since a cruiser flew past with lights flashing, and in the distance, a halo of illumination emanated from the sheriff's property. *It sure looks like I have your attention now. Time for stage two.*

CHAPTER TWENTY-SEVEN

A welcome cool breeze lifted Kane's hair and brought with it the aroma of pine forests. He took a few steps away from the cottage to enjoy a lungful of clean air. He reluctantly strolled back to the front door and glanced over at Rowley. The young deputy's hair was stuck to his face with sweat. It was way past two in the morning and Rowley had worked non-stop to clean up the cottage with him after Wolfe had gone home to be with his kids. They had spent most of the night scrubbing down walls and hosing away blood.

Kane straightened his aching back and yawned. "That will do, I'm bushed. Thanks for your help, Jake."

"It smells okay out here now at least." Rowley dropped a sponge into a bucket and peeled off rubber gloves. "Do you think Deputy Wolfe will be able to save the newspaper articles?"

"Yeah, he'll photograph them. He has software to bring out the print." Kane removed his gloves. "I'm sure we'll be able to get copies via the library archives, if all else fails."

"Great." Jake pushed a hand through his brown wavy hair. "I'll head on home now."

"And upset our sheriff?" Kane smiled at him. "She invited us to sleep over and trust me, the hot chocolate and cookies waiting for us will be worth it." He winced. "I'd love to sleep in my own bed too but the cottage still has *eau de* death." He indicated to Duke asleep in the bushes. "Even the dog won't go inside." He grinned. "So are you staying?"

"Okay. Do you think she is in danger from this crazy?" Rowley rubbed his dimpled chin. "Although you look like the target at the moment."

Kane shrugged and stared at Jenna's house. "Someone followed her into her house undetected, so they're good, real good. It has to be the same person who called me. I think they are sending me a message to leave them to administer street justice."

"We are all investigating the murders. Why target you and not the sheriff?"

"I guess because I've been interviewing women who suffered abuse as a child." Kane collected the scrubbing brushes and dropped them into an empty bucket. "The killer believes I get a thrill out of hearing them speak about child abuse."

"And you're a man." Rowley stood with his fists balled on his narrow hips. "The sheriff told me about your early morning workouts so I gather she can handle herself pretty well."

"Jenna could take most people down single-handed but that's not the problem. Whoever managed to get inside her house moves like a shadow and they are fit. They took off running at impressive speed after they sprayed my house with blood." He glanced at Rowley. "Don't worry. I doubt Jenna will let anyone get the better of her again."

"I haven't seen her fight but she sure doesn't mess around when she's making arrests." Rowley grinned. "She took on Rockford when she found him creeping around her house and he is a big guy."

"She isn't weak but Rockford had lost the element of surprise. He woke her and she was able to grab her Glock and deal with the asshole." Kane sucked in a deep breath then coughed out the chemical taste in his mouth. "It's the ones you don't hear that are the most dangerous. Surprise attacks kill more people than by other means. I'd say if an intruder had a knife and got the jump on any of us, they could inflict a lot of damage." He sighed. "Just to be safe, I'd like to make sure her security system is fully functional and I'm too exhausted to deal with it now. Fixing the lights was easy."

"I'd say she'll be asleep anyway." Rowley glanced over to Jenna's house. "I need to take a shower and get out of these stinking clothes, but it feels strange doing that at your boss's house."

Kane chuckled. "I know what you mean. You're welcome to use my spare room to shower and change if you don't mind the smell?" Seeing Jenna's shadow move in front of the window, he lifted his chin. "We'd better get a move on. She is awake and no doubt waiting for us."

"Okay, thanks, I appreciate it. I'll grab the bag from my car." Moments later, Rowley followed him inside and glanced around. "It's bigger than it looks from the outside."

"Yeah, I gather it was built for the ranch manager some hundred years ago." Kane led the way down the passage then pointed across the hall. "Everything you need is in there."

Fifteen minutes later, Kane sat at Jenna's kitchen table sipping hot chocolate. His head throbbed and he had inhaled enough chemicals to drop an elephant. He raised sore eyes to her face. "I'll be glad to hit the sack. It's been a long day. I'm starting to look like my dog." He rubbed the hound's head.

"I won't be able to sleep." Jenna nibbled on the cookie she had dipped in her hot chocolate. "My mind is in overdrive trying to figure out what the hell is going on." She sipped the beverage and her gaze bore into him over the rim of the cup. "I'm used to killers doing the deed then getting the hell out of Dodge, not dropping by for a visit and making threatening calls." She directed her attention toward Rowley. "I would really like to find out if the vigilante suspects know each other. The support group idea is something we need to explore." She sighed. "I feel like we're going round in circles. Did you find any associates of the murder victims?"

"We've found a few people who knew the murdered men but none of them are friends. All say the same thing: They didn't socialize." Rowley's dark gaze lifted from his cup. "There has to be a link."

"I think it's obvious." Kane shrugged. "We have three murder suspects, all victims of child abuse. All the women, including the young girl Zoe, mentioned the men wore masks. That is the link. The men are the same group of people and have been doing this for years."

"Why do you think all the suspects are involved?" Rowley placed his cup on the table and yawned. "You made mention in the murder books that all the suspects were in town on the same day."

"I did wonder if the women contacted each other but how would they know their names? The courts and media withhold the names of abuse victims." She drummed her fingernails on the polished wooden tabletop. "Unless the vigilante followed the newspaper stories about missing kids. If they turned up alive, maybe they contacted them later in life?"

"So, we could have a group of women killing the men who hurt them?" Rowley looked interested. "The motive is there. They would want to stop them before they hurt another kid."

"You could be right. Whoever called Kane and vandalized his house has given us a clear indication there is a group of men kidnapping, molesting, and murdering kids." Jenna grimaced. "I want to find out who is in this pedophile ring; then we'll be able to catch the killer before they strike again."

"Easier said than done." Kane swallowed the bile creeping up his throat. "They could be operating right here in Black Rock Falls under our noses."

"Exactly. I hope Wolfe has a list of the missing kids from the newspapers by morning. From what I could see they are a spread from neighboring counties."

The idea of so many kids dying by the hands of child molesters sent a jolt of adrenaline flooding through Kane. The weariness subsided and his mind zoomed in on the facts of the case. "Yeah, and going way back, some ten years or so. It's going to be one hell of a job tracking down cold cases and we'll be up against jurisdiction problems."

"I don't give a damn about jurisdiction." Jenna shot him a cold glare. "I'll contact the other sheriff's departments personally and ask for their cooperation, which *will* be given. The local judges will offer up search warrants without a problem if we have probable cause." She nibbled on a cookie. "We have to break this pedophile ring for two reasons: one to stop the vigilante, and two to prevent another kid from being kidnapped. I want a round-the-clock investigation. I have Walters taking the 911 calls on Sunday. I'll hold a meeting on Monday morning to allocate the workload but we will need to go into the office in the morning and keep moving on the investigation. Sorry, guys, can you make it in before ten?"

Kane nodded in agreement. "The new deputies seem very efficient and I'm sure they can hold the fort with Walters while the rest of us do the grunt work."

"Yeah, I agree." Jenna reached for another cookie. "I want to be right in the middle of this investigation. I should have been with you when you interviewed the vigilante suspects but I didn't want to lose the opportunity to speak to Zoe."

Kane shook his head. "With two cases on the go, you had little choice but to split the workload. We covered lot of ground and have Angelique Booval to interview on Monday. Maybe we can speak to the Blackwater social worker as well. They might be able to give us a list of support groups in the area."

"I can't imagine a killer attending a support group." Jenna pushed a lock of black hair behind one ear and sighed. "Then I have no idea what type of crazy we're dealing with this time."

"This year, I've seen different types of killers." Rowley glanced at Kane. "From what you say, this type of lunatic comes in many varieties."

Kane yawned and covered his mouth. "Yeah, there are many different classes of killer."

"Knowing what type they are makes a difference." Jenna glanced at Rowley, placed her cup on the table, and stretched. "They are all crazy, and the vigilante is another rung up the ladder to what we've been used to of late."

"Would you class a man who kills in a rage, say when he finds his wife cheating on him, the same type of killer as the man who murdered the schoolgirls last summer?" Rowley ran a hand through his hair, making it stand up in all directions. "You said he was a psychopath, so what is the difference?"

Kane wanted to sleep but he owed Rowley an explanation. "In very simple terms: In a crime of passion, like your first example, the men are blinded by fury so really didn't know what they are doing. If it is a wife or lover who has hurt them they usually attack the face. They usually show remorse or are shocked they have killed someone. A psychopath may or may not plan a murder but they have no feelings toward their victim. The killing satisfies a selfish need in them, and most of the time in their minds they don't see murdering as wrong. Some of them truly believe it's normal to kill people."

"That's terrifying." Rowley sipped his drink. "From what you said about the vigilante, they know what they are doing. I would say they are well-planned revenge murders." His face went blank as if deep in thought. "So, this is someone who doesn't fit neatly into either category?"

Kane leaned forward. "Most psychopaths are driven by a trigger. Something bad that happened to them as a child. My guess is our killer is female and suffered abuse as a child. She may have heard or seen something that triggered the killing spree. Taunting me is another trait because they believe they have superior intelligence and can outwit us. They can't. Eventually they make mistakes. The first one was contacting me and the second was coming here tonight."

Jenna's eyes flashed. "And the third was underestimating me."

CHAPTER TWENTY-EIGHT

Sunday

Jenna had woken at eight and strolled out of her room the following morning dressed in her workout gear. She went to the kitchen following the delicious aroma of fresh coffee. She found Kane looking as fresh as a daisy, nursing a steaming cup of joe. "Good morning. Thanks for making the coffee."

"My pleasure. I've repaired your alarm as well but you might want to ask Wolfe to give it an upgrade." He smiled. "I thought you'd want to work out, so I went home, fed Duke, and changed. Oh, and Rowley headed home. He will meet us at the office at ten. He had to feed his dog too."

"Where is he? Duke, I mean."

"Asleep in his basket. I think we kept him up too late last night." He chuckled deep in his chest. "Do you know he snores? Truly, and he runs in his sleep."

Jenna poured a cup of coffee and added the fixings. "He looks good now. I can't believe he is the same dog, and not a vicious bone in his body. After being mistreated I thought he would be different."

"He is a hound dog; they're not known for having a bad temperament. He is gentle and very clean. Whoever gave him to the shelter must have been nuts." Kane smiled warmly. "I haven't had a dog since I was a kid. He's great company."

Jenna smiled at him, liking the glimpse into his secret past. "He is lucky to have you."

"Thanks." Kane leaned his wide frame back in the chair, making it creak in protest. "If we go into the office early, maybe we can be done in time to look at those horses?"

Jenna finished her coffee and stood. She needed a good solid workout to clear her head. "Maybe. Are you ready for me to kick your ass?"

"Lead the way." Kane's blue eyes sparkled in amusement. "I guess you can try."

Before she left home, Jenna called Wolfe and discovered he had wasted no time in collecting the information from the newspaper articles. "That's great news. You must have worked all night."

"Yeah, I worked last night but if you're going into the office this morning I'll email it to you, unless you need me to report for duty, ma'am."

"Just send the list and we can discuss anything else on Monday." Jenna frowned. She did not intend to steal his entire Sunday with his kids. "I think you've done more than enough this weekend. Thank you, I appreciated you putting in the overtime."

"It's all part of the job, ma'am. I'll see you on Monday unless the killer strikes again."

Smothering a yawn, Jenna dragged a hand through her hair, not sure if she had brushed it, and sighed. "I hope not. See you on Monday."

She disconnected and gulped down her third cup of coffee in an effort to drive away the exhaustion. The cases had gnawed at her and she had tossed and turned before falling asleep. The workout with Kane had been brutal, and now she had fallen into the slump from the adrenaline rush. She filled her takeout cups with coffee and headed for the door, glad to see Kane waiting in his black rig for her. His offer to drive her into the office had been most welcome and she would enjoy the company.

She opened the door and noticed Duke's head hanging over the back seat. She looked at Kane and raised one eyebrow in question. "Is he a new recruit?" She slid into the seat and deposited the travel cups in the console.

"Do you mind?" Kane looked chagrined. "I did promise to take him for a walk in the forest. You do know he can track a person by their clothing."

She gazed at Duke's bloodshot eyes. "He doesn't look as if he has the energy to keep his eyes open let alone track anyone."

"He is fitter than you think." Kane's mouth twitched up at the corners as he started the car.

She fastened her seatbelt. "If we can process all the information we've collected for both cases for Monday morning before lunch, I'll come with you to look at the horses, but I want boots on the ground until we solve these cases."

"Sure, I'll be glad of the company." Kane smiled at her. "I'll be interested to see what info Wolfe got from the old newspapers."

Jenna stared out the window at the green fields flying by, not really listening. All she could think about was finding Zoe locked in the cage. She understood the fear of being at the mercy of brutal men. Her flashbacks were a constant reminder. When Kane cleared his throat in an unnatural way, she glanced over at him. "Sorry, did you say something?"

He repeated the question.

"Yeah, we'll have names of missing girls and where they lived at least." She sighed. "They seemed to have vanished into thin air."

Kane flicked her a glance then returned his attention to the road. "The earlier cases— opportunistic I'd say, maybe by snatching kids walking home alone. We know pedophiles frequent online chat rooms to procure kids. They often like to share experiences as well but these men are being extra careful."

"As we've drawn a blank on the murder victims' associates and the FBI have come up with zip, we can't move forward on the murder cases until we interview Angelique Booval and the Blackwater social worker. I figure we should start by following up on the missing kids' cases from the newspaper cuttings left in front of your cottage. Now we have access to statewide databases, we can check each name." Jenna pushed her hair behind one ear. "If any of them are alive, they might have information we could use."

"What about Jane?"

"I'm still waiting for the all-clear to visit her again. Now she has had time to get over the shock, she might be able to give us some more information."

"I hope so. I think finding the journalists who wrote the stories would be beneficial. Writing an article on a missing kid would be hard to forget." Kane turned onto the highway and they followed a slow-moving tractor. "They often have theories they can't print about suspects. It would be worth following up on them just in case we get a lead on the pedophile ring."

Jenna picked up her coffee cup and sipped, allowing the rich brew to run over her tongue. "Good idea, but as those missing girls came from all over the state, I'm going to run Price and Dorsey through the Montana Sexual and Violent Offender Registry and see if they have been active in other towns. They often list known associates as well." She glanced at him. "We know about Stewart James Macgregor, the magician, and I'm sure I received an email when he was released from jail. I didn't red-flag him because he was classed as reformed and a minimal threat."

"They can't be reformed." Kane snorted in derision. "It is a sexual preference they'll never change." He pulled up outside the sheriff's department and lifted the other cup of coffee from the console. "Rowley has already arrived and it looks like Webber has volunteered as well."

Jenna heaved a sigh of relief. "Great, we need all the help we can get." She slid from the car and headed for the door.

She walked to her office, passing Rowley chatting to Webber. "In my office, deputies."

After waiting for her deputies to sit down, she went to the whiteboard and picked up the marker then split the board in two down the center. "We are dealing with two cases. They are intertwined but we need to take a separate approach to both of them." She wrote *Vigilante killer* on one side of the board and *Pedophile ring* on the other then listed the victims and suspects.

She turned to face them. "I'm going to run the names of the vigilante killer's victims through the Sexual and Violent Offender Registry. With any luck, if they have committed an offense anywhere in the state, the arresting officer will have a list of known associates." She moved back to her desk and sat down then turned on her computer and waited for her emails to download. She located the file Wolfe had sent her and printed four copies. "Deputy Wolfe has emailed me a list of the names of the missing kids, dates, and the names of the journalists involved with the cases." She lifted the copies from the printer and scanned them. "Okay, we have six kids. Rowley, you take the top three, and Webber, you take the last three. Feed the names into the state database and see if you get a hit. You will be looking for juvenile missing persons' reports. Next, I want you to find a contact number for the reporter. You would be surprised how useful they can be if you speak to them off the record." She pulled out her notebook and checked the list she had made overnight. "Kane, I want a list of all known associates of Lizzy

Harper and Pattie McCarthy; maybe throw Angelique Booval into the pot as well. Find out if they are involved in any clubs or groups."

Not one of the deputies made a sound, and apart from the strong scent of a variety of aftershaves, she would not have known they were there. She looked up from her notebook at their unblinking stares, handed the copies to the deputies then sighed. "What are you waiting for? Lives are at risk, get a move on." *Maybe I need to start cracking a whip.*

CHAPTER TWENTY-NINE

Dread had hung over Chris Jenkins like a storm cloud the moment the image of Amos Price flashed onto his TV screen, and the feeling had gotten worse with the news of the cops finding Ely Dorsey's dead body in a motel. His fingers had itched to call Bobby-Joe, but keeping to the code they'd devised to prevent any outsiders from discovering their friendship, he climbed into his SUV and headed up the mountain road to Bobby-Joe's house.

After parking some way from the locked entrance to Bobby-Joe's private road, he headed on foot to the old, dilapidated cabin. As he walked through the pine trees, he did a slow scan of the area to make sure Bobby-Joe was alone. Satisfied, he dashed across his front yard and entered the house by the back door. The kitchen was empty, dirty dishes overflowed the sink, and the place stunk of garbage and stale beer. "Bobby-Joe. Where are you, man?"

"Here in the bedroom. I'm talking to my honey."

Chris wiped the sweat from his brow and strolled into Bobby-Joe's bedroom. Bobby-Joe was seated at the computer and typing a response to someone in an online chat room. "We need to talk. Did you see the news?"

"Yeah, just a minute." Bobby-Joe typed some more then spun around in his seat. "Man, I have this sweet thing on the hook and I've found the perfect place to take her. A cabin reasonably close to the road and no one goes near the place this time of the year. I could park on the fire road and walk there." He grinned widely. "She is already willin' to meet me. Would you believe she is coming on her bicycle?" He chuckled and winked at him. "If you're looking for a nice place, we could maybe meet up there with both girls then bring them here. I have plenty of room in my cage for two lovelies."

"Yeah, but unlock the damn gate so I can drive here. It's one hell of a walk."

"I'll give you a key. Most people who see your SUV will think it's me anyway. It's the same make, same color but stop cleanin' the damn thing if you plan to come here. A clean rig don't look right." Bobby-Joe chuckled.

"Sure." Chris nodded, surprised Bobby-Joe was still making plans to kidnap another girl. Concerned by his friend's laid-back attitude, he swallowed hard. His friend was unpredictable and acted as if Amos and Ely showing up dead meant nothing. "Are you thinking of taking another girl now, so soon after what's happened?"

"Yeah, of course, and I *know* you want one of your own. Now that Amos's girl is unavailable, I'm getting anxious."

Chris stared at him, not able to understand why he was so calm. "The cops found the girl? Holy shit. I thought you went over there. Why didn't you bring her here?"

"Because I thought he would be coming back and I didn't have the keys to unlock the damn cage." Bobby-Joe stood and ambled into the kitchen. "I didn't know he'd dropped dead. Heart attack, I expect, fat bastard." He took a couple of beers from the refrigerator and handed him one. "Don't worry, the kid won't be able to identify us, and we made sure we left nothing there. It's cool." He sighed. "You down with my plan or what? We take two at the same time and bring them here. I have plenty of tranquilizers. We'll work out the time. You meet your girl at the cabin first and half an hour later, I'll get mine to arrive. They won't be able to get away from both of us."

"Yeah, yeah, I'm in."

A rustling noise came from outside the open window and Chris spun around. His heart pounded with fear. "Did you hear that? Maybe the cops are out there."

"Man, you're jumpy." Bobby-Joe gave him an exasperated look and leaned out the kitchen window. "There's no one out there apart from a few chickens scratchin' around." He pulled his head in then took a long gulp of his beer. "You need to grow some balls. No one comes here. It's safe, so stop worryin'."

Chris swallowed the fear strangling his voice and tried to lean casually against the counter. "I'm being cautious, is all."

"Sure you are."

"What do you think happened to Ely?" Chris opened the bottle and frowned. "Two of our friends dying in the same week. It doesn't make sense. Do you think someone is hunting us down?"

"Nah, you really believe a young girl could kill either of them? Ely died on the job." Bobby-Joe sniggered. "One of the paramedics who transported his body to the ME's office spoke to me. He said he was naked and wearing a condom. I guess his new girl split; no one mentioned finding her at the motel." He sighed. "He's dead so it don't matter if she saw his face."

Chris pushed a hand through his hair. "What about Ely's girl?"

"I sneaked down the mountain on foot and took a look at his cabin through the binoculars. The house has crime scene tape across the door." Bobby-Joe sighed. "The cops have her as well."

"Shit! She could identify us. I'm sure of it." He took a long drink then wiped his mouth with the back of his hand. "The news never mentioned her."

"They took her to the hospital." Bobby-Joe sank into a chair at the kitchen table. "Ely didn't feed her much and as she was chained up the cops will order all sorts of tests. I doubt she could identify us. Think about it: We've been careful and covered our faces since the little bitch escaped." He shrugged. "We haven't touched Ely's girl in ages. We're home free with her, no evidence. The cops will blame Ely and he's dead." He smiled. "We're fine. Stop worryin'."

Panic closed Chris's throat and he gaped at his friend. "I know you went to his place recently and you work at the hospital. What if she recognizes you?"

"Nah, the chances of me running into her would be slim." Bobby-Joe sipped his beer. "The doctors will keep her in the hospital for ages. The cops get to interview her after the psychiatrist clears her. I've seen the process before and it will be days before they release her." He sighed. "I never went near her without the mask, it's cool."

"She'll sure as hell recognize the tattoo on your hand, and your green eyes are distinctive. Once she tells the cops, they'll be on you like flies on shit."

"My eyes maybe." Bobby-Joe sighed. "The tattoo, I always keep covered and have done since the girl escaped from here. The hospital believes I have an old wrist injury and I need to wear a brace. So my hand is covered and usually I have surgical gloves on as well when I'm working." He shrugged. "I don't take chances."

Why the hell was he taking it so calmly? Any minute the cops could break down the door and haul their asses off to jail. "It's too much of a risk to bring any new girls here. We'll have to find another place."

"No way. The cops can't come on my land without a warrant and they can't connect us to Amos or Ely."

"What happens if Ely's bitch gives the cops your description? It will be all over the news. How many people do you know at the hospital? One of them will call the cops for sure. The cops will stick a clown mask on you and she will identify you. Shit, anyone who knows you could."

"Yeah, maybe, but she wouldn't have given a statement yet. Like I said, the doctors have to clear her before they allow the sheriff to

talk to her. My guess is the sheriff will show up sometime tomorrow."
Bobby-Joe leaned back in his chair with a thoughtful expression on
his face. "The cops always make sure people of interest are on the
seventh floor, and they only have a deputy on duty during the day.
At night, they lock down the wards but I have access to all areas. I
can fix our problem easy enough."

Terrified, Chris stared at him. "What are you going to do?"

"I know the movements of the night shift at the hospital. By
midnight there is only one nurse on each ward. I can easily put her
out of action. I'll get there just before the nurses on that floor are due
to take a break and slip something into the coffee pot and the hot
water urn just to be sure." He sniggered. "The CCTV cameras are on
the main entrance. I'll go in via the back door—I have a swipe card."

"Which the cops will be able to trace."

"Nope." Bobby-Joe chuckled. "You remember the old cleaner
who had a heart attack about three months ago? I have his card. I
took it from him when he collapsed."

Chris eyed his friend's relaxed demeanor. "Yeah, then what?"

His mouth curled into a sadistic grin. "I'm gonna pay the stinking
bitch a visit and kill her."

CHAPTER THIRTY

Curled in the damp soil under a bush growing beneath Bobby-Joe's kitchen window, she flicked away a spider determined to crawl into her mouth. By the tremble in Chris's voice, he recognized a threat was on the loose and he was in the line of fire. *They should be frightened of me. Very frightened.*

If the sheriff had found two girls and taken them to the hospital, she needed to discover which one Bobby-Joe planned to murder. She heard voices again and very carefully eased out from under the bush. Straightening, she pressed her back against the wall beside the open window. The wooden slatted shutters on each side of the window would hide her from view.

The voices drifted out to her and she listened, too nervous to breathe.

"I can't remember the name of Ely's girl. He used to call her 'bitch' every time I went to visit." Chris cleared his throat. "How are you going to find her?"

"I *know* her name." Bobby-Joe sniggered. "I heard Ely call her Jane the last time I went to see him. I don't know how much she remembers about her old life; she must be seventeen or so by now."

"Yeah, I remember she called him 'Daddy'." Chris swore under his breath. "He was a sick son of a bitch. With us it was different."

"Yeah, that's right, you 'love' kids, don't you?" Bobby-Joe's sudden harsh voice made her skin crawl.

Yes, I bet you do. With her pulse thumping in her ears, she crept away from the house. Rage welled inside her. Dammit, if she had thought to bring her gun she could have stormed into the cottage and shot both of them. No, a quick death would be too good for them. She must stick to the plan. *I'll make them pay.*

Once well away from Bobby-Joe's cabin, she jogged up the footpath, heading toward the falls. At the top of the mountain, she clambered over a pile of rocks to the small parking lot cut out of the mountainside the tourists used before the rock fall blocked the road. She hesitated and scanned the area but the place was deserted. She rested for some time, mulling over what the men had said then made her way back over the mass of fallen boulders to a cleared area half a mile down the mountain where she had parked her car.

Sitting in her car, she sipped from a bottle of water and gazed out at the expanse of blue sky. To her right, the falls crashed down the mountainside, creating a dozen rainbows. A soft breeze moved the tops of the pine trees, and the masses of wildflowers sat in patches of brilliance against the boulders. The scene was a photographer's dream. She turned her head to look at the mountain's many peaks. In all directions, pine trees marched up the sides of the rock face in green splendor. How she wished her memories of Black Rock Falls could be different. What secrets this forest held. She slipped from the car and went to run her palm over the rough bark of a massive pine. The trees at the edge of the road stood in a row like sentries guarding the way to the falls.

It was a shame monsters roamed the forest.

CHAPTER THIRTY-ONE

After spending the morning searching through the Sexual and Violent Offender Registry for all known offenders in Montana, Jenna then checked the statewide database of fugitives to see if the victims' names came up. Stu Macgregor was the only name that did. When Kane knocked on her door, his arms laden with takeout, she glanced at the clock. "Oh, I didn't realize it was so late." She stifled a yawn. "Ask Rowley and Webber to come into the office and we'll discuss our findings over lunch."

"I don't think our search yielded much information, I'm afraid." Kane placed the bags on her desk then headed to the door. "Bring your food with you, and your notes. We'll eat with the sheriff."

Once everyone had settled, Jenna glanced at her deputies. "I found zip on our victims and a bit of info on Stu Macgregor. Price and Dorsey haven't had as much as a parking ticket. What have you found?"

"Not much, only what we know already. Amos Price, Ely Dorsey, and Stu Macgregor all worked for Party Time; they often went to the same gig. I spoke to the owner of the establishment and he has never received a complaint against them. He informed me as far as he recalls not one of the men working for him has a spider tattoo on his hand. He said he would likely refuse to hire someone with something that might disturb the kids." Kane took a sip of his coffee and sighed appreciatively. "I looked into our murder suspects as well. Apart from the molestation as kids, I can't find a link between them at all. They all went to different schools and have different occupations. I checked social media to see if they have any friends in common and came up empty. In fact, they had hardly any friends at all, and Lizzy Harper hasn't got an account. She is a real loner. I guess we'll have to wait until Monday to speak to a social worker about possible support groups. That is the only other link I can think of right now."

"Rowley, what did you find?" Jenna munched on a turkey sandwich. She had not realized how long it had been since breakfast.

"All the missing girls on my list are still listed as missing. I had to check all over the state but most of these are from the three surrounding counties. I left messages for the journalists to contact me if they had an update on the stories but the missing persons' files would be up to date." His dark eyes moved over her face. "I contacted two of the girls' parents in Blackwater. The cases were all seven to ten years ago. I checked their alibis for the time of death of our victims to rule them out. I asked what they remembered about the days or weeks prior to their kids going missing. All had taken their daughters to a party in the week before their disappearance."

Jenna nodded. "That's very interesting, so the Party Time link is definite. Have you narrowed it down?"

"Yeah." Kane's gaze rested on her. "They employed four clowns and two magicians in the last ten years: The two we know are involved, and the Booval brothers. The other magician died last year." He raised one eyebrow. "The manager mentioned the FBI was all over them this week as well, so I gather they are working statewide on the pedophile ring or they would have notified you." He shrugged. "So it seems none of their employees are part of the pedophile ring."

Damn. The leads were running through her fingers like water. She glanced at Webber. "Anything to report?"

"Nothing on my list of missing girls." Webber cleared his throat. "I found an arrest report on Lizzy Harper but nothing we don't know about already. The other missing girls on my list are still missing. I didn't have any luck contacting the journalists at all." He sighed. "There is a mention in the Blackwater files about the Angelique Booval case and the conviction of Stu Macgregor but her file is sealed as well."

Jenna let out a long, disappointed sigh. "Dammit, I hoped we would find something. Thanks for coming in today. Go home and get some rest. Walters is on call today and I'll only contact you in an emergency."

She noticed the way Kane remained seated. She flicked him a gaze. "Is there anything else?"

"Yeah, now we're finished for the day, are you ready to leave?"

Collecting the food containers and stuffing them in the garbage, she nodded. "Yeah, a break will do me good but keep it short, okay? I want to re-check everything before we head out to Blackwater tomorrow." She collected her notepad and cellphone. "Do you mind going over a few things on the ride out to the ranch?'

"No, ma'am." Kane stood and stretched. "Do you want to go home first and change?"

Exhausted and with the case weighing heavy on her mind, she met his gaze. "We don't have time to go home and change. Going for a ride is out of the question." She glanced down at Duke, lounging at Kane's feet. "Sorry, Duke, maybe next time, okay?"

"Are you feeling okay, Jenna?"

"Yeah, it's just my head is reeling from all that's happened." She shrugged. "I'm not sure what help I'll be—I don't know a thing about buying horses. I'll be useless at offering an opinion."

"That's okay." His voice had lowered to the caring tone he used when she became angry with him. "I'll pick out a suitable mount for you. What color do you prefer? I don't want to buy something you'll hate."

Laughter bubbled at his serious expression and the tension of the day lifted from her shoulders. She grinned and tapped her bottom lip as if trying to make up her mind. "Well, let me see, black goes with everything, but then so does white."

"I hope we can find something to suit you." Kane's lips curled into a smile. "We'll be able to take them today. The stables are ready and I have a horse trailer."

Jenna stared at him. "You have a horse trailer?"

"Yeah, I had it delivered to Gloria's ranch on Friday." He rolled his broad shoulders and suddenly looked abashed. "She is very, ah, accommodating. Rowley introduced her to me the other day in Aunt Betty's."

Jenna headed for the door. "Really? You've never mentioned meeting her before."

"I didn't think it was a relevant part of the current caseload, ma'am." He attached a leash to Duke's collar and straightened.

She noted the high color in his cheeks and bit back a snort of laughter. "That's why you want me along, isn't it? So she doesn't hit on you again."

His expression had closed into his professional persona and he ignored her question. After working with Kane for almost a year, she knew by his face that the subject of Gloria Smithers was not open for discussion. *Hmm, maybe he likes her.*

As they headed out to Gloria Smithers' ranch, Jenna looked through her notes. None of the victims' associates were involved in the case. The victims had no social life, no friends or workmates they hung out with at weekends. Every person they spoke to led to another dead end. Apart from the fact the two murder victims worked at Party Time, they had nothing to prove they as much as spoke to each other outside of work. It made sense that if a group of men visited the girls on a regular basis, they would have been friends for some time. The men in the group trusted one another and obviously planned each meeting with care. The fact they had been very careful not to allow themselves to be recognized in any of the images they had found made her wonder just how many men were involved. The girls mentioned four men, but she could not be sure if they were the same four men. She rubbed the tip of her nose. The only conclusion she could come up with was the men met years ago, maybe as teenagers, and yet nothing her deputies had discovered pointed to anything other than the two working for Party Time. She had to dig deeper. *But where?*

She glanced at Kane. "Do you think the killer was either a victim of abuse or a relative of one of the girls they molested?"

"So far all the relatives we've found have sound alibis for the time of death of both victims." Kane shrugged. "Although we are assuming the six missing girls we know about are the extent of the pedophiles' activities; there could be more. Then add the fact it is all assumption; we don't have proof any of these missing girls were involved with our victims." He sighed. "The killer being a victim of abuse is the more likely case."

Jenna scanned her notebook as if the proof she needed would suddenly jump out at her. "Revenge is the only motive for Price and Dorsey I have. The problem is, all missing kids are still missing, which leaves us with the three women molested as kids: Lizzy Harper, Angelique Booval, and Pattie McCarthy."

"Pushing them for information will be difficult; maybe you'll have a better chance. They don't want me to speak with them."

She let out a huge sigh. The masks were significant. If the group of men used the masks as a regular disguise, it would have started from the get-go and would have left a lasting impression on the girls. Her three suspects held key information on the identities of the others in the group of molesters, although getting them to admit or identify any of the men involved was proving difficult. Her thoughts turned to Angelique Booval. The interview with her the following day might give her the breakthrough she needed to solve the case.

She glanced at Kane, who appeared deep in thought. "Did the Booval brothers mention anything about their sister's whereabouts during the murders?"

"They did mention she was in town but apparently she won't go near them in costume; clowns frighten her." Kane's head remained face front, staring at the road. "Another suspect was in town that day as well. I saw Pattie McCarthy heading away from Stu Macgregor, who was wearing a clown costume. Maybe she doesn't like clowns either."

Jenna stared at him in surprise. "That's not a reason to kill someone. Many people hate clowns—it's a real phobia."

"Sure is. It goes by the name of coulrophobia but I don't think that particular phobia is what our killer suffers from." Kane's blue gaze met hers for a few seconds before returning to the road. "In my opinion, the vigilante has a form of PTSD and something triggered an episode and set them off on this killing spree."

"I can relate to that. In fact, I'm not surprised the murders happened when we have a festival in town. Entertainers are all over: the ones in the park and the magician on the sidewalk. I need to find out if Price and Dorsey worked the streets in some capacity last week as well." She made a note in her notebook. "I'll find out if Party Time knows anything."

"I checked that already." Kane sighed. "Party Time isn't involved in the street festivals. The local town councils organize and pay the entertainers."

"Okay." She looked back at Kane. "So we know Harper and McCarthy were in the vicinity at the time of both murders and

Angelique Booval was in Black Rock Falls the day Ely Dorsey died. We need to know if Booval was in town the day Price died."

"We'll ask her in the morning." Kane turned into a driveway. "Here we are now."

Jenna glanced up as they entered a sweeping driveway with white fenced areas of land each side containing numerous horses. "This place is huge."

"Yeah, Gloria has a few different breeds here, I gather." Kane drove to the steps of a white ranch of considerable size. "She has picked out a few mounts we might find suitable."

The moment the car pulled up at the front steps, the door flew open and out stepped a voluptuous woman in her late twenties with flowing red hair and wearing jeans so tight if she had varicose veins, Jenna would have been able to see them. As Kane slid from the driver's seat, the woman grabbed him and kissed him on both cheeks.

"Dave, how wonderful to see you again." The woman linked her arm with his as if she had known him for years. "I'm so glad you could make it."

"So am I. Do you mind if I bring the dog along?"

"Of course not, silly." She beamed up at him.

Jenna climbed from the SUV and went to Kane's side. "You must be Miss Smithers. I gather you have some horses for sale?"

"Ah, yes." Kane turned and gave her a stony look. "Gloria, this is Sheriff Jenna Alton."

Gloria hardly acknowledged Jenna's presence but towed Kane toward a big barn set some way from the ranch. Jenna could hear them chatting in low voices and her instinct told her to get back in the car and wait, but she pushed down her bubbling resentment toward the woman and caught up to them. She forced her lips into a smile. "Do you live here alone, Miss Smithers?"

"Of course not. How could I run a place like this alone?" Gloria turned her attention back to Kane. "There is a black gelding I think will be perfect, and a choice of two mares. The bay is very quiet, for the more inexperienced rider." She shot an almost pitying glance at Jenna. "Then there is a white Arab; she is a little headstrong but sound."

Jenna could not help herself and touched Kane's arm. "I like a horse with spirit."

"I'll have Arnie saddle them for you." Gloria led the way into a massive barn and detached herself from Kane to speak to one of her staff.

Jenna turned to him. "Nice lady. I wonder why she's not married."

"I have no idea." Kane's mouth turned down and he bent to rub Duke's ears.

"She likes you." Jenna stared after Gloria. "Why don't you ask her out on a date?"

"She's not my type, and for the record, I have no intention of dating anyone." Kane's eyes rolled skyward. "I'm here to buy a horse." His lips twitched. "You *do* know the meaning of the word *schmoozing*, right? Being nice to the right people when you want something is how things are done around these parts." He turned his gaze back to the returning Gloria and smiled. "Trust me, I'm an expert."

CHAPTER THIRTY-TWO

Jane Stickler stared into the shadows in her room at the hospital. The quiet was driving her crazy. The sheriff's department had closed the entire floor she was on, and during the day, a deputy sat on duty beside the elevators. The nurse had insisted she was safe overnight as the hospital restricted access to the wards. Yet only one nurse sat at the nurses' station all night and most times reading a book.

Apparently, no one could find her but her stomach ached at the thought of the interview with the sheriff in the morning. Ely was dead, so why did they need any more information? She chewed on what was left of her nails, wondering what they would ask her. Embarrassment heated her cheeks. She could not tell them everything—it was just too awful. The drugs the doctors had given her made her brain slow and she couldn't think straight. She glanced at the digital readout on the clock above her bed; it was after midnight and she had dozed for three hours after taking the medication, but now fully awake, she just wanted to go home.

She wondered if her room would be the same or if her parents had thrown out her things. They had been strange when they arrived. They looked so much older and she hardly recognized them. It was as if two strangers had walked into her room. She had been so excited to see them and desperately needed a hug but they had not so much as touched her hand. In fact, they seemed ashamed of her, sitting well away from her as if she had some contagious disease.

Her mom hadn't mentioned taking her home at all and left without saying when or if they would return.

Thank God, Adam had arrived soon after the sheriff dropped her at the hospital. Her brother left her for an hour then returned laden with everything she would need: nightgowns, toiletries, and clothes. Sure, some of the things were a little big, but she had not had anything of her own to wear in eight years. Her brother had grown up to be a very kind man and had offered to take her to his house in Black Rock Falls.

A noise in the hallway caught her attention and she looked through the glass panel in the door, expecting to see the deputy who walked past and peered at her on the hour every day. Panic hit her like a blow to the gut as the dim lighting hit a clown face. Ely was coming and he would kill her for telling the sheriff about the others. Frozen with terror, her gaze fixed on the man strolling slowly along the passageway. No, it could not possibly be *him*. The sheriff had told her Ely was dead but his words filled her head as if he stood next to her whispering in her ear. *If you say a word to anyone, we will find you. There is no place to hide. We will kill you and your family.*

Heart racing, she gasped for breath and slipped from the bed. She had to get away. After pushing the pillow under the covers to make it appear she was sleeping, she ducked under the bed and lay on the cold tile. As the door pushed silently open, the man moved into the room. She heard him breathing. The blankets came off the bed in a whoosh and the man swore.

"Where are you, bitch?"

His feet moved inches from her nose, and she let out a gasp. The next moment, the hideous smiling face peered at her.

"Get out from under there and get into bed or I'm taking you back where you belong."

She recognized the voice as one of the men who used to visit her, the mean one with the green eyes. She backed away. "I'll scream and the nurse will come."

"No one is coming. All the nurses are having a nice sleep and you are the only patient on this floor. The other kid went home." He leaned in and grabbed her by the hair. "Do as I say and I'll be nice, or you'll suffer. Your choice."

Trembling with fear, she eased out from under the bed, the smell of him bringing back a rush of terrible dark memories. "Let go of me and I'll do what you say."

"I know you will." He stepped back a pace. The grinning red lips stretched wide on his white face sent tremors of disgust through her.

A shaft of light lit up the room and a small figure dressed in black with their face covered in a ski mask stood in the doorway.

"Who the hell are you supposed to be?" He turned away. "Get out of here, kid."

As the figure moved into the room leaving the door wide open, Jane inched her way around the foot of the bed. If she could make it out of the door, she could find help.

Without warning, the figure lunged toward the clown, and Jane heard a voice.

"Run!"

She didn't wait and hurtled toward the door. The clown's large hands grasped at her nightgown but she slipped away and edged out into the hall.

"Leave her alone." The figure stepped in his way. "Run and don't look back."

The clown bellowed with rage and Jane heard a loud thump as he plowed a fist into the stranger. "I'll deal with you next, kid."

Terrified, she forced her legs to move and ran out the door then pelted down the dimly lit corridor toward the nurses' station. The place was deserted, and behind her, she could hear the clown swearing at the woman. *I need to get help.*

Her feet clad only in socks slipped on the polished floor and she bounced off the walls in a desperate attempt to get away. Safety was not far but seemed to be miles away. She screamed as loud as possible. Someone must be around in a hospital and might hear her. "Help me! Help me!"

Her screams echoed down the empty corridors but no one came. Desperate for help, she ran past the doors to the other rooms, peering through the small windows, but no other patients occupied the rooms. She remembered something her brother had told her earlier—she was in a ward on a floor all to herself. For her own safety. Breathless, she ran for her life and slid to a stop, gaping in disbelief at the nurse behind the counter. The night nurse lolled back in her chair, eyes closed. Jane banged her fists on the desk.

"Wake up, I need help."

The woman did not move.

She slapped at the counter, sending papers spilling to the floor. "Help me." She stared at the nurse, waiting for her to take a breath.

The nurse's chest did not move.

Had he killed them all?

Desperate to get away, she glanced in all directions. The elevator doors loomed in the distance, the metal glistening like the pearly gates. If she could make it to the elevator, she might get away. She took off at a sprint. *I can make it.*

She turned to see him strolling slowly toward her, his grotesque mask grinning.

"I'm coming." He chuckled deep and low. "I'm going to kill you."

Her chest tightened and her heart beat so fast it nearly burst through her ribs. His footsteps sounded behind her, and with each measured step, he taunted her.

"You can't get away from me."

He was gaining on her but she still had time. She slid into the wall beside the elevator, dragged in a breath, and slammed her trembling palm on the button on the panel beside the door. Machinery whirred and lights lit up on the screen showing the floors. The elevator was on the bottom floor and she was at the very top. "Come on, come on." She pounded the button and stared at the readout as it seemed to creep up the floors in slow motion.

Five more floors to go, three more to go, two more. It was moving fast now.

He was faster.

"Got you." He slammed her into the wall, forcing the air from her lungs.

The elevator doors slid open. Too late; he had her. She could not breathe. His weight pinned her like a butterfly to a collector's board. Before she could fight back, he spun her around and wrenched her arm out, and something sharp pricked her flesh. She tried to say something but her mouth refused to work. She stared into his pitiless green eyes and shuddered at his disgusting red grin. *I'm going to die.* The world tilted then folded in at the edges.

CHAPTER THIRTY-THREE

Flat out on the floor of Jane's hospital room, she gasped for breath and rolled into a ball. Pain shot through her stomach. She might have known Bobby-Joe would use his classic move on her and punch her in the guts. At least Jane had got away. She would not fail to kill him next time they met, but right now she needed to get away before he came back to kill her.

The sound of dragging came from outside the door. With one arm wrapped around her ribs, she stumbled to her feet then slid into the shadows behind the open door. Moments later, Bobby-Joe entered the room, dragging Jane by the hair. He hoisted her onto the bed, and through the crack in the door, she watched him tuck her under the blankets. The man was careful, wearing a mask and surgical gloves, and would not leave a trace of evidence. When he looked under the bed and glanced around the room, she held her breath. One on one, he would kill her.

"Dammit, now I have a kid stalking me. Not that I have to worry. I'm a ghost." He chuckled then went back to the bed and stared down at Jane "I told you, no one gets away." Bobby-Joe turned away and sauntered out of the room.

She waited until she heard the elevator doors close then peered around the door and stared in horror at Jane. Her face was sheet-white. She moved close to the bed and checked for a pulse in Jane's neck. Nothing. He had killed her. Anger raged over her like a tidal wave. "I'm so sorry."

Her first priority would be to get out of the hospital. She peered cautiously out the door then, rather than take the elevator, turned the other way and headed for the fire exit. Her ribs hurt and she had learned an important lesson. The next time she met up with Bobby-Joe, she would be carrying a weapon.

CHAPTER THIRTY-FOUR

Monday, week two

After finishing his workout with Jenna, Kane headed out to the stables to tend the horses. He inhaled the satisfying smell of fresh hay. It reminded him of his childhood and his misspent youth in a small country town before joining the marines. He smiled at the memories. Both animals had settled in well overnight and snickered in greeting at his arrival; they had accepted Duke as well, which was a bonus. He rubbed the horses' silken noses and spoke quietly to them before moving them out to the corral.

He was mucking out the stalls when he heard Jenna's voice calling his name. "I'm out back."

He pushed the wheelbarrow toward the barn and met her. "Something wrong?"

"Yes, very wrong. Jane died overnight." Jenna's mouth formed a thin line. "The doctors have no idea what happened. She was fine when the nurse gave her meds at bedtime."

He rolled the wheelbarrow into the barn then removed his gloves and dropped them onto a table. "Who was with her? Any signs of a struggle?" He wiped sweat from his brow with his forearm.

"Not that the doctor noticed. She died in her sleep, or so it seems." Jenna stood with one hand resting on her service weapon. "It sounded suspicious to me so I sent Wolfe to take a look at the body. If he thinks a post is necessary, we'll have to get her parents' permission for an autopsy."

He nodded in agreement. "It does sound suspicious, especially as we'd planned to interview her again soon. Problem is, who would kill her? The vigilante is killing the pedophiles not the victims."

"The thought crossed my mind as well." Jenna worried her bottom lip, turning it rosy-pink. "Although, from what the vigilante has told us, the men involved murdered a lot of kids—maybe one of them killed Jane?"

Kane met her gaze. "Yeah, but only we know what she told us. If she was murdered and her killer knows anything about hospital procedure for traumatized patients, he would assume Jane would need a doctor's clearance before we interviewed her." He rubbed his chin. "He would also need access to the hospital at night."

"Yeah, which tells us it's more than likely one of the men in the pedophile ring works at the hospital." Jenna flicked him a worried glance and started toward her house. "Get ready. I want to get to the hospital, and we have to visit Angelique Booval in Blackwater today. We'll go in your car."

The memory of her exhilaration the last time she drove his car drifted across his mind. He gave her a long look. "Do you want to drive?"

"What, *me* drive 'the beast'?" Her lips twitched into an almost smile. "As much as I'd like the chance to put the pedal to the metal on an open road, I'm not sure if your nerves could handle it." She eyeballed him in almost a challenge. "She is your *baby*, after all."

He lifted his chin. "My nerves are fine."

"I'd rather have your mind on the case than my driving." She turned to go then stopped and looked back at him. "I'll fix breakfast. Can you be ready to eat in fifteen minutes?"

The idea of a cooked breakfast made his stomach rumble; of late he had settled for cereal. He smiled at her. "Yeah."

After breakfast, Kane drove to the office and Jenna was unusually quiet. He glanced at her to see her chewing on her lip, a habit she had when deep in thought. "Problem?"

"I'm just going over the cases. Jane dying is too coincidental. She managed to survive just fine chained to a damn wall, and the moment she is safe she dies in her sleep? I'm not buying it, not at all." She glanced at him. "The problem is if foul play was involved, the crime scene would have been destroyed by now. There would have been nurses and doctors all over the room."

"Not necessarily. Wolfe is very good at his job."

"Yeah, I know, but it took a lot of convincing to persuade the doctor to leave the body in situ." She flicked him a glance. "I insisted we regard any death involving a crime as suspicious, and he finally agreed to seal the room and wait for Wolfe to arrive. He'll be there by now, so will have some answers by the time we get there."

"He'll know if it looks suspicious."

"Another thing." Jenna turned in her seat to look at him, filling the air with her honeysuckle fragrance. "I have a gut feeling this vigilante is involved in more than we give her credit for, and I'm sure it's a woman. The blood on your doorstep, the phone call. The more I think about it, it just seems like the actions of a vengeful woman."

Kane cleared his throat. "Yeah, I'm sure too the profile fits a woman. She wanted to give her motive for murder and send a warning to back off from interviewing the women. What else do you have?"

"I think she is playing us like a chess game." Jenna leaned toward him with an excited edge to her voice. "Think about it. She is giving us clues and telling us these men are guilty of murder as well as being in a pedophile ring, but by doing this, she is directing our investigation. She must know that after we read those newspaper articles we'd be talking to any women who have been molested in the last ten years." She threw both hands in the air. "We are heading out of town today—why? Because we need to follow up on Angelique Booval, who is a prime suspect. But what if Angelique had nothing to do with the murders and the vigilante is just getting us out of town so she can kill again?"

Kane shrugged; she did have some valid points. "Maybe, but assuming Jane died as a result of homicide, if the vigilante was watching the movements of the men concerned, why didn't she stop Jane's murder?"

"I don't know, but if my theory is correct, both the other men on her list live in Black Rock Falls."

"I think that's a given." He turned the vehicle onto Stanton Forest Road and headed toward the hospital. He glanced at the forest with the mountains towering in the distance and found it hard to believe such a beautiful vista could hide so many crimes. Since his arrival in Black Rock Falls, the seemingly harmless little town had revealed a bottomless pit of secrets, none of which so far had led to anything but death.

Kane dragged his thoughts back to the now. "It's a nuisance that we have to go back into town to open the office; it will add more time on our trip to Blackwater and I said we'd be there before two."

"I'm way ahead of you." She flopped back in her seat and her attention moved away from him. "Rowley is in charge of the office today, I called him earlier." She cleared her throat. "Have you noticed how big he is getting? He asked me if I could supply bigger shirts. Of course, I ordered them at once. He must be working out. Do you have the time to show him some of your unarmed combat moves?"

"No need." He slowed the car to make a bend then glanced at her. "He works out at the gym in town and has joined a martial arts dojo."

"Why the sudden need to build himself up? He is a very capable deputy."

Kane bit back a grin. "He is seeing someone and women bring out the best in men."

"Oh, I see." Jenna's cheeks pinked. "I guess he is still dating Alison Saunders?"

Kane drove through the hospital gates and parked in a reserved space out front beside Wolfe's cruiser. He met her gaze. "My lips are sealed."

CHAPTER THIRTY-FIVE

The smell of the hospital surrounded Jenna as she walked with some trepidation toward Jane's room. Outside in the hallway, her brother Adam sat on a chair with his face buried in his hands. She moved to his side and laid one hand on his shoulder. "Mr. Stickler, I'm sorry for your loss. Is there anyone I can call for you?"

He lifted his pale, tear-streaked face and looked at her then shook his head. His expression held so much pain, Jenna's stomach cramped.

"I just want to see her." Adam scrubbed at his eyes. "Why won't they let me see her?"

Jenna gave Kane a nod to go ahead and speak to Wolfe. As the Black Rock Falls County Coroner, Wolfe would have to make the call to allow him to view her body. She sat down beside Adam and swallowed the lump in her throat. "It was so strange for her to die in her sleep. I thought it best for our coroner to take a quick look just to make sure no one hurt her."

"I have the awful feeling someone did." He wiped his eyes with his sleeve. "She was just fine when I left her last night, really happy. She wanted to live here in town with me." His bloodshot eyes blinked and his gaze moved over her face. "One of the men who kidnapped her has killed her. She told me they threatened her and said if she said a word to anyone they would kill everyone she loved."

Astonished that Jane had spoken to Adam about her ordeal, Jenna took the opportunity to push him a little more. Any information she could discover would be a bonus. She stood and went to the coffee machine a few feet away and purchased two cups of coffee. After handing one to Adam, she sat down. "I hope you like it white with two?"

"Yeah, thanks." Adam clutched onto the cup as if it were a life preserver and glanced at her. "I hope the assholes come and try and kill me." His head turned and he stared straight into her eyes. "Jane told me what they did to her. I can't believe she survived eight years with them. They chained her to the wall, for Christ's sake."

Jenna held his gaze. "We know there were at least four men involved and two of them are dead. Did she give you any clues about the others? I know they wore masks but any small clue might help us to track them down."

"One had green eyes." Adam snorted in anger. "When they first took her, she said she thought he was a fairy because he had fair hair and his eyes were green, emerald green." The nerve in his cheek twitched. "And a spider tattoo in the web of one hand. From what she told me he was a mean son of a bitch, cruel and merciless. She was terrified of him."

Wanting to keep him talking, Jenna put down her cup then took out her notepad and jotted down a few details. "Anything else you can remember?"

"I'll never forget what she said to me last night." He rubbed a hand over his face and blinked as if still seeing her. "She said since you found her, bits of memories have been coming back. She thinks there could have been four men. Two were of similar build but one of them was real quiet. The others teased him but she did remember something significant about him."

Pen poised above the notepad, she leaned toward him, anxious to hear every word. "Which was?"

"He had a scar on his knee like mine." Adam placed his coffee cup on the chair beside him and rolled up one leg of his jeans to display a long scar running up the center of his knee. "I came off a horse when I was a kid and crushed my knee so bad it had to be replaced. My father's health insurance covered the surgery but Jane said these men always appeared to be short of money. They argued about putting in money to pay for her upkeep. So the fact he had such expensive surgery has to be important."

Jenna let the facts roll around her head. A rodeo rider came to mind then a thought hit her. "He could have been in a car wreck."

"Exactly." Adam rolled down the leg of his jeans. "A big claim like that would still be on record with an insurance company." He rubbed the back of his neck. "She said they all wore masks and latex gloves but she could see the tattoo through the glove." He swallowed hard and looked away. "She said they took photographs. Disgusting freaks."

Jenna winced at his aggressive stance and stood. "Okay, thanks. I promise you, we will find these men."

Relief flooded over her at the sight of Kane coming from Jane's room. When he waved her over, she looked down at Adam. "It won't be long now. I'll go and speak to Deputy Wolfe."

"He looks tense. Problems?" Kane raised one dark eyebrow and led the way into the room.

"He is angry and does not believe for one second she died in her sleep." Jenna moved to Wolfe's side and stared down at the emaciated figure of Jane Stickler, trying to ignore the scent of death hovering in the room. "Have you come to a conclusion?"

"Yeah." Wolfe moved the overhead light so it illuminated the corpse. "She has needle marks in her arms but they could have been during administration of drugs by the nurses. So usually a full toxicology screening wouldn't be necessary but I figure someone overdosed her. I have the list of what the hospital gave her during her stay and nothing could have killed her."

Jenna shot him a glance. "A hunch isn't homicide; you must have found something else."

"Look here." Wolfe moved the light so it shone on the top of Jane's head. "See the bruising? That is fresh and not in the initial report. I had reason to believe someone dragged her by her hair, so I checked the room and found many of her hairs under the bed and by the door. I suggest checking the hallway for hairs and dusting the nurses' station and the elevator control panel for fingerprints."

"Okay." She glanced at Kane. "Grab Wolfe's kit and get me some evidence."

"Yes, ma'am."

Jenna moved her attention back to Wolfe. "What else have we got?"

"Jane's socks look brand new but are soiled as if she was walking around." Wolfe's gray eyes narrowed. "She has a bundle of new socks on the chair over there. Why wear dirty ones to bed? Then there is this…" He flicked back the sheet and pushed up the girl's nightgown to display red marks on her knees. "Classic friction marks. She was dragged face down."

A wave of apprehension hit Jenna and she swallowed the lump in her throat. "Do you believe she tried to run away from her killer?"

"Yeah, he could have chased her down and subdued her then dragged her back by her hair. Sometime during the struggle, he administered a hot shot then put her back to bed."

Jenna's head spun with the news. "How the hell did someone kill her in the hospital? Where were the nurses?" She paced the room, shaking her head in disbelief. "I want answers. Do they have CCTV cameras on each floor?"

"No, they are at the main entrance and the emergency entrance." Wolfe covered the body. "I already asked."

"I'll have to speak to the nurse and everyone on duty in the wards last night." Jenna headed for the door just as Kane came back in. "Find anything?"

"Nope, the nurse on duty said the cleaners did this area before the body was discovered but I did find out something interesting. One of the nurses used the water from the hot water urn for tea in the break room and passed out cold. She is still asleep and the doctor thinks someone put sleeping pills in the water. I told her to make sure no one touches the urn so we could get a sample."

"You mean someone drugged the entire staff last night?"

"On this floor and the two below, yes. It makes sense they did—apparently, the night shift on those floors usually take a short break to make coffee or whatever at eleven thirty, and it's rare to have more than one nurse on duty overnight. If anything happens to a patient, she only has to call down to emergency to get assistance." Kane leaned his wide shoulders against the wall. "Whoever did this knows the shift times and when the nurses take a break."

Jenna scratched her head. So much to do and time was running out. *Delegate.* "Wolfe, if you're taking blood from the people on duty last night who could have been drugged, can you question them as well and see if they noticed anything unusual?" She sighed. "This is way too big for us; we'll have to call in the FBI again to carry out a full investigation. I want to know if the pills we found on the victims and the drug used on the staff came from this hospital. You can trace packaging and the batch numbers from missing inventory out of the hospital pharmacy can't you?"

"Yeah, not a problem, I'll contact them. I'm going to be hanging around for hours waiting for documents to be processed. The hospital has to complete a ton of forms before they'll release the body."

She let out a long sigh. "I'm convinced it's an inside job. It's obvious a member of the pedophile ring works here or knows someone who does."

"Unfortunately that doesn't help much." Kane cleared his throat then gave her an apologetic look. "Anyone who spent time in here as a patient for any length of time would be used to the shift changes as well."

"I'll speed things up a bit by taking blood samples from the nurse on duty last night and we'll need to go confiscate the urn." Wolfe rubbed his chin, making a rasping sound over his blond stubble. "I'll have to do an autopsy." He pushed a gurney closer to the bed then threw Kane a pair of gloves. "Help me get her onto the gurney. It stinks in here. I'll put her in the room next door for her brother to see her." He flicked a glance at her. "Can you distract her brother for a few minutes? He is in her file as next of kin. Obviously, her parents gave him the honor. Get him to fill in a permission form. There is one in my kit."

"Sure, but before I forget… Did Price or Dorsey have a scar on their knee? It would have been significant, maybe the same as knee replacement surgery."

"No, they had nothing unusual apart from the scar on Dorsey's stomach, and the birthmark on his neck Zoe identified."

"Then the one with the scar on his knee is still out there." She looked at the girl with deep compassion. "I have to find her killer; she deserves justice."

CHAPTER THIRTY-SIX

Jenna waited as her two deputies used the sheet to lift Jane onto the gurney. She noted the way Wolfe covered her with a fresh sheet and almost reverently smoothed her hair.

"If you take Adam down to the nurses' station to sign the forms, we'll move her." Kane rubbed at the black stubble on his chin and glanced at her with a look of detachment. "He might refuse to sign the permission forms."

"He'll sign." She bent to search the pockets of Wolfe's bag. "He wants to know what happened to her."

After collecting the required form, she headed out the door. She found Adam Stickler in the same position and touched him on the shoulder. "I'll need you to fill out a few forms if you don't mind? Come down to the nurses' station with me."

She sighed with relief when he followed her without question. The poor man was so pale she thought he might collapse. "The ME has a few concerns, as you do, about Jane's death. He would like to do an autopsy but we'll need the next of kin's permission."

"I'm her next of kin as of yesterday." Adam gave her a disgruntled stare. "My parents are embarrassed and were too cowardly to tell her they didn't want her living with them." He let out a half-choked sob. "They won't have to worry now, will they? You know, I haven't bothered to tell them she died. I'm not sure if I ever want to see them again."

Jenna blinked back the tears stinging the backs of her eyes and rested a hand on his arm. She did not know what to say to him. "Do you want me to speak with them?"

"Would you?" He straightened and looked down into her eyes. "Deputy Wolfe is the new ME, isn't he? Is he good? Will he be able to find out what happened?"

"Yes, he is the best I know." She led him to the nurses' station and placed the paperwork on the counter. "If you'll sign these forms, I'll take you to see Jane."

With the signed forms in one hand, Jenna took Adam into the room to view and formally identify his sister's body. Kane and Wolfe stood to one side, their faces grim. Beside her, Adam allowed the tears to fall and held his sister's hand for a long time.

"I'll take care of her for you." Wolfe stepped forward and laid one large hand on Adam's shoulder. "Go home and get some rest."

"Did she suffer?" Adam's mouth turned down.

"No." Wolfe led him to the door, his voice low and compassionate. "She went to sleep."

Jenna watched the two men walk out the door and turned to Kane. "Do you know what her murder means?" She dashed a hand through her hair. "We're chasing smoke and shadows. Whoever did this is running scared of the vigilante and the law. He killed Jane because he thought she could identify him and maybe others in his group of perversion."

"Which means Zoe could be next on his list."

Jenna pulled out her cellphone. "I'm calling Zoe's father to give him the heads up. I'll call the sheriff there as well to keep him in the loop."

*

In the hallway outside Jane's room, Jenna made the calls. She decided to inform the Blackwater sheriff she would be interviewing a potential suspect in his jurisdiction as well. She smiled at Kane when the Blackwater sheriff offered her his full cooperation to solve the case. "Yes, I do believe the pedophile ring is widespread, and from the list of missing girls I sent you, there may be other counties involved." She put her cellphone on speaker and moved closer to Kane.

"Oh, I'm on the case, Sheriff. I've had my deputies working all weekend checking out cold cases from ten years back. I'll be chasing down leads to any street entertainers as well. We have a few clowns coming through at odd times of the year. If we find anything, I'll call you."

"Thank you." She disconnected and turned to Kane. "That's good news and we have the go-ahead from the Blackwater sheriff. I didn't want to tread on anyone's toes."

When Wolfe strolled toward her wearing a concerned expression, her stomach dropped. *What else is wrong?* She lifted her chin. "You look like the sky before a storm, what's up?"

"Being here in the hospital clicked something in my mind." He glanced at Kane. "Do you have the images you took of the bottle of pills found in Amos Price's truck?"

"Yeah." Kane pulled out his cellphone then scrolled through the images. "Here." He gave Wolfe the phone.

"Dammit, I missed it." Wolfe held up the image of a bottle of pills with a printed white label on the front with *Diazepam 5mg* written in black. "See this bottle? This is a bulk bottle supplied to hospitals. When a doctor prescribes medication, there is a patient's name, dosage, number of pills, and doctor's name on the label."

Jenna swallowed the bile in her throat. "So whoever killed Jane has access to the hospital pharmacy."

"It's something I'll notify the FBI about when I contact them. We found drugs of the same type with both our other victims. It makes sense one of their group is supplying them." Wolfe rubbed the back of his neck in an agitated manner. "Something else—when I was organizing for the removal of the body, the pathologist working in the morgue informed me that after eleven at night, access to the hospital is by a swipe card or via the emergency room."

A rush of excitement hit her. "So they'll have a record of anyone entering the hospital?"

"Yes and no." Wolfe's brow creased into a frown. "You'll be able to get a printout of the people entering the hospital using a swipe card but not the names of patients in emergency because of confidentiality laws, but we do have the CCTV footage. All we need is a court order, but if Jane's killer worked here, he would make sure he would avoid the camera or be in disguise. To go to this much trouble to kill her he would be taking every precaution." He met her gaze. "I spoke to the office. They'll email you a list of people who used their cards overnight and a list of employees."

"Thanks." She chewed on her bottom lip. "How long before you start the autopsy?"

"I'll start as soon as the body arrives at my office. Although, I won't have the toxicology screen results back for about three weeks. If she died of a drug overdose, which I suspect, it points to someone with knowledge of the administration of drugs. I mean, for instance, an overdose of insulin would kill. It doesn't have to be a narcotic. We shouldn't discount we could be looking at an underground drug supply in town."

"I understand drug trafficking, Wolfe. Now you're moving into my area of expertise." Jenna nodded. "The FBI investigators will do a complete audit of the drugs. Make sure we are kept in the loop; I want to know if the drugs came from here." She thought for a few minutes. "If that's all, we're heading over to Blackwater to interview the Booval girl."

"Nothing more I can think of, ma'am." Wolfe nodded.

"If you're finished here, ma'am, we should be going." Kane moved to her side. "It's an hour's drive at least and you mentioned wanting to speak to the local social worker as well. If we leave now, we'll have time to grab some takeout on the way to interviewing Angelique Booval."

She heard his stomach rumble and sighed. "I'm ready. I think you burn up calories faster than anyone I know."

"Nah, I just like food." Kane grinned.

"I'll travel down with you in the elevator." Wolfe pushed the paperwork under one arm then bent to pick up his bag. "I have to make arrangements with the hospital administrator to remove the body."

As they walked into the confined space, Jenna turned to Kane. "You're the profiler on my team. We have two killers running us around in circles. I need more information to catch them. What can you tell me?"

"The vigilante we know is a woman set on revenge and is not a danger to anyone else in the community. She has one goal and that is to wipe out the men who killed the girls in the newspapers." The nerve in Kane's cheek twitched. "The person who killed Jane has gone way past being a pedophile or a child killer. Child molesters who kill are not necessarily psychopaths. They often kill the kids out of fear they will identify them and then they feel remorse. The person who killed Jane must be the mean one the girls mentioned. He is a completely different killer and has definite psychopathic tendencies. He likes to frighten and intimidate his victims. He is a dangerous man and we need to stop him before he kills again because next time, it's going to be nasty."

CHAPTER THIRTY-SEVEN

She was having one of those days that never ended. It felt as if she had been driving for hours without a break. She had time for lunch before going home. The smell of freshly brewed coffee and donuts hit her with a blast of delicious aroma as she stepped inside the local café. She collapsed into a seat in the back corner and bit back a moan. Battered and bruised from Bobby-Joe's assault, she had dressed in a long-sleeved blouse to cover the injuries to her forearms. Her stomach ached and his punches had bruised her ribs but she offered the waitress a wide smile and ordered her meal.

"You look pale today. Are you feeling okay?" The waitress filled her cup with coffee.

"I'm just tired. I had a hot date last night." She winked at her. "Can you leave the coffee pot? I'm still half asleep."

"Lucky girl." The waitress placed the coffee pot on the table. "I'll be right back with your order."

She smiled at her, glad Bobby-Joe had not marked her face. His blows had been swift and immobilizing before he'd caught and murdered Jane. The idiot must have believed she would be waiting around for him to kill her as well. Anger shook her hands and she clutched the coffee cup. Only a fool would rush out to get revenge with injuries, and she was no fool. She would deal with him soon enough. With the law crawling all over Black Rock Falls, she would have to bide her time a little longer and concentrate on eliminating an easier target.

She sipped her coffee, deciding the best way to activate the next step of her plan. The sheriff would likely leave the two new deputies and Rowley to run the office in her absence and distracting them would not be a problem but Deputies Kane and Wolfe would be another matter. *One simple call will take care of the sheriff and her two faithful dogs.*

It had taken some months to set up her different identities in the chat room to lure the monsters but Bobby-Joe had still not taken the bait. She did have another on the hook and spoke to him as often as possible online. The idea of watching him die filled her with a rush of excitement. A tingle went through her as she pictured him writhing in agony. There could be no better feeling than watching the terror in his eyes as his life leaked away. She stabbed the steak on her plate and lifted a rare piece to her lips. The smell of blood filled her nostrils and she smiled. She had to admit she enjoyed killing the monsters. *Maybe too much.* Her mind went to the hunting knife she had purchased at a yard sale. It was as sharp as a razor blade. *It will do nicely.*

CHAPTER THIRTY-EIGHT

Kane set the GPS in the car for the address of the social worker Jenna had called and headed toward Blackwater. They traveled for over an hour without speaking, Kane content to listen to the soft music on the radio and to take in the view. The long straight blacktop spread out for miles like a black snake slithering through the green countryside. Here the forest followed one side of the road with pine trees like giant fence posts guarding the way to the mountains. As they rounded a long sweeping bend, the majesty of the Rocky Mountains came into view, spread out in a line, jagged peaks stretching up to the blue sky. Along the other side of the road was flatter terrain. Wildflowers grew in abundance amidst the scrub and when caught in the wind appeared to move across the grasslands in waves of color.

He spotted a few ranch houses in the distance but this part of the county was isolated. He turned to Jenna, who had not taken her attention from her cellphone since they left. "The views are spectacular out here."

"Yes, I know, but I wouldn't travel out this way alone." Jenna flicked him a faraway glance. "I can't imagine how you drove all the way here from DC in the middle of winter, you must be crazy."

He chuckled. "Even I'm not that crazy. Although it would have taken about three days in summer, I wasn't going to risk it in winter. I was in Helena before I came here. I had things to arrange, and I needed to purchase a decent vehicle. I wanted to have it customized before I attempted to drive to Black Rock Falls." He met her confused gaze with a smile. "For the record, you never asked me how long I'd been traveling. It took longer than I expected due to the recent snowfall. That's why I arrived in town so late."

"Oh, after hearing where you came from originally, I figured as you love this SUV so much, you must have driven it from DC." She held up her cellphone. "I've been going over our case files. If we decide Angelique Booval is our vigilante, we are going to have a problem. We can't arrest her in Blackwater; we have no jurisdiction."

Kane drummed his fingers on the steering wheel. "Why is this a problem?"

"If she is our killer, and realizes she is a suspect, she might leave the state; then we'll have a bigger problem." Jenna regarded him with a serious expression. "It wouldn't look so suspicious if I interviewed her alone. I'll wear my com device so you'll hear the interview and can prompt me if I forget anything vital."

"Okay, but if you took a Blackwater deputy with you then they could make the arrest if necessary." He glanced at her then moved his concentration back to the road. "We'd have to go through due process to bring her back to Black Rock Falls anyway, but I'm sure the Blackwater sheriff will do what he can to help."

"Good idea but she'll have to be a female deputy."

He shrugged. "After the disturbing interview I had with Lizzy Harper, I think you're right." He cleared his throat. "You mentioned profiling people to find suspects. Lizzy Harper is on the top of my list for being the vigilante. She radiates anger and has killed before. Sure, we need to pinpoint her whereabouts at the time of both deaths, but we do know she was in town when both murders were committed."

"Oh, she's on the top of my list, and Pattie McCarthy is running a close second." Jenna snorted. "She looks fit enough to run the distance from my house to the road. Both of them are vindictive enough to have thrown blood all over your front door and threatened you over the phone."

The voice on the GPS told them to take a right at the next intersection and Kane slowed the SUV to take the corner. She was correct: The women had become defensive the moment they laid eyes on him. Both appeared to be fit and able to sprint if necessary. He nodded in agreement. "Yeah, and both live in town."

Signs of habitation came into view and soon the GPS advised him he had reached his destination on the right. He pulled up in front of a brick building and did a visual sweep of the main street. "Rowley said the sheriff's department is across the road from the community health center, which is right here."

"Yeah, I can see it, down there on the left past the pizza place." Jenna unbuckled her seatbelt and turned to him. "Go and speak to the social worker and I'll head down to see the sheriff; it will save time."

"Okay." Kane pushed open the car door and stepped onto the sidewalk. "Do you mind calling me when you're ready to leave?"

"I could just meet you back here?" Jenna gave him an inquisitive stare.

Kane cleared his throat. "You know social workers, always trying to psychoanalyze everyone. I might need an escape clause."

"Ha! Sure, I'll call." She headed down the street, shaking her head.

As Kane entered the building, he heard police sirens wailing and kept walking. *Not my problem.* He spoke to the woman at the desk then strolled along the passageway to find the room number. To his surprise, the door was open, and seated on a sofa inside was a willowy blonde, engrossed in a magazine. Her carefully made-up face lifted in his direction and she crossed her long, tanned legs. His attention lingered on the white stilettos, with straps around the ankles, and the long bare thighs peeking from beneath a tight white skirt. He dragged his gaze away and knocked lightly on the door. "Ah, Miss Simpson? I'm Deputy Sheriff Kane from Black Rock Falls. Do you have time for a quick word?"

"Yes, of course. Deputy Rowley called to tell me someone would be dropping by this morning."

"I have someone in my department who suffered trauma earlier in the year. We have nothing to help in Black Rock Falls and I was wondering if you have any support groups in the area?"

"That depends on the trauma."

Kane clasped his hands in front of him. "Kidnapping, attempted rape, and murder."

"Male or female?" She eyed him critically. "It makes a difference. You see, women often refuse to open up in front of men."

Kane gave her his best concerned stare and leaned forward in his chair. "Female, and it will take some convincing to get her to attend but I want to try."

"Then you must try to persuade her to make an appointment with me. We do have various help groups but what you are describing requires specialist help." She smiled but the humor did not go to her eyes. "Group sessions, if any, are held under the supervision of a therapist in the strictest of confidence."

Kane could see from her defensive posture he would get no information from her. "I see. I will speak to her and ask her to contact you." He stood. "Thank you for your time."

As he strolled toward the front door, he heard a deep voice issuing orders through a megaphone and took in the chaos happening in the middle of town. Deputies' cruisers blocked the street and in the middle of the road, a man held Jenna to his chest with a pistol pressed against her temple.

CHAPTER THIRTY-NINE

Time seemed to stand still as Kane pushed his way through the gathering crowd with their cellphones held high, seemingly unconcerned for their own safety. "Move." He pushed a man to one side and elbowed his way to the front of the crowd. After a year of fighting the effects of PTSD, the last thing Jenna needed was a maniac holding a gun to her head. Something was going down and she had neglected to call him. He noted Jenna's Glock was missing from her holster and ground his teeth. What the hell had happened? No way would she give up her weapon.

Catching sight of a gray-haired man holding a megaphone over the roof of a cruiser, he shouldered his way to his side. "Are you the sheriff?"

"Yeah." The man turned to look at him. "Sheriff Johnson, and you must be Deputy Kane?"

Kane's attention did not move from Jenna. "Yes, sir. What's the situation?"

"The man with the gun robbed the convenience store and took a pregnant woman hostage. Sheriff Alton gave me her sidearm and, without a word of explanation, marched over there and demanded to take the place of the hostage."

Kane gaped at him in disbelief. "She did what?"

"Oh yeah, she is a feisty one and she is gonna get herself killed." Johnson gave him a disparaging stare. "The man is Rick Horal. He got out of jail not three days ago."

Kane frowned at Sheriff Johnson. "Has he done this before?"

"Yeah, he is a repeat offender. Never hurt anyone before but he went down for armed robbery."

Kane met the man's gaze. "I'd like permission to take the lead on this one. Sheriff Alton's safety is my responsibility and I'm trained in hostage situations."

"She thinks the sun shines out your ass and said you'd be by before he shot her." Johnson gave him a long, unreadable look. "Heard you shot one of the Daniels boys right between the eyes during your *negotiations*."

Ignoring the hostility, Kane moved his attention back to Jenna. She appeared calm and stared at him then lifted one elbow and made a halting gesture with the other hand. He figured Jenna planned to take the gunman down alone. He shrugged, not wanting to offer any signal to the gunman, and flicked a glance at Johnson. "I do what's necessary."

"Well then, go rescue your sheriff. My men will follow your lead. I have a vest in my car. I'll send someone for it."

Kane noticed the slight tremble of the gunman's hand, the finger resting above the trigger, and the sweat beading on the man's top lip. *He is losing it.* "No time."

"It's your funeral." He motioned his men to his side and spoke to them in hushed tones. "Deputy Kane has experience in hostage situations so listen up."

Kane turned to them. "Stay back and don't get trigger happy. Leave him to me. I don't want Sheriff Alton hit."

As if ice-cold blood slid through his veins to heighten his perception, Kane surveyed the situation, taking into account the position of all the players and every possible outcome. He had to make himself the target and allow Jenna to solve the problem. The idea of not trusting her with his life despite the gun to her head and recent flashbacks did not come into the equation. *I trust her. She won't fail.*

*

Dammit, I can't have a flashback now. Cold sweat dampened Jenna's shirt and the slight tremor in her hand often came without warning. She had gotten herself into this situation and she was more than capable of getting herself out.

Seeing Kane in the crowd had settled her, and she concentrated on his face, mentally willing him to draw the gunman's attention and allow her to do her job. Worried he might believe her to be in mortal danger, which she was to some extent, she hoped he understood her signal to back the hell off. When Kane moved almost nonchalantly from the cover of the cruiser without wearing a Kevlar vest to protect him, she wanted to scream at him to go back. Instead, she took a deep breath to focus and calm her nerves. She noticed the hard line to his mouth and flicked her eyes toward the group of deputies standing behind the cruisers. It was obvious he did not want the Blackwater deputies involved in the situation.

They had trained together for almost a year now and run through many similar scenarios. She had the ability to take down the gunman without his help, but with a pistol pressed against her temple, she needed a distraction, and it seemed Kane had volunteered. When he met her gaze and gave her a slight nod, she flicked her eyes hard to the right. Once the gun was away from her head, she would strike out with deadly force.

To her relief, Kane understood her frantic gesture. He moved out into the open, keeping to the man's right, and held up his hands. If Rick Horal aimed his weapon at him, she would get a split-second chance. She ground her teeth and forced her trembling knees to calm. The training to slow her heartbeat and remain in control, which Kane had reinforced in her over the past months, fell into place. *I am in control and I'm going to take down this son of a bitch.*

She held her breath as Kane's movement caught the gunman's attention.

"Hey, Rick, what's all this about?" Kane shook his head slowly. "I hear it's not like you to take a hostage."

"You ain't a Blackwater deputy and you got no say in what I do."

When the muzzle of the gun moved away from her temple, Jenna got her feet under her and casually as possible lifted one elbow level with Horal's stomach then closed the palm of her other hand over the fist. *Ready when you are, Kane.* When Kane's gaze flicked back to her, confidence flooded through her. If Kane could make the gunman angry enough to draw fire, she would strike.

"Yeah, maybe, but that's my sheriff you have there, and the mayor of Black Rock Falls would have my badge if I allowed you to shoot her." Without hesitation, Kane took another step forward. "It's not too late. Hand over the gun, and the sheriff won't have you charged with kidnapping her."

"No one is gonna let me walk away, and I'll kill her if you take one step closer."

"That would be a stupid thing to do unless you plan on dying today?" Kane moved another few paces to the right. "Right now, we can work this out, but the moment your finger moves to the trigger, your brains will be all over the street before you have time to take a breath." He smiled at him. "That's a promise, and look behind me—you have the entire Blackwater Sheriff's Department just waiting to shoot you full of holes. You can't win."

"Yeah, well, maybe I'll take you out first. The sheriff here ain't got no weapon and she ain't no threat to me." Horal stepped behind Jenna, using her as a shield. "They won't risk shooting her, will they?" He moved the pistol away from Jenna's head and lifted his outstretched arm to aim it at Kane.

She had a millisecond to save Kane's life. As if in slow motion, Kane hit the ground, drawing his Glock out of its holster in one fluid motion. Jenna slammed her elbow into Horal's guts. As the gunman cried out in pain then bent in agony, she brought up her thigh and slammed his face into her knee. His nose shattered with a satisfying crunch and she stepped to one side as he folded, dropping his pistol. The chop she delivered at the base of Horal's skull sent him sprawling face down on the blacktop, screaming for his mama. Disgusted as the smell of urine burned her nostrils, she stepped over him and kicked his weapon out of reach then bent to draw his arms behind his back and cuffed him.

After dragging the gunman to his feet and handing him over to Sheriff Johnson, Jenna ignored the congratulations or bemused stares of the deputies then retrieved her weapon. She nodded to the sheriff. "I'm not pressing charges against him but you might want to ask the pregnant lady."

"Thanks for your help." Sheriff Johnson tipped his hat.

Jenna waited for Kane to brush the dust from his uniform then glared at him. "Didn't you hear the sirens?"

"Not until I'd left the social worker's office." The nerve in Kane's cheek twitched. "I'm surprised you got involved in a local matter. Were you aware the gunman just got out of jail for armed robbery?"

She gaped at him in astonishment. "A pregnant woman had a gun to her head and Johnson was acting like it was a day at the beach. Dammit, Kane, if I died no one would give a shit. That woman has a family."

"I'd care."

Noticing the other deputies watching them with interest, she headed to the other side of the road, away from the dissipating crowd. "Drawing his fire without wearing a vest is suicidal. Do you have a death wish or something?"

"No. I trusted you to bring him down and you did." Kane shrugged and his concerned gaze moved over her. "Are you mad at me, ma'am? I figured I was following orders."

Adrenaline still surged through Jenna's veins and her heart had not slowed but exhilaration thrummed through her. The PTSD flashbacks had crippled her in similar situations, but the rigorous training Kane had put her through had paid out in silver dollars. She looked up at him, not sure what to say. As usual, he had placed his own safety above her own. "No, but you broke the protocol *you* insisted we all follow. Why the hell weren't you wearing a vest?"

"No time, ma'am." Kane walked with her along the sidewalk. "I assessed the situation. The guy was shaking so bad, I knew once he turned the gun on me, he wouldn't have been able to hit the side of a barn." His lips twitched at the corners. "He sure underestimated you. Wham, bam, bam." He punched the air. "Did you see the faces on the Blackwater deputies?" He laughed.

Although thrilled by his compliments, Jenna kept her face expressionless. "Okay, I admit I *was* expecting you to show and draw his fire."

"I'll always have your back, Jenna." He glanced at her. "You would have done the same for me."

CHAPTER FORTY

"Well, that was a waste of time." Jenna peered at her lunch, the café in Blackwater didn't come close to the delights served at Aunt Betty's Café.

"Yeah, social workers are all much the same." Kane shrugged. "I thought she might at least tell me that support groups existed in the area."

"Never mind." Jenna sipped her coffee. "I spoke to Sheriff Johnson about Angelique and he will have a female deputy waiting outside her residence at two. He did mention her case, mainly what he knew about the abduction, but nothing about what transpired during the court case. Same as what we've been up against; it was closed court."

"Yeah, and we have no chance to get a judge to grant access either as we don't have a shred of evidence against any of our suspects. Did he mention if he noticed any change of behavior in her?"

The adrenaline rush had left a headache in its wake and Jenna rubbed her temples in slow circles. "Yeah, he said she'd been *different.* She used to attend church every Sunday with her parents and that stopped. She keeps to herself, has few friends, and works part-time in the library here and in Black Rock Falls." She glanced at Kane. "She prefers to work after hours. As far as he knows, she restacks the shelves and does the odd book repairs."

"That would be why she was in Black Rock Falls the day I interviewed her brothers." Kane pushed his plate to one side and leaned back in his chair. "I wouldn't mind betting she was in town at the time of the murders. It would be easy enough to check."

Jenna finished her coffee. "I agree." She pushed to her feet. "I wondered why she specified a time for us to speak to her. I guess she isn't working today. I'm not sure I would like to drive from here to Black Rock Falls to work part-time. She can't be making much money." She dropped bills on the table and frowned. "I'm concerned about a motive. As far as we know, Stewart Macgregor was the only person named in her case. If she is our vigilante, what is her reason for killing Price and Dorsey? If she'd planned to kill someone, wouldn't she go after Macgregor first?"

"We need to find out if anyone else was involved in her abduction. After all this time, she might be prepared to talk." Kane pulled out his wallet and matched her pile. "I don't believe for one second any of these men acted alone. She was able to identify Macgregor and his house but if there were others involved, perhaps she couldn't identify them and kept quiet."

Jenna led the way to the door and they strolled to Kane's black SUV. "I asked Sheriff Johnson if she mentioned anyone else was involved at the time. All she remembered is the clown at the party. She was a little girl. Think about it, Kane. They kept her in a cellar for three days; it would be dark, and to a small traumatized kid, any man with a clown face would look the same."

"That's a point you could bring up with her. She will most likely clam up; they all do, but we have to find out if she was abused by the same group of men." Kane unlocked the car and climbed behind the wheel.

Jenna slid into the passenger seat. "I'll do my best."

Kane pulled up beside a neat brick home set in a row of similar houses not far from Blackwater's main street. A cruiser waited outside, and on their arrival, a middle-aged deputy climbed out to greet them.

"Don't forget your com device." Kane's forehead creased into a frown. "Tell the deputy to keep well back then you won't appear so threatening. Maybe explain she is here as you don't have jurisdiction to interview her."

Jenna attached the earbud and waited for Kane to fit his own then tested the reception. "Okay, let's get the show on the road."

She pushed open the door and slid onto the road then strolled to greet the deputy. "Thanks for coming."

"My pleasure. I am Christine Parkes. What do we have, ma'am?"

Jenna explained the situation and headed toward the stoop in front of the neat house. A curtain moved then footsteps came and a woman with graying hair peered at her. "Yes, what do you want?"

"I'm Sheriff Jenna Alton from Black Rock Falls and this is Deputy Parkes. I've come to speak to Angelique."

"It's okay, Mama." A petite woman with long, flowing black hair came to the door. "Pierre called and explained why they are here. It is nothing to worry about. I'll speak to them in the living room." Her accent held a hint of French. "Can you watch my cookies so they don't burn?" She looked at Jenna. "Come in."

Jenna followed her into a room awash with color. Bright yellow walls and pale blue sofas dominated the room. Floral scent filled the air from a vase overflowing with flowers on a coffee table. The chairs sat around a modern fireplace. Jenna took a seat and Parkes stood by the door to observe. The mantel held photographs of generations of a large family. From the images, Jenna noticed Angelique had hardly changed from the photograph she had seen of her at twelve years old. *You look too sweet and innocent to be a killer. What happened to you?*

"My brother mentioned you are looking for pedophiles." Angelique sat in the chair opposite her and frowned. "Why would you think I would know any?"

Jenna offered her a smile then took out her cellphone, found the photographs of Price and Dorsey, and held it up for her to see. "These men were found murdered recently and we've discovered both worked as clowns with the same company as Stu Macgregor." She noticed the girl's face had paled. "At their homes, we discovered girls they had kidnapped."

"That's awful but I don't know anything." Angelique rocked back and forth in her seat, clearly agitated.

"I know what happened to you." Jenna lowered her voice to a conspiratorial whisper. "Could there be any chance that the man who molested you could have been more than one man?"

"What do you mean, more than one man? I don't understand."

Obviously, she needed to be blunt. "Tell me about the man who kidnapped you. How many times did he visit you in one night?"

"Oh my God." Angelique's hands went to her face. "I went over this in court."

Jenna pushed a little harder. "I'm sure you did but I am not allowed to view the files and I have reason to believe at least four men are abusing girls. Two are dead and we need to arrest the others involved. This has been going on for at least ten years and you might have vital information. Will you try and think about that time again to help the other girls?"

"Two are dead? If it has been ten years, I'm not surprised—people die every day."

The cold look in Angelique's eyes sent a shiver down Jenna's spine. "Someone murdered these men."

"Maybe they deserved it."

Jenna cleared her throat. "Where did Macgregor hold you?"

"In a dark room, a basement. When he came down, he only had a flashlight and he'd shine it on me."

"You identified him, so he never wore a mask?"

"He had a clown mask, but I knew he was the magician because he took me from the party." Angelique let out a long sigh. "He has a tattoo on his arm as well. It is a heart, blood dripping, with an arrow through it." She chewed on her nails and frowned. "I saw it at the party, and when he took me, he had pushed up his sleeves."

"Can you answer the questions I asked before? It may be very important to my investigation. Did he visit you once or twice or many times?"

"I can't believe you're asking me this." Angelique gripped the edge of her seat and her knuckles went white. "Many times, all the time. He would go away for a few minutes then return."

"How many times, say in one evening?"

"Oh, I don't know, maybe six or eight." Angelique blinked a few times as if recalling the horror. "That's impossible for one man, isn't it?" She rubbed at her face. "I was so frightened and at first I was tied to the bed and blindfolded. I begged him to take off the blindfold and said I couldn't breathe. I'm sure I saw flashes before he removed the blindfold. I think he took pictures of me, the sick asshole." She lifted her angry gaze to Jenna. "Yes, I guess there could have been more, but they did not have fat guts like those men in the images on your cellphone. Macgregor was twenty-two, I think, at the time. If there were other men, they didn't say anything to me and all I could see was a grinning clown mask."

"Do you remember if they smelled different?"

"Smelled different? How does a stinking man smell? They all smell the same… I don't know." Angelique's eyes flashed with anger but Jenna could see the frightened child cowering within.

"Okay, that's all about that for now, but if you can recall anything at all, give me a call." Jenna handed her a card. "I understand you work at the Black Rock Falls Library part-time and here as well. When are you usually in Black Rock Falls in case we need to speak to you again?"

"I'll be working there all week from tomorrow. Before it was odd days: Monday through Wednesday, and Friday." Angelique changed back into the sweet-tempered woman who had greeted them without missing a beat. "I'm moving there in the morning. My brothers have a house just out of town. It's such a long drive back and forth from here."

"You'll be moving in with them?"

"No, I already have an apartment on the outskirts of town. Living there, I can avoid the festivals. I received a settlement after the court case so I don't need to work, but I love books and it's nice working in the library after hours."

Jenna smiled. She had admitted being in town at the time of the murders; all she needed now was to pinpoint the times. "What time are you usually in town?"

"Oh, I get there by lunchtime. I like Black Rock Falls. I look at the stores, have a meal at Aunt Betty's Café. I don't have to be at work until closing." Angelique smiled. "It's not a difficult job, and some days it only takes me an hour to stack the shelves. People don't read that many books anymore, it is all about e-books now. Once I've finished, my time is my own."

Time enough to commit murder. Jenna pushed to her feet. She did not have enough evidence to obtain an arrest warrant. "Well, that's all we need for now. Thank you for all your help. We'll see ourselves out."

Jenna thanked Parks for her help then climbed into the front seat of Kane's vehicle and looked at him. "What do you think?"

"She ticks all the boxes."

She pulled out the earbud and sighed. "Yeah, I agree, and her mood swings almost like a split personality, but she is tiny, maybe five two, and doesn't look capable of killing anyone let alone a man the size of Ely Dorsey."

"Says the woman who just took down a lunatic with a gun, who weighed at least two hundred pounds." Kane flicked her an amused glance.

She welcomed his ego stroke. Kane did not hand out compliments often. "We'll head back to the office. Wolfe will be doing Jane's autopsy by now. Once we update the case files and include an incident report on what happened today—" she let out a long sigh "—we should be able to leave by five for a change."

"Hallelujah."

CHAPTER FORTY-ONE

That evening, in her bedroom, she laughed to herself as she turned on her computer. The latest news bulletin stated the sheriff had made no further statements about the mysterious deaths of Amos Price and Ely Dorsey, or the death of Jane Stickler. She had the Black Rock Falls Sheriff's Department running all over the state, and one phone call to Deputy Kane tomorrow from a payphone would have them all scampering up the mountain to look for graves. Everything was going to plan.

She entered the chat room and signed in as Needy Girl then waited. After a few moments, she noticed his username, Eighteen and Lonely, in a list, and a message box opened up moments later.

She ran her fingers over the hunting knife and smiled. Her time spent running the blade over a whetstone had been worth the effort. The edge glistened under the overhead lights, reflecting patterns around the room. She took a firm grip on the handle and practiced an upward thrusting motion. The knife fit snugly in her palm. The guard at one end would stop her hand slipping in the blood and onto the blade.

There would be a lot of blood.

She would need to strike fast and hard because if she missed, he would kill her without a second thought.

I will not miss.

Allowing each potential scenario to percolate through her mind, she wet her lips, confident she had a plan to kill a monster. A message popped up on her screen.

Hey, Needy Girl, do you like clowns?

CHAPTER FORTY-TWO

Tuesday, week two

Jenna stepped out on her porch and blinked into the sunshine. She slipped on her sunglasses and surveyed her domain. The rain overnight had refreshed the lush vegetation surrounding her land in various shades of green. The air had the fresh-cut hay smell she loved, and inhaling deeply, she strolled down the steps and headed to the corral. She had not had time to breathe let alone enjoy the two horses Kane had purchased, but she found them groomed and glossy, munching the overgrown grass. She wondered what would happen when they ate all the grass, because Kane had not mentioned using any of the other paddocks.

"Hey, Jenna, admiring the horses?"

Jenna turned at Kane's voice. I have to admit they are beautiful creatures but a lot of extra work for you."

"I don't mind; it doesn't take that long to groom them and muck them out." Kane leaned his tanned forearms on the top rail of the corral and smiled. "I feel peaceful when I'm with them and I can get my mind straight." His attention followed the moving horses. "There are so many angles to consider with these new cases, I need time to reflect."

"I agree but I do my best figuring in bed." She took a position beside him. "I'm looking forward to having the time to take a ride. You do know all the surrounding paddocks up to the line of trees are on my land so if you need it for the horses, go right ahead."

"Thanks." He looked down at her. "I'm done here—are you ready to go?"

"Yeah, I just have to lock up." She met his gaze. "I'll follow you into town."

"Sure." His mouth twitched at the corners and he touched his hat before ambling to his vehicle.

She stared after him. Their workout this morning had been brutal and she had staggered into the shower with her legs shaking. Often Kane would return after he had showered and eat breakfast or drink coffee with her and mull over the caseload, but this morning he was a no-show. His mind worked on cases differently to her own; he often kept silent until he had digested all the facts then spit them out in a long monologue. She barked her ideas at everyone expecting them to collect the evidence she required.

After setting her house alarm and picking up a travel cup of coffee to drink on the way, she climbed into her vehicle and followed Kane's black SUV to the office.

She pulled up in her usual space, noting Wolfe had arrived. She hoped he would have the findings from the autopsy on Jane Stickler. Her stomach gave a little twist as she slipped out from behind the wheel and headed for the front door. The bright sunny day had suddenly turned ominous. Hearing about the last moments in a young girl's life was not on her list of favorite things to do.

She greeted Maggie with a wave. It was unusual seeing a line of people waiting at the front desk. To her surprise, her deputies—with the exception of Walters, who was now working part-time—appeared to be hard at work in their cubicles. She glanced at her watch, wondering if she was late, then noticed Rowley waiting by her office door with a perturbed expression. *Has everyone arrived before me this morning?* "Morning, did you want to speak to me?"

"Yes, ma'am, if you have a moment?"

She removed her weapon and slipped it into the desk drawer with her keys then sat down and looked up at him. "What can I do for you?"

"Yesterday, I sent Webber out to investigate the complaints we've received about dogs running loose in town. Ah, Kane mentioned them being dangerous and all."

"Yes." Jenna drummed her fingernails on the desk, and the action made Rowley's face pale.

"Well, seems he wrote about twenty tickets or more. I was on the 911 call-out last night and people were calling me at all hours complaining about him." His cheeks pinked. "I thought you should know, ma'am."

Annoyed idiots too stupid to keep their dogs under control had blocked the emergency line with stupid calls, she pushed to her feet. "Good job. Those dogs are becoming a hazard, and as to the people waiting to pay their fines, leave them to me." She strode past him and headed for the door then stopped. "Tell Bradford to help Maggie on the desk until we clear the backload."

The line of people waving tickets glared at her as she approached. She cleared her throat. "Listen up, folks." She waited until all eyes had turned to her. "We are currently doing a blitz on dogs. Many are running on the roads causing accidents and others are forming packs. If they bite a child, the owner will be held responsible." She ran her gaze over them all. "Secondly, if anyone calls 911 without a true emergency, I will personally write you a ticket for falsely reporting a crime. Do you understand?"

Not waiting for a response, she turned on her heel, and seeing Wolfe and Kane at the coffee machine, she headed through the office to speak to them. "Do you have an autopsy report on Jane Stickler for me, Wolfe?"

"I have a preliminary report. The toxicology screening will take weeks before I can give a positive cause of death but I have discovered evidence of interest that might point to our killer."

"Okay, we'll wait for Bradford to finish on the desk then I want everyone in my office for an update." She flicked a glance at Kane, who was busy making coffee. "Can you grab me one of those?"

"Sure thing."

She walked back to her office and pulled down the whiteboard. She entered the information on Angelique Booval to the list of suspects for the vigilante murders then added a new column for Jane Stickler. After staring at the lack of information, she heard Kane's voice behind her.

"The troops were busy while we were out yesterday. They tracked down more information on the victims. I mean the first two victims, Price and Dorsey." He handed her a cup of coffee. "Rowley has been working hard and interviewed the people who last saw them alive."

"That's great." She sipped her coffee then smiled. "I was starting to think they were phantoms."

She waited at the whiteboard for her deputies to take seats in her office then placed her coffee cup on the desk. "Okay, Rowley, you have some information to share—you can start."

"I received a couple of calls last night on the crime info line we set up with the local news channel." Rowley made a show of going through the folder on his lap. "Amos Price was seen at a party on the Sunday before his death. Sam Button hired him for his son's birthday party over in Blackwater. It was a word-of-mouth engagement and didn't go through Party Time. The second sighting was on Monday, he went into the convenience store. The one near the library on Main Street. He purchased chocolates, a bottle of bourbon, and condoms. The checkout guy, Pete Sadler, said he paid cash. He remembered him, as he had a baseball cap pulled down low on his head and looked suspicious, so he was watching him on the CCTV camera. I have a copy and it's Amos Price." He cleared his throat. "He is wearing the same clothes as when we found him."

"Was he alone?" Kane turned in his seat to look at Rowley.

"Unfortunately, yes. I could clearly see his truck in the video taken from the camera outside and no one was waiting for him inside."

Jenna made notes on the whiteboard. "So we can place Price's murder on Monday?"

"No, because he was picked up driving by on the CCTV camera on Tuesday as well."

She glanced at him. "Do you have a time?"

"Yeah, two thirty." Rowley flipped back through his notebook.

"That is great work, Rowley." Jenna smiled at him. "Anything else on Dorsey?"

"The motel owner was the last person to see Ely Dorsey alive. He remembers seeing his vehicle drive past the office. He had nobody with him. I spoke to the owner of Party Time and he said Dorsey had taken time off work, said he needed a few days to repair some things in his cabin. He spoke to him about ten the day of his death."

"I have something too." Wolfe raised one blond eyebrow. "I spoke to all the nurses on duty at the hospital and the doctors. Jane Stickler had three visitors: her parents and her brother. The nurse on night duty picked up her coffee as usual at midnight then chatted with two other nurses for a few minutes before returning to her desk. She remembers feeling sleepy but nothing until she woke around four in the morning. She went to check on Jane but only shone her flashlight on her. She thought she was asleep. It wasn't until she went back at five to take her vitals before the shift change that she found her deceased."

Jenna made more notes on the whiteboard as her deputies spoke. "So, we can assume her killer was in the hospital before midnight to drug the coffee."

"Yeah." Wolfe's forehead creased into a frown. "There lies the problem. I called the hospital administrator and insisted he give me a list of the people who entered using their cards. One of them is dead and has been dead for some time. I would say the killer has his hospital access card."

Oh, wonderful, another curveball. Jenna rubbed her temple. If anything could go wrong to make the case more complicated, it would. Her day was getting better by the second. "Why can't we have simple murders? Why is everything that happens in this town so darn complicated?"

CHAPTER FORTY-THREE

Bobby-Joe Brandon's week could not get any better. He sat at Chris's kitchen table with his hand wrapped around a bottle of beer and rubbed his thumb over the condensation. He grinned at his friend. "It was easy; nothin' had changed. As usual, the deputy on duty went home when they secured the ward. All I needed was the swipe card and I had access to all areas. As I had expected, the drugs worked on the night nurses on the floor below as well. It worked slowly so they would all believe they had dropped off to sleep. Hell, it happens all the time on the graveyard shift. They won't report fallin' asleep on duty now, will they?" He sipped his beer. "I found the girl's room easily enough. The bitch tried to run but I caught her before she escaped in the elevator. You should have seen her eyes, man." He grinned at his friend. "She was shit scared of me. I gave her a head start to make it interestin' and she was at the elevator door pounding the buttons. Those elevators are so slow, and when I came up, I hit every floor on the panel to send it back down. It was movin' so darn slow, I could take my time and enjoy watchin' her. I wish it could have lasted longer but I needed to get out of there. I slipped a needle into her arm and bang, she was dead."

"What about the person you saw in the room? Can they identify you?" Chris looked like he was going to spew. "We can't meet the girls now. It's too soon after the murder. It will be all over the news the moment we take them, and they will see the connection. Shit, she was Ely's girl, they'll know everything by now."

"Stop actin' like a baby. Who could possibly connect us to a murder? Ely's girl didn't speak to the cops; she didn't get time. Nobody recognized me at the hospital and I left no prints. I covered up good walkin' in and even added a limp just in case. Soon as I was clear of the CCTV cameras outside, I wore a doctor's jacket I found in the dirty laundry, gloves, and my clown mask in the elevator." He sipped his beer. "You are stupid if you think he's a threat to us. I hit him hard in the guts and made it quite clear I would kill him. He didn't see anythin' and took off before I'd gotten the girl back to the room. He was just a kid and probably hid in the hospital until dark to steal drugs; he won't tell anyone." He snorted. "What can he say? 'I was stealing drugs and a doctor dressed as a clown hit me for being in a patient's room?' Who would believe a story like that? They'd probably arrest him for murder."

"If you're sure it's safe to meet the girl, I'll go. I don't want to lose her—it's taken me days to get her to cooperate. I don't want to mess it up." Chris wiped a hand over his sweaty face. "I'm meeting her on the trail to the cabin today. She is coming on her bicycle straight from school. I'm leaving my rig on the fire access road—it isn't too far to carry her, or she might walk if I can convince her I'm taking her home."

"I'll leave my truck there as well. Good thinkin'." Bobby-Joe chuckled. "Mine is riding her bicycle too. She usually rides home from school so no one will suspect anythin'. She is tellin' her mom she is visitin' a friend. I told her I would take her home afterward. She is real keen." He wet his lips and let out a long sigh. "Man, it's been a long time since we've had two in the hole. I took a few sick days. I couldn't work knowin' I had two honeys at home."

"I only have two days off work." Chris eyed him suspiciously. "Mine will get there first. Now don't you go ruining her before I've had my fun. I want at least the weekend with her before you invite any of your friends over."

Bobby-Joe lifted his beer in a salute. "You got it, but you know, if you'd taken the time to build a decent cellar in this dump, you could have kept her here."

"I'm too close to the next cabin and someone would hear her or see her."

"Maybe, maybe not." He reached into a pocket and pulled out a bottle of pills. "You'll need these. One will make her manageable and two will put her to sleep." He slid the bottle across the table. "You know, I figure today is shapin' up to be the best day of the week."

CHAPTER FORTY-FOUR

Holding the meeting and going over recent events was a prequel to listening to the dreaded autopsy report. What made it worse was Jenna had rescued Jane Stickler and felt a connection to the girl. She had made sure the doctors had located her in the special ward assigned for injured prisoners. She had left Walters on duty all day. The only access to the hospital wards overnight was via a card *unless* someone sneaked into the hospital by way of the ER, but they could leave undetected via the fire exit. This made no sense, as a patient would require a nurse or paramedic to admit them into the ER.

Only a handful of people knew Jane was at the hospital, and her greatest threat, Ely Dorsey, was dead. They had no leads, and the only person unaccounted for who had entered the hospital in the time leading up to her death had been dead for months. It had to be someone with access to the dead man's card but he had no living relatives and his personal effects shed no light on the theft.

After returning to her desk, listening to her deputies' reports, and making sure they updated the case files, Jenna turned her attention to Wolfe. She had to know the truth about Jane. "Are we ready for the autopsy report on Jane Stickler?"

"Yes, ma'am." Voices echoed around the room.

"Go ahead when you're ready, Deputy Wolfe."

Wolfe gave her one of his ice-cold glances and placed a pile of photographs on the desk in front of him. "Do you want me to read my full report or do you want the abridged version?"

Her gaze slid to the stack of photographs and she swallowed hard at the images then turned her attention back to Wolfe. "The short version will be fine."

"Firstly, the toxicology reports will take at least three weeks, maybe more. Add to this the changes in blood chemistry after death and what drugs were administered at the hospital, it is going to be difficult to pinpoint what drug was actually used." Wolfe's mouth formed a thin line. "I have reason to believe this was a homicide as there are too many injuries to assume a nurse gave an unintentional overdose of medication at the hospital." He glanced down at his notes. "I have numbered the photographs to give you a clearer picture of my findings." He passed Jenna an image of what she assumed was the back of Jane's head. "I found substantial bruising on the head. As you can see in the image, I removed a section of the hair to reveal the extent of damage. Further investigation shows a substantial hematoma beneath the scalp consistent to the killer dragging the victim by her hair. The extent of the bruising, swelling, and blood clotting suggests this happened while she was alive." He slid another image to Jenna.

Jenna stared at the images and her stomach rolled. The excited and very much alive girl she had met was now an exhibit of cruelty. "Could this have happened before we found her?"

"No." Wolfe's expression was serious. "There is nothing on her chart from the hospital, and the doctor's initial examination was complete. She listed a scar on the scalp, so she would have hardly missed the substantial damage I found." He passed another three photographs across the table. "The victim has burns on her knees consistent to being dragged over tiles; her calf is dirty on one side and her nightgown was bunched up with marks on the front. I believe the killer dragged her by her hair face down, likely unconscious." He cleared his throat. "I spoke to the nurse on duty, who gave her a sedative at eight that night, not an injection, and yet she has a fresh and very ragged puncture wound in her forearm. More of a tear than an injection site. I believe she knew her killer, ran from him, and was caught, injected with something to knock her out cold, then dragged back to her bed. By the swelling and bleeding beneath the scalp, I would say death occurred a short time after her killer returned her to bed." He met Jenna's gaze and his cold expression remained unaffected. "If she had lingered more than a few minutes, the hematoma and swelling would have been significantly more pronounced."

Although her stomach knotted into a tight ball, Jenna stared at the photographs in an effort to take a clinical approach. In death, Jane needed her help just as much as she had alive. "Anything else?"

"Yeah." Wolfe's lips turned down and his eyes flashed in anger. "She suffered prolonged torture. Her time as a sex slave to four men must have been brutal. Her right arm shows misaligned untreated fractures to the radius and ulna." He pointed to his forearm. "She has cracked ribs and internal scarring." His face darkened and he flipped over another image. "And this."

Nausea rolled over Jenna as she stared at the scarring over the girl's back. "The only people who would benefit from her death are the two remaining men in the pedophile ring. I figure they were worried she could identify them, but all we have to go on is a spider tattoo and a scar on one knee. In this town many of the hockey players or rodeo riders would have scars on their knees."

"We searched high and low for a man with a spider tattoo and found no trace. The Black Widow biker club split up ten years ago. You would imagine if he worked at the hospital someone would notice it." Rowley scratched his head, making his brown hair stick up in all directions. "Could the tattoo have been one he stuck on or something?"

"It's a possibility. Doing something like that would throw us off his track." Wolfe shrugged and glanced back at his open file. "Although everything Zoe told us has been correct: the appendicitis scar and the birthmark on Dorsey's neck. She has amazing recall considering the stress she suffered."

"Yes, but she wouldn't likely spot the difference between a fake and a real tattoo." Jenna chewed on her bottom lip. "Everything points to Jane's killer being involved with the hospital. He managed to get inside after hours unseen and leave without a trace. We have cleared everyone who used the employees' entrance bar the person who used the dead man's swipe card. The employees' entrance doesn't have a CCTV camera, so we have no idea who used the dead man's card." She scanned her notes. "We have the drugs to consider. The pharmacist confirmed the bottles we found in Price's truck and Dorsey's cabin were from the hospital supplies. Our mystery killer works at the hospital, has access to drugs, and is likely a nurse. Yet, after extensive interviews, not one person on the damn staff knows a man with a spider tattoo and if it's the other pedophile we don't have a description."

"We called everyone who works at the hospital." Rowley's eyes narrowed. "It doesn't make sense. We went further as well—delivery services and even asked the mortician. This person is a phantom."

Jenna shook her head. "Not a phantom, very clever. I think we have to examine every nurse at the hospital personally. One of the people you called could have lied, right? I know it will be tough going but we have no choice. I'm sure Jane's killer is an associate of Price and Dorsey. Rowley, get the list of people working here divide it between you, Bradford, and Webber."

"Yes, ma'am."

"Two things." Kane leaned his broad back into the chair, making it groan. "Rowley could be right, it could have been a stick-on tattoo: Many criminals use them to throw the law off their tail. And why didn't he try to kill Zoe? If he works at the hospital as you say, he could have poisoned her food, for instance, and if he has access to drugs as we assume, he could have tampered with her meds."

"She wasn't medicated." Wolfe flipped through his notes. "According to the doctor who treated her, he was happy to have her treated by the family's GP in Helena. He wanted to wait for the blood tests to come back to make sure she wasn't suffering from any STDs and did recommend a course of antibiotics for a chest infection."

"Okay, so he didn't try to kill her, but she had to be a threat, so if he is part of this circle of predators, why didn't he try?"

"You have a point." Jenna drummed her fingernails on the table. "Jane had a secure environment, or so we thought, and Walters was there checking everyone in and out during her stay. Maybe he didn't get a chance to attack Zoe."

"He couldn't have gotten near her." Kane stretched out his long legs and sighed. "Her parents never left her side. I doubt he would have had the opportunity to put anything in her meals. From what Walters said, her father purchased takeout for her most of the time." He glanced at Wolfe. "Is there anything else we need to know about Zoe?"

Wolfe lifted his gray gaze. "Apart from malnourishment, she appeared to be quite stable and lucid considering her ordeal. I was able to view the doctor's notes after the parents gave me permission."

"What I'd like to know is how the vigilante killer became involved." Rowley had been listening intently and looked at Jenna. "At first, I thought it might be a father of one of the missing girls, but they have alibis, so why did the vigilante give us the newspapers? What message is the killer sending us?"

Jenna smiled at Kane. "This is your field of expertise."

"Sure." Kane rubbed his large hands together as if on the brink of receiving a wad of cash. "I'm pretty certain our killer is a woman. She gave us a motive for her killing spree, maybe to make us back off because in her mind she is doing the right thing, like putting out the trash. She wants us to know how many kids are involved and the period of time the pedophile ring has been in operation. She is giving us clues to find them, not her."

"So she figures you'll go easy on her?" Webber flashed Jenna a white smile.

"She has murdered two men and it wasn't in self-defense." Jenna pressed both palms on the table. "She will be treated the same as anyone else we suspect is guilty of murder."

"How do you think a jury would consider her crimes?" Bradford's soft voice sounded strange amongst Jenna's usual meeting of all-male deputies. "Do you think they'll go easy on her?"

"I'm not here to worry about what a jury will think." Jenna glared at her new deputy. "I know this case is conflicting; of course we all want these men brought to justice. Never forget our job is to bring them in and let the courts decide their punishment. I don't want any of you thinking you can go easy on the vigilante killer. That may be the last mistake you ever make."

"There is one thing for certain." Rowley's eyes scanned her face. "The vigilante knows who is involved in the pedophile ring."

Jenna nodded in agreement. "She obviously found a link between the men we haven't been able to discover. Apart from the two victims working at Party Time, their tiny ring of friends and associates came up clean. She has to be involved somehow, but all the girls we assume they kidnapped apart from Zoe and Jane are still missing. She can't be a victim; we need to look elsewhere." She sighed. "If we had the names of the other men in the pedophile group, we might be able to save the next person on her list, but I doubt anyone will admit to abusing children in exchange for our protection."

Kane's cellphone rang, disturbing her train of thought, and she stared at him. "Take that outside, will you please?"

"Yes, ma'am." Kane stood, answering the call as he strolled through the doorway, then turned and held up one hand for silence. He walked back into the room wearing a concerned expression. "What do you want?" He placed the cellphone on the table and a distorted voice came out of the speaker.

"I gather by now you have figured out the missing girls in the newspapers are still missing?"

"We have. What is your interest in these cases?" Kane leaned over the table and his concerned gaze locked on Jenna.

"You should be looking up in the mountains."

"I'm listening."

"Head up to Craig's Rock and you'll need to check out Old Corkey's place as well. It's about five minutes away from there downhill."

"Did you murder Amos Price and Ely Dorsey?"

The line went dead.

What the hell is going on here? Jenna swallowed hard. "Rowley, have you heard of Craig's Rock or Old Corkey's place?"

"Yes, ma'am, they are way up in the mountains. Not a place people visit because of the bears. It's way off the hiking tracks; you won't be able to drive up there. Ride maybe, but it will be a long hike off the main track along the falls."

"Okay, get Webber and Bradford organized for the nurses' interviews, I'll need you with us. I'll take the GPS and the satellite phone." She shot a glance at Kane. "Will your friend Gloria be able to supply us with extra horses?"

"I can ask." Kane picked up his cellphone and headed out the office.

"I have my own horse and trailer. If you can hire another horse from Gloria, make it a gelding and they will travel okay together," Rowley called after him.

"Can you ride, Wolfe?"

"Sure." He stood. "I'll collect my gear."

Jenna pushed to her feet. "I'll call in Walters to hold the fort." She tapped her bottom lip, took a deep breath, and looked at Rowley. "Soon as you have organized the interviews with the hospital, go and get your horse. We'll meet you at Gloria's." She turned to Webber. "When you're done at the hospital, remain in the office unless there is an emergency." She grabbed her weapon and pocketed her cellphone then picked up the keys and dropped them into his hand. "If we aren't back by five, lock up."

"Sure thing, ma'am."

Jenna strode out of her office and looked up at Kane. "It looks like you're getting a ride in the forest after all." She pushed her hair behind one ear. "Bring old Duke. He might be able to help."

"Yeah. He'll be an asset." Kane's expression was solemn. "This ride is not really what I had in mind. If the caller is the vigilante, she might be sending us off on a wild goose chase to get us out of town."

Dread washed over her. "You mean so she can kill again?"

"Uh-huh. That's exactly what I mean."

CHAPTER FORTY-FIVE

Excited did not come close to how Chris Jenkins was feeling after speaking to Bobby-Joe. His shabby, run-down cabin with its squeaky front door and dripping taps did not appear quite so bad. He stepped onto the porch to gaze into the surrounding forest and wanted to shout out. It was a beautiful day after the rain. Perfect for meeting the girl. He grinned and went back inside. *I am one lucky son of a bitch.*

Having his friend close by would sure make things easier if he had any trouble getting her to his SUV. He laughed to himself. She would be *his* property, and the income she would provide from members of their special group would make his life more comfortable. He would not miss Ely and Amos; in fact, once Stu had gone to jail, they had insisted on kidnapping the girls and he ended up paying his dues just to get involved in the action. Now Chris would be calling the shots.

He figured his girl would be the first of many. If he had two in Bobby-Joe's cage, he would be able to purchase a cabin higher up the mountain. Many of the older doer-uppers were for sale and some already had root cellars. If he had two or three girls in his own cellar, he would become a very rich man. He chuckled and strolled into the kitchen to prepare a bottle of pop. His girl had made a point of asking him to bring pop and bourbon. It was an unusual request but who was he to argue? And the alcohol would make the drugs work faster. *Then she will be mine.*

As he crushed the pills and added them to the drink, his mind filled with what he would need to take with him. He had anticipated meeting her for some time and wanted to have time alone with her before Bobby-Joe arrived. He frowned. He had no choice but to go along with his odd behavior. Without Bobby-Joe's hidden cellar, he would not be able to keep his girl. He wondered what her name was and sighed. It did not matter anyway as Bobby-Joe's rules did not allow anyone to call the girls by their names. He said it was too easy to slip up if the cops arrested them, and if they did not know their names, they would pass a polygraph.

He replaced the lid on the bottle and put it back in the refrigerator then headed for his bedroom. His heart pounded with anticipation of finally meeting her and he had to force his mind to focus on what he needed to take in his bag to the meeting. He already had cleaning materials in the SUV. After taking two girls to the small cabin, they could not risk leaving any evidence. The forest rangers usually went by to check them, and with two girls missing, if they left the place in a mess, the rangers would call the cops. He pulled on a pair of surgical gloves before tossing the box into his bag. He knew the drill by heart; everything he touched could leave a fingerprint. He tossed a couple of large towels, condoms, and a change of clothes into the backpack. A box of chocolates and his clown mask. He stood back and surveyed the room then picked up his camera and stuffed it in the bag. It was much safer than using his cellphone.

He turned and glanced at the clock and his stomach gave a squeeze. He had time to eat then he would head down the mountain to Black Rock Falls and take the back road into Stanton Forest. He wet his lips in anticipation of what was to come and grinned at his reflection in the mirror. *I'm coming.*

CHAPTER FORTY-SIX

After stopping to rest the horses and have a bite to eat, Kane mounted his horse and adjusted his backpack. Duke had kept up with their slow pace and seemed to be having the time of his life. He was a great companion and had stuck to him like glue. *I'm glad I kept him.* When Duke returned to his side, he smiled at him. "Good boy."

The picturesque ride up to Craig's Rock would have been easier if they had gained access to a private road leading higher up the mountain, but the gate was locked and well signposted with "Keep the hell out" written in red. As Rowley insisted the mountain folk might shoot first and ask questions later, rather than cause a problem, they had taken the dangerous trail up beside the falls. Riding single file with a massive drop on one side of the rock-strewn pathway, the horses showed reluctance to move at times, but as the path reached closer to the summit, Kane enjoyed a spectacular view of the entire valley. Far below, the town seemed insubstantial against the miles of open ranges on one side and the massive pine forest on the other.

At the top of the trail, Kane noticed a group of eight or so cabins set in the woods, quite close together. He rode up to Rowley. "Are those the fishing cabins Mayor Rockford used to own when he lived here?"

"Yeah, he used to hire them out to tourists." Rowley removed his hat and pushed his fingers through his damp hair. "You would be surprised how many people come here to spend weeks hiking through this forest in the summer. I guess they camp most times but then arrive here to spend a few days fishing before they make the trek home." He pushed his hat back onto his head. "I gather the real estate office handles the bookings now."

Kane surveyed the cabins then shrugged. "I guess but it's one hell of a ride up here to fish. How much further is Craig's Rock?"

"A few minutes, if the GPS is correct."

They took an animal track through the forest with Rowley out in front, using the GPS for navigation. It would be easy to become lost in the dense mass of pine trees; apart from up or down, every direction appeared the same. Without the sunlight spiking through the branches, the tall, unforgiving, rough trunks appeared sinister. Kane moved closer to Jenna and she turned and gave him an enquiring look. It was obvious by her virtual silence most of the way, her mind was back on Black Rock Falls and the vigilante.

"I need a word, Wolfe." Jenna waited for him to catch up to her. "I guess there's a remote possibility we'll find a grave. I doubt we'll find anyone alive up here. If so, we'll need a forensic anthropologist. Do you know anyone?"

"I have a team on standby." Wolfe nodded at her. "Don't worry, I have everything covered. If we find anything, I'll make an initial assessment—for instance, confirm the bones are human and what approximate age—then arrange to have the Helena team come up here tomorrow. We'll need their expertise to discover how long the bones have been there; we might be looking at a burial, hundreds of years old."

"Yeah, I understand. You work with flesh and fingerprints to discover the cause of death and identity and they look at things like moss or mold on the bones, animals in the area, and determine sex and cause of death in other ways."

"Exactly." Wolfe's face cracked into a smile. "I've studied the field but it is a different degree. For instance, they'll be able to extract DNA from teeth, if any are intact, and arrange carbon dating if it's an old burial."

Kane looked into the never-ending vista of trees. "It's going to be difficult getting a team up here with the equipment required."

"Not necessarily." Wolfe scratched his blond stubble. "I had a good look around when we took a break and I'm pretty sure they could land a chopper on the top of Black Rock Falls. There is a large flat area on one side of the mountain far enough away from the falls to be safe."

"I wish I'd known that earlier." Jenna held her back and groaned. "Although, asking the mayor to pay for a chopper might be pushing my luck."

Kane urged his horse forward. "That won't be our problem if it is more than we can handle; the Helena forensics team will take over. As the girls are reportedly missing from all over the state, they'll want to be involved from the get-go, and so will the FBI."

"Maybe, but they're not excluding us." Jenna's expression was determined. "This is our case in my county and I plan to solve it." She moved ahead of him along the trail. "I'm just holding my breath nothing happens while we are on a field trip."

"Walters said he would go into the office. You have three capable deputies on duty and they'll contact you if anything happens." Kane rode beside her. "We can't do anything in town. If the vigilante is going to strike, she'll do it anyway." He shrugged. "If we had a clue who she picked out for her next victim, we could have placed him in protective custody, but we don't. All we can do is wait and hope her killing spree is over."

"Maybe if she has led us to the grave site, we will discover enough evidence to find the girls' killers and bring them to justice." Jenna sighed. "Then she might be satisfied and stop killing the men responsible, but if she figures sending us up here will get her off the charge of murder, she is sorely mistaken."

Kane nodded in agreement. "She would be underestimating you if she believes you'll ever give up chasing her."

"Yeah, and playing the victim card with me won't work."

"Craig's Rock is in front of us now, which makes Old Corkey's cabin some ways west from here. It's close to private property, so we'll have to be careful." Rowley turned around in his saddle and brushed at the sweat trickling down his temples. "Orders, ma'am?"

"We'll dismount and spread out on foot. Stay in sight. I hear there are bears in this area, so stay alert." Jenna slid off her horse and winced as she landed. "Take the bear spray just in case."

Kane dismounted and took in his surroundings. A trail led through the dense pine trees and the jagged rock face peeked out between them. "I think it would be this way. I would not risk walking through poison ivy; I'd use the animal trail." He gave Jenna a long look. "This is a very remote place. Why send us here?"

"Well, it may be a hoax, but we won't know until we take a look." Jenna strode away, back straight and head erect.

"I wouldn't mind betting those cabins have something to do with the missing girls." Wolfe moved beside Kane and his expression turned murderous. "You mentioned Rockford's son was doing time for having child pornography. Maybe we need to pay him a visit in jail?"

"That's a thought but the FBI investigation turned up zip. I doubt he was involved and trust me, during the court case he would have given up his soul to avoid jail time."

Thinking of Mayor Rockford's extensive estate before his son went to jail, Kane turned to speak to Rowley. "Hey, Rowley." He removed his shades and pushed them into his shirt pocket. "Those cabins are miles from anywhere—how did Rockford maintain them? I couldn't see him trekking all the way up there to change the sheets."

"There used to be a road that ran down the other side of the falls. It met up at the top near the cabins. Many folk stayed up here on weekend fishing trips. There was a trailer that came every weekend through summer, sold everything from milk to hot dogs." Rowley removed his hat and wiped his sweat-soaked face with a cloth. "After the rockslide, I doubt Rockford came up here to check out the cabins. The hikers had to fend for themselves, I guess." His brow furrowed. "There are people living all over up here, scattered around the national park areas and all have private roads off the mountain, but they pretty much keep to themselves. Most are self-sufficient and don't leave their properties more than once or twice a year."

A memory of Lizzy Harper flashed through his mind. "Hey, hold up a minute." He waited for Jenna to turn around. "When was this rockslide?"

"I'm not sure—about six years ago, maybe longer." Rowley's brow wrinkled into a frown. "Why?"

"Wolfe was wondering if the cabins have anything to do with the missing girls and I recall Lizzy Harper mentioning her father took her fishing on the weekends. That's where he molested her and no doubt had other men involved as well."

"Then once we've checked around here, we'll find Old Corkey's place then check out the cabins." Jenna pushed back her hat, allowing her dark hair to fall over her cheeks. She raised both eyebrows. "Come on, let's go, it's getting late and it will be hard enough riding down the mountain in daylight. I don't fancy tackling the trail beside the waterfall in the dark."

"We could stay in the cabins." Rowley's expression was hopeful.

Kane opened his mouth to say something but Jenna beat him to it. "Have you lost your mind?" She glared at Rowley. "Not one chance in hell."

Duke had run ahead with his drooling tongue flopping out the side of his mouth. The crashing through the undergrowth stopped and he gave out three barks then whined.

"I hope he hasn't disturbed a bear." Kane followed the dog through the trees and came out on the edge of a small clearing.

Duke came to his side and nudged his leg, clearly agitated. Kane surveyed the immediate area and swallowed hard. *Oh, shit!* A skull's hollow black eyes stared at him as if pleading for help. The bleached white skull lay on one side with green moss growing over one cheek. A foot away, the top of another peered out of the leaf mold as if hiding. Long fine bones littered the open space nestled beneath Craig's Rock. Nothing could be worse than finding the graves of murdered children. He schooled his expression to cover the welling emotion and turned away as Jenna came toward him. "I'm afraid it's a mass grave, ma'am."

CHAPTER FORTY-SEVEN

On the way to meet the next monster, she took the old back road, which ran between the end of town and the lower edge of Stanton Forest. It snaked its way through the south side and ended in a large circular area for cars or trucks to turn around. Emergency services used the road and it acted as a firebreak just in case a wildfire sparked into life. After driving her car down a track, some distance from the trail he had mentioned, she parked behind a clump of bushes then slid from behind the wheel and dragged a bicycle out of the trunk. She made sure she had everything she needed then covered her vehicle with a camouflage sheet. With the keys in the ignition, she could make a quick getaway if everything went to hell.

A sound startled her; if he spotted her now, he would know it was a setup. She turned slowly, staring in all directions, but nothing but the breeze moved through the tall pines. After removing her hat and allowing her hair to drop to her shoulders, she replaced it, pulling the front down to cover her eyes. With her large sunglasses covering most of her face, he would think she was fourteen for sure. Now if her monster, or Eighteen and Lonely as he called himself, drove past her on the road, he would not suspect a thing.

The idea of killing him excited her and terrified her at the same time. The fact she enjoyed watching them die frightened her sometimes. She pushed away the fear and embraced the gnawing need inside her to rid the world of predators.

She pulled a backpack onto her shoulders, mounted the bicycle, and headed down the road. As she turned the bend, she heard a car and hid in the bushes. A car went flying by her, and to her horror, Bobby-Joe Brandon was behind the wheel. *I can't take on two men at once.*

Indecision plagued her. Stay or leave? What should she do now? She stared after Bobby-Joe but the SUV kept on going and disappeared around a bend in the distance. Not long after, an identical SUV drove slowly up behind her, and she turned on her seat then stopped pedaling. A man climbed out of the vehicle wearing a clown mask, and every instinct to run screamed in her. Fear gripped her. If he had planned on Bobby-Joe as his backup, she had made a fatal mistake.

"I'm Eighteen and Lonely. Are you Needy Girl?"

Although slightly muffled, the one thing she recognized was voices. This man trying so hard to hide his identity was Chris Jenkins.

Trying to act nonchalant and keeping her head down so the cap shadowed her face, she nodded. "I thought the clown mask was a joke. I didn't really expect you to wear one."

"I wanted you to be sure you'd found the right guy. The woods can be dangerous." Chris rounded the hood of the truck and his gaze drifted over her.

Glad she had the sunglasses as a disguise, she stuck out one hip in a pose she had noticed many teenage girls use. "Well then, now you know it's me, why don't you remove it?"

"Ah, because I like to play games." He chuckled. "All girls like to play games. You do, don't you?"

"Then I'm keeping on my sunglasses." She put one hand on her hip and snorted. "I thought we were going to have sex. Have you changed your mind?"

"Nope but I want it to be fun and memorable. Anyone can do it like your parents." He moved closer but did not attempt to touch her. "I'm gonna make it special."

"Okay, but let's get on with it. I'm hot and thirsty." She shrugged. Acting impatient often put them off guard. They did not want to lose their prize. "Is the cabin far?"

"See that trail just up there yonder?" Chris pointed to a track about six yards away on the right. "It's just down there. Do you want to hop in my ride and I'll drive you there?"

I'm not that dumb. "I'll ride my bicycle if you don't mind." She could feel the knife in the sheath pressing into her ankle and its presence spurred her on. "Why don't we walk the rest of the way?"

"I'll do whatever you want but I don't want to leave my vehicle here. I want to make the cabin nice and cozy for us. I have the liquor you wanted and the chocolates." He pulled his bag from the truck then gave her a long look. "You sure are pretty. I can't wait to see more of you. Wait here, I'll park up there a-ways and walk back." He dropped his bag, jumped into the SUV, and drove away.

Not long after, she watched him jog back to her, still wearing the clown mask, and it made him look ridiculous. When he reached her side, breathing heavily, he picked up his bag. "I told you I wouldn't be long. Ready for some fun?"

She swallowed the bile rushing up her throat and forced her mouth into a smile. She had to act naive and not afraid but right now, she wanted to get as far away from him as possible. *Dammit, I have to stop messing around and kill this son of a bitch.*

Chris's hand trembled as he touched her back. "This way, down this track." He led the way into the forest.

The idea of Bobby-Joe being close by worried her but she bit the bullet and asked the question burning on her tongue. "I saw another SUV go by just before. That man won't bother us, will he?"

"No." Chris's hot palm ran down her back. "I promise, he won't come anywhere near the cabin. It's just you and me. I'll take good care of you. You can trust me, darlin'."

A cool breeze rustled the trees and she snapped back to full alertness. She must play the part. The plan played through her mind, each step she needed to take. She hoped he would do exactly what she expected. So many things must fall neatly into place and if she made one mistake and did not strike at the first opportunity, she would be the one to die.

She climbed off her bicycle and leaned it against a tree. Taking a deep breath, she followed him inside the cabin. At once, he dragged out the contents of his bag and covered the bed with a plastic sheet and a large towel. When she noticed her staring at the bed, he chuckled.

"We don't want to make a mess and upset the rangers or they'll lock these cabins and we'll have no place to meet." Chris moved closer and peered at her through the hideous smiling mask. "Why don't you take off those glasses, sit down, and relax. We'll have a drink." He chuckled.

She kept her head down, acting reluctant. "Okay, but I want to see you first." She removed her backpack and sat at the table.

"Sure." He stepped back and pulled his T-shirt over his head but the mask remained intact. "I'll do whatever you want." He tossed the shirt onto the table then undressed. He strolled over to the small table and took a bottle of pop from a cooler. He opened it and held it out to her. "You should have a drink, it will help you relax."

The smell of him, aftershave and sweat, accosted her nostrils. She took the drink and pretended to sip it. "That's a bit strong." She coughed dramatically. "You look different from your photo, older."

"Sorry to disappoint you. Drink some more, it gets better the more you swallow." He loomed over her. "Then take off the sunglasses, I'm anxious to look at you." He moved closer and stood in front of her.

"I'm fine and the glasses stay just like your stupid mask." She put the bottle to her lips again, watching him closely, then placed it on the table. "I'll have to take off my shoes first." *I don't want your blood all over them.*

A shiver of disgust went through her as he ran his hands over her shoulders. She bent in front of him to untie her laces then tossed her shoes some distance away. Before she straightened, she closed one hand around the hilt of the knife attached to her ankle. The bone handle felt warm and comforting against her palm. With a roar, she pushed upward and plunged the knife under his ribcage with the force of eight long years' rage. The sharp blade slid into him like butter, missing bone and slicing into his heart. She pulled back and thrust again, cutting deep. As a hot scarlet spray soaked the front of her shirt, laughter bubbled up inside her and she dragged off his mask.

"Hello, Chris."

He made a gurgling sound and blood trickled from his mouth. He staggered, clutching at her with his rough hands. She winced as his fingers bit deep into her shoulders and she pulled off her sunglasses. "Look at me, you son of a bitch. I want to watch the life go out in your eyes."

He let out a feral moan and his eyes widened in stunned surprise. She twisted the knife. "Does it hurt?"

Without a second thought, she spread her feet, dragged the sharp blade out, and forced it deep again. His eyes, now slightly unfocused, stared at her face and his grip lessened. She watched his mouth trying to form words but she did not give a damn what he wanted to say. His lungs were filling with blood and life was ebbing away.

She dragged out the knife and grinned at him. "Don't tell your mommy, this will be our little secret."

CHAPTER FORTY-EIGHT

Apprehension fell over Jenna like a shroud as she walked into the picturesque clearing. She hoped Kane was mistaken and the bones he had discovered belonged to animals. The temperature dropped considerably as she entered a shadowed, horseshoe-shaped area surrounded by a sheer rock wall rising hundreds of feet into the air. The air was still and held a damp, earthy fragrance. Underfoot, a coating of twigs and pine needles crunched with each step. She peered into the darkness waiting for her eyes to adjust. Protected from the weather, she considered absently how the secluded area would have made a superb camping ground until her attention moved to the pathetic stark white remains scattered in the long grass. "Oh, dear Lord. Stand back, everyone. Wolfe take a look and see what we have here."

Her gaze moved to Kane on his knees peering intently at something. His dog sat obediently on the tree line watching his master as if waiting for a command. "What do you have there, Kane?"

"It's a locket." Kane's expression was grim. "I recognize it from one of the photographs of missing girls." He glanced over at Wolfe, who was suiting up in coveralls. "Maybe you should start here."

"I'll do a preliminary examination but by the weathering of what bones we can see, I won't be able to determine the age of the remains by usual methods. There is no smell either, which would make me assume the remains have been here for some years." Wolfe threw a bundle of coveralls to Kane. "Suit up. We'll need to mark out a grid, make a sketch of the area, and take some pictures. Then I suggest we look for Old Corkey's cabin."

Jenna left them to it and did a slow visual scan of the area then turned to Rowley. "We'll mark out the perimeter of the crime scene." She moved back a few paces and removed her backpack then took out a roll of crime scene tape. "Start way over there, attach the tape, then come back to me."

By the time they had finished attaching tape to trees, Wolfe was waiting to speak with her. She strolled toward him. "How many?"

"It's too early to tell but there are three skulls visible, so the killers buried them in very shallow graves. I can see plastic sticking through the grass in places and they marked each grave with a rock. There are three rocks." Wolfe stood hands on hips, his face expressionless, a façade he seemed to drop down when on a case. "Once the area is photographed and I've made a rough sketch of the positions of the bodies, I will make up a grid. It is easier to have a term of reference when excavating a site of this size." His gray gaze slipped to the gravesite then back to her. "Once we have finished the preliminary examination, I'll have more accurate information to relay to the FSD in Helena."

Attempting to keep her own professional persona, though the horror of what lay a few feet before her had shaken her to the core, Jenna nodded. "Okay, but if you want to find the other burial site, we will need to keep track of the time. It's not safe traveling these trails after dark and those graves will still be here in the morning. Tell Kane and Rowley how you want the grid set up. I have rolls of tape, string, and bright orange flags in my backpack." She gave the backpack a kick with her toe. "I'll take the photographs."

"Yes, ma'am." Wolfe turned away and spoke to Rowley.

"The locket belongs to a girl named Jodie King." Kane pressed an evidence bag into her hands then held up his cellphone to show her a picture. "She is wearing it in this image and it's inscribed on the back: *To Jodie, love Mom and Dad*." He cleared his throat. "She went missing eight years ago."

Within fifteen or so minutes, she had the photographs and her deputies had the grid set up. Jenna stood to one side with Rowley watching Wolfe and Kane move from one grid to the other. She had attended grave excavations before but not on this scale and found she had a morbid fascination in the way Wolfe worked. Using a small trowel and a brush, he removed fallen leaves and other debris from each grave, made notes, measured any bones lying on the surface, and ran a commentary into a small recording device. She checked her watch and another hour had flown by in an instant. By the time Wolfe and Kane had flagged three graves, the sun had slipped low in the sky.

To her relief, Wolfe stood and walked carefully from the crime scene with Kane at his heels. She waited for them to remove their coveralls and gloves then walked toward them. "Do you have a preliminary report?"

"Three shallow graves, three skulls are visible, two show no signs of trauma, and one shows indication of blunt force trauma. From the bones scattered over the general area, there is evidence of animal intervention, but there are also the same injuries I found on Jane Stickler. Untreated broken bones, which would indicate the killers kept at least two of these children for some time, at least six weeks after the injury." Wolfe let out a long, weary sigh. "This site is going to take some time to excavate. It may be months before we discover the identity of these kids."

Anger reared at hearing about the atrocities the kids had suffered, but she pushed down the rage welling inside her. *I have to find the men who did this.* "Contact Helena and ask them to assist our investigation."

"Yes, ma'am."

Jodie King's locket weighed heavy in her hand. She lifted her gaze to Kane. "How did the vigilante know about this place?" Jenna stared at the dirt-smeared locket, her mind racing. "She must have been involved somehow. I wonder if one of the men kidnapped her. From what we know about Lizzy Harper's father, he took her to a fishing cabin up here somewhere—she could have witnessed Jodie's murder and overheard where they planned to bury her body."

"Do you think we have found our vigilante, ma'am?" Rowley's dark eyebrows raised. "I mean, do you think Lizzy Harper is our killer?"

"Everything points to her being involved."

"She is on the top of my list but maybe she only witnessed *one* of these kids' murders." Kane rubbed his chin, his face pensive. "The timeline doesn't fit for Jodie, but then we don't know how long Lizzy's father abused her or how long they kept Jodie alive before they killed her. Lizzy won't give us any information."

"With what we have so far, I might be able to convince the DA to issue an arrest warrant. If not, I'll organize surveillance." Jenna bent and pulled an evidence bag from her backpack, labeled it *Jodie King*, then dropped the smaller bag inside. "If it is her, I don't want any more murders on my watch."

"If we could find the rest of the ring, we might be able to stop the vigilante before she strikes again." Kane rubbed the back of his neck and gave a weary sigh. "If we had one single connection to link our murder victims we might have a chance."

"They can't be far away if the vigilante is stalking them in Black Rock Falls. The cabins are the common denominator in all these cases and all are located in Stanton Forest." Jenna chewed on her bottom lip. "What other clues do we have, Kane? We found two girls in cabins in the mountains. Lizzy Harper told you her father took her fishing and they stayed in a cabin at the top of Black Rock Falls." She waved a hand around, encompassing the area. "The fishing cabins are walking distance from here. I'm convinced they have a hideout close by." She stared at the failing light. "Dammit, we need more time."

"If we go straight to Old Corkey's cabin and check it out, we'll have time to ride up to the fishing cabins and take a look. It's not that far out of our way." Kane raised one black eyebrow in question at Rowley.

"Ten minutes, I guess." Rowley pulled the GPS out of his pack and scanned the screen. "Maybe a lot less as we're riding. Old Corkey's is in that direction." He pointed into the forest. "The fishing cabins are above us and to the right. I'll scout around for a trail." He headed for his horse.

As usual, she could depend on Rowley's local knowledge. She shot a glance at Wolfe. "Did you contact the Helena forensics team?"

"Yes, ma'am. They'll be able to pick us up from the Black Rock Falls Hospital helipad at seven in the morning and bring us back here." Wolfe waved a hand toward the gravesite. "I have covered all the remains. The crime scene should be fine overnight. There is nothing of interest for any wildlife."

When Rowley rode up moments later, Jenna walked to meet him. "Find a trail?"

"Yes, ma'am. It's not five minutes away. We would have spotted it but it's hidden by the trees."

Jenna gathered up her belongings then straightened and stared at her deputies. "What are you all waiting for? Grab the gear. I want to arrive at the fishing cabins before dark."

They followed Rowley's lead and soon a dilapidated cabin came into sight. Jenna scanned the area. "It looks like it's abandoned."

"No doubt." Kane had dismounted and was following Wolfe to the front door. "We'll take a look, ma'am." He turned to Duke. "Stay, boy."

Jenna waited for a few moments, watching the door expectantly. Wolfe came out first, removing his surgical gloves, then Kane shut the door and walked toward her. "We have bodies wrapped in plastic under the floorboards, but from the dust, no one has been here for some time."

"I'll have to come back in the morning with lights—its pitch-dark in there." Wolfe's brow creased into a frown. "From what I can see, there are three bodies. I'm going to need help. The two experts Helena are sending with the chopper will not be enough. It may take a day or so to organize; we are talking about two different teams and equipment. This can't be rushed."

"Pull in anyone you need." She glanced at her watch. "I doubt anyone will disturbed them overnight. We should move out or we won't have time to check the fishing cabins."

Six bodies. Could these be the missing girls in the newspapers? Jenna swallowed hard and turned her horse back up the mountain.

CHAPTER FORTY-NINE

Warm blood soaked her shirt and trickled down the front of her jeans. She stared at the knife, sticky against her palm. It had taken seconds to kill him and yet the room already stank of death. At her feet, the last twitches of life left Chris Jenkins' body. He lay sprawled on his back, a fixed startled expression on his face. She bent over him and stared into his eyes. "See what you made me do?"

A stark clarity of mind engulfed her, removing the emotion and hate she felt for the monster. Once she had killed him, the gnawing rage melted away like ice in the sun and left behind a warm glow of contentment. She straightened and peered around the room, trying to retrace her steps. The sheriff would search the cabin and she must make sure she left no hint of her existence behind, not one hair or fingerprint. She found a bucket close by and removed her clothes then pushed them into the bucket. A threadbare towel hung over the edge of the sink and she wrapped it around one hand to turn on the faucet. The pipes made a gurgling sound and discolored water ran into the basin. She washed using the sliver of soap someone had left behind, but without a mirror, she had no idea if any blood remained on her face. After scanning the floor, she wet the towel and rubbed it over her footprints then let the water run for some time to make sure no trace of blood remained in the trap. She turned off the faucet, dropped the towel in the bucket, then dressed in clean clothes from her backpack.

After wiping down the chair with the monster's T-shirt, she added the bottle of drink to the bucket. She took one last look around the cabin, pulled her cap down low on her head, and pushed on her sunglasses; with her backpack over one shoulder, she picked up the bucket then headed for the door. She used the T-shirt to turn the knob, dropped it on the floor, and elbowed the door open. The moment she stepped outside, she stared into the startled face of a young girl pushing a bicycle. She let the door swing shut behind her and waved the girl away. "Run! The man in there has a knife, he tried to kill me."

Concerned she might be identified, she brushed past the terrified girl and grabbed her own bicycle, but before she had mounted, the girl came flying by, pedaling fast. After riding to the end of the trail, she stared both ways and saw the girl heading in the opposite direction to where she had left her car. Goosebumps rose on her skin as a wave of apprehension washed over her. The girl was heading in the same direction as Bobby-Joe had driven. There was nothing at the end of the road as far as she was aware and perhaps by now he had turned around and headed home. The idea of him being so close nagged at her. *Why is he in the forest? Did the monsters plan to meet two girls today?*

To her relief, the girl turned left, taking a hidden path away from the main trail, and the forest swallowed her. Many animal paths weaved throughout Stanton Forest and she probably knew of a shortcut back to the main road. Turning in the other direction, she pedaled hard, glad to find the small clearing where she had left her car. Once she had stowed the bicycle and the bucket under the tarpaulin in the trunk of her car, it took her a few moments to remove her baseball cap and brush out her hair. She checked her face in the mirror, added some lipstick then headed back to town.

The heavy weight she had carried for so long was finally getting lighter. *One to go.*

CHAPTER FIFTY

Bobby-Joe had waited for thirty minutes and was getting restless. She should be arriving soon and he wanted to be waiting for her at the cabin. He drummed his fingers on the steering wheel of his truck then decided to pay Chris a visit. If he walked in on him and his honey, so what? He picked up a bottle of drugged pop then slipped from the seat and depressed the key fob to lock the doors. After taking a quick look around just to make sure no one lurked in the shadows, he strolled toward the cabin. As he turned the bend, he noticed a white sedan moving away at speed in the distance. He cursed under his breath; if Chris had invited anyone else to the party without telling him, there would be hell to pay. *I'm running this show, not you, asshole.*

Movement caught his eye in the dense forest and over the birdsong came the distinct sound of crying. He turned slowly, peering in all directions. "Hello, is someone there?"

"M-me, I'm here." A girl pushed out the bushes, tears streaming down her face. "You didn't c-come from the cabin, did you?"

Bobby-Joe stared at her in disbelief. *Oh, this is my lucky day.* "Me? No, I parked my truck some ways up the road." He indicated behind him with his thumb. "My dog jumped out the back and headed this way, I've been lookin' for him. Have you seen a brown dog come by?"

"No." The girl rubbed at her eyes.

"What happened to you?" Bobby-Joe kept his distance, not wanting to spook her. "It's not safe for young girls to be walkin' alone in the forest."

"I came to meet someone at the cabin." She sniffed and her tear-filled eyes moved over him. "I met a girl back there near the cabin. She said there was a bad man in there with a knife, so I ran away but then I fell off my bicycle. The wheel is all bent out of shape."

Bobby-Joe frowned, wondering what the hell Chris was doing. At least Chris had an advantage over him right now. The upset girl could identify him but Chris would have been wearing his clown mask. He had his hanging out of his back pocket. He sighed. *Too late now. It looks like this one is coming home to stay.*

His mind ran through a few scenarios of what to do with her. She was scared and he had to appear to be a safe option. All he had to do was persuade her to get into his truck. "Oh, there are some nasty men around. Like I said, it's not safe in the forest. I guess I had better look for my dog in the other direction. I don't like the idea of being stabbed today by some lunatic." He made to turn away then stopped and looked at her. "Do you want to walk with me?"

"Okay." She followed him. "What's your dog's name?"

"Deefer."

"That's a stupid name." She wiped her nose on a tissue then coughed.

Bobby-Joe thought all his birthdays had come at once. He figured she was the girl he had groomed for months, but now Chris had spooked her, and any chance of convincing her he was the man she planned to meet would be a waste of time. She would connect him to the maniac in the cabin. He would have to play it cool and held out the bottle of pop. "Wanna drink? I haven't opened it yet so it hasn't got cooties."

"Thanks, I'm very thirsty." She removed the top and took a long drink. "It will be dark soon. Is there a trail out of the forest up this way?" She held the bottle out to him.

Bobby-Joe shook his head. "Nope, and you have the drink. I have more in my truck."

"How am I going to get home?" She drank again then looked up at him. "I'll get lost out here and I might run into the man with the knife."

"You might."

"Will you help me?" She moved closer and grabbed his arm. "Please?"

Excitement rushed through him. She had walked straight into his arms. He could not believe his luck. His truck was a few yards away. The drugs would kick in soon enough and she would be his. He smiled at her and held out his hand. "Don't worry your pretty little head, darlin'. I'll take care of you."

"Thank you but what about your dog?" Her eyes had become wide and innocent.

He swallowed hard and forced his body to relax. *Be nice, she is on the hook.* "I'm sure he can look after himself. Getting you home is more important."

"Maybe I can come back here tomorrow and help you look for him?"

Bobby-Joe bit back a grin of triumph. "I'd like that." He waved a hand toward his vehicle. "My truck is over there. I'll drive you home."

When she took his hand and smiled at him, a rush of euphoria swept over him. This one he would keep forever.

CHAPTER FIFTY-ONE

Wednesday, week two

The following morning, Kane sat in his cubicle and stared at the case files, wondering if he had lost his edge. The killer had eluded him and the men involved in the pedophile ring seemed to move through life like ghosts. Every step into the investigation he took, he came up with dead ends. He agreed with Jenna and considered Lizzy Harper to be the prime suspect for the vigilante. Although a woman small in stature, she was in good shape from the heavy workload she endured as a cleaner. Lizzy Harper had murdered her father, so there could be no question of her having the guts to kill, and they had the tie-in with the fishing cabins. He ran through the transcript of her interview for the third time. Yes, she hated men, but she seemed to him to be angry with everyone. If she was the vigilante, what was her motive? She had already killed the man who molested her.

The only explanation he could contemplate was that her father exposed her to the men in the pedophile ring. Although, they found no signs of anything unusual in the old fishing cabins—no cellars or anything significant enough to believe a group of pedophiles had used them—but after so many years, anything was possible. He doubted Lizzy would identify the cabin where her father molested her now, because during the court case, she had had the opportunity to implicate other men but had remained silent. Yet he had proof another man was involved. Lizzy's son was not the product of incest. *Who is the kid's father?* He checked his email inbox again, hoping to see the DNA results on the vigilante's two victims. If there was a match to Lizzy's son, then they had motive to bring her in for questioning.

His fingers itched to call Wolfe but Jenna had sent him with Webber to the gravesites with the Helena forensics team. With a killer on the loose, she had insisted he and Rowley remain at the office following up leads. He scrolled through the contacts on his cellphone, found the number of the pathology laboratory Wolfe used, and called them. He gave the required information and waited, and waited. Ten or so minutes later, the laboratory technician came back on the line.

"I'll send the results through to the Black Rock Falls ME's office now."

Annoyance rippled up Kane's spine. "Include the Black Rock Falls Sheriff's Department in that email. I need that information yesterday and the ME is somewhere on the top of the mountain."

"Sure, sending it now."

Kane stared at his computer screen and refreshed his inbox three times before the email came in with attachments. He opened the file and bit back a whoop of excitement. At last, the evidence they needed. Amos Price was the father of Lizzy Harper's son. He pushed to his feet and grabbed Rowley by the shoulder. "With me."

"We have a breakthrough in the vigilante case."

When Jenna lifted her gaze to him, he grinned. "We have enough evidence for an arrest warrant for Lizzy Harper. The DNA results came in and Amos Price is the father of her son. This proves he was involved, so we have motive. She was in the area at the time of the murder and has a key to the house where Alison Saunders found his body."

"Thank God. Now we can stop her before she kills again. Good work." Jenna smiled at him. "Write it up and give the paperwork to Rowley to take over to the courthouse. I'll call the DA to move things along faster then I'll track down her current location."

"Yes, ma'am." Feeling jubilant, he strode out the door and headed for his cubicle.

The paperwork did not take long and he handed the document to Rowley and sent him on his way. After spending the next hour making calls and updating his case files, he glanced up as Maggie, obviously distressed, left the front desk and bolted into Jenna's office. *What has happened now?*

Jenna came out and waved him into her office. He picked up his notepad and walked into the room, closing the door behind him. Jenna was on the phone to the media, giving details of a missing child for an Amber Alert. He had only caught the end of the conversation and waited expectantly for her to explain. After replacing the receiver, she dropped her head in her hands and stared at him with an expression of remorse but said nothing.

He frowned at her silence. "Who went missing?"

"A thirteen-year-old girl, Sandra Doig. I have notified the National Crime Information Center to enter her on the Missing Persons File and put out a BOLO. All local counties will be on the lookout for her and will issue an Amber Alert. I also made a call to the FBI Child Abduction Rapid Deployment Team, so help is on its way." She gave a tired sigh. "I've just finished speaking to the media. They will release her details immediately, so let's hope we find her quickly. She told her parents she was having a sleepover with her friend yesterday but didn't show for school this morning." Jenna pushed her fingers through her thick black hair. "Her mom wouldn't have known only she went by the school to give her some lunch money. The friend said she didn't go home with her."

This town is becoming crime central. Kane pushed to his feet. "Did she call her other friends?"

"Yeah, Maggie asked all the right questions when Mrs. Doig called. The girl's mother said it is usual for Sandra to sleep over with Peta Braun, they are BFFs and Mrs. Braun makes sure they don't stay up all night." Jenna chewed on her bottom lip. "The principal asked the kids over the intercom and a couple of them saw her heading away from the school toward the back road to Stanton Forest after school yesterday."

The memory of the murders they had investigated earlier in the year ran through his mind. "That's not good. I hope we don't have another killer stalking the forest."

"I'm more worried about the current very active pedophile ring."

"Yes, and the local pedophile who has been working in town during the festival." Kane swallowed the bile rushing up the back of his throat. "Ask Maggie to arrange for a member of the family to bring something Sandra has worn. It's going to be difficult searching the forest and Duke can track by smell."

"Yeah, her husband is on the way with a pair of her socks. I already thought of Duke." Jenna's eyes narrowed. "We need to move on this now. I am assuming this is another kidnapping by the same men. Now that Zoe is unavailable, they would need another girl. I'll call Rowley and tell him to get back here ASAP." She pursed her lips. "Stu Macgregor is the only known predator in town we are aware of at the moment—find him."

"Yes, ma'am." He rubbed his chin. "I'll call the town council and see if he is working in the area."

"Okay. Did you locate Lizzy Harper?"

He could almost see Jenna's mind turning over; she had so many things to consider and was prioritizing at an amazing speed. "Yeah, she and her mother are cleaning a house on Clifton Drive. She should be there until five."

"Good, and she has no idea she is on our radar. Once we receive the arrest warrant, I will send someone to pick her up, but right now Sandra Doig is our first priority. I want to be speaking to Macgregor in five minutes." Jenna waved him away and reached for her phone.

With Deputies Wolfe and Webber at Craig's Rock with the Helena forensics team, the office was shorthanded. Kane returned to his desk and immediately called the local council, and after the operator passed him from one department to the other, he managed to establish that the magician was working on the street across from the park not far from the sheriff's office. Kane leaned back in his chair, recalling his earlier conversation with the man. He pushed to his feet just as Rowley came through the front door carrying a folder and went into Jenna's office.

He followed him inside then waited for Jenna to stop speaking to Rowley. When she turned her gaze on him, he cleared his throat. "Stu Macgregor is working across from the park. That seems to be his spot during a festival. I spoke to him there last week."

"Okay, we'll speak with him first." She turned to Rowley. "While I'm out, put Bradford on the desk to help Maggie with incoming calls from the public about the missing girl and make sure she keeps me up to date with any developments. You speak to Mr. Doig; he is bringing in something of Sandra's we can use for scent."

"Yes, ma'am." Rowley marched out of the room.

The call panel on her desk lit up and she flicked an apprehensive glance at him. "This might be information on the missing girl. Go and speak to Macgregor. It will be quicker to walk."

"Sure." He held up one hand. "I'll need the girl's details."

"I've already sent all the information to your phone." She lifted her chin and her eyes bore into him. "I'll pick you up at the park when I'm finished here and we'll go door to door, starting from where

Sandra was last seen. I'll get Wolfe and Webber back here and they can bring in Lizzy Harper."

"Okay." Kane headed for the door.

The sun hit him full in the eyes as he stepped out onto the street. He reached for the sunglasses in his top pocket and moved through the milling crowds enjoying the festival. The schools had closed for one day the previous week but the number of kids underfoot staggered him. He dodged a group from the local kindergarten class waving sticky fingers and smiling at him with toffee-apple-stained teeth. This week many entertainers, buskers, clowns, and magicians had set up in the parking lots in front of the local stores. He picked out Stu Macgregor surrounded by kids and he pushed down his anger. Would he go to work as usual if he had a kidnapped kid at home in his cellar? Could he be procuring kids for other pedophiles? *Probably.*

Predators, like psychopaths, had the ability to appear normal and most times wore the façade of a person of trust and likeability. Although he had found psychopaths to be extremely clever without feelings toward their victims, most pedophiles truly believed they loved the children they molested. They acted on their sexual perversion. The problem he had as a profiler was the two types of personality often crossed. He could be dealing with a pedophile with psychopathic personality who craved sex with children but had no conscience when it came to hurting or killing them.

He moved to the front of the mass of people watching Stu Macgregor run through his performance. The man noticed him at once and Kane noticed his hands shake a little during his final trick. When the magician announced he would be taking a short break, the crowed moaned as one then started to wander away. Kane walked up to him and stood, hands on hips. "Do you drive over from Blackwater each day or do you have a place here in town?"

"I leased a house. It's a run-down place outside of town on the way to the falls." Macgregor busied himself with his props, not meeting Kane's eyes. "Why?"

Kane watched his body language with interest. *He is worried.* "I thought Stanton Road was upmarket."

"Not Stanton Road, way past there up the highway near the Triple Z bar. It's an old bunkhouse on Weller's Road."

Kane leaned closer. "Did you take a little girl up there last night?"

"No." Macgregor still refused to look at him. "I don't know nothing about a little girl going missing."

"I didn't say she went missing, did I?" Kane glared at him. "Pack up your things. We're going to take a ride to the sheriff's office. You can wait in a cell while we search your place."

"You don't have a warrant to search my place."

Kane moved so close he could smell the man's sweat. "You're on parole, I don't need one and I have enough to detain you on suspicion of kidnapping."

He pulled out his phone and relayed the information to Jenna. "Give me your keys. You are a registered sex offender and a girl is missing." He gave him a little push toward the sheriff's department. "Start walking unless you want me to cuff you in front of all the kids."

CHAPTER FIFTY-TWO

For once, she was in a good mood. She had the day free to enjoy the Fall Festival. After wandering through town avoiding the milling people, she spotted Stu Macgregor, but right this minute he was the least of her problems. He had never touched her or any of the girls and was a broken man after his time in prison. The court case had taken up all his cash and his family wanted nothing to do with him. The deputies had him on their radar. Not that she had left him out of her diary. She had recorded every detail she could remember in that time, along with details of her recent murders, because as sure as hell, Sheriff Alton would not allow her to walk free for much longer.

Over lunch in Aunt Betty's she savored the memory of watching Chris's life slip away. With glee, she allowed each detail to percolate through her mind. Killing him had been satisfying and she had enjoyed the heat of his blood gushing over her. The smell of death intrigued her with its many facets and she almost wished she had the time to roll in it like some barbaric heathen. She let out a contented sigh. Yes, her plans to kill monsters were going along just fine.

She glanced up at the TV, and the noisy crowd enjoying their meals seemed to vanish from view. Her chair clattered to the floor and she dashed from her table to the counter to catch the breaking news on TV. She gaped at the image on the screen of the young girl she had seen outside the cabin yesterday. When she read the "Missing girl" banner splashed across the screen, anger curled in her belly, making her hands shake. Her heart raced and she could not drag her eyes away from the TV, then Susie Hartwig's voice brought her back to reality.

"Dear Lord, won't you look at that poor child." Susie frowned up at the TV. "I sure hope she hasn't fallen into one of the swimming holes and drowned."

There are worse things that can happen to a girl in Black Rock Falls. She gathered herself and glanced at Susie. "I hope not. Can you turn up the volume so we can hear what happened?"

"Sure thing." Susie moved behind the counter.

The stern face of the news anchor filled the screen. "Thirteen-year-old Sandra Doig was last seen leaving Black Rock Falls Middle School by the back gate on her bicycle yesterday. If anyone has seen Sandra, please call the number on your screen."

Holy shit, what happened to her? Chris was dead and could not hurt her. The forest was deserted and the road empty when she left. Sandra should have made it safely to the highway. In fact, she had not given her a thought since leaving Stanton Forest. The memory of seeing Bobby-Joe driving past flashed into her mind and she wanted to scream in anguish. *Oh shit, Bobby-Joe has taken her to his cabin.*

A trickle of sweat ran annoyingly between her shoulder blades but she could not move her attention from the TV. Her gaze slid to Susie, who looked at her with a puzzled expression. She tried to relax and think. Her plans for Bobby-Joe had been complex, but with the sheriff's department climbing all over the mountain not far from his secluded cabin, she had little chance of torturing him to death, and nothing else would do. He would pay for what he had done.

She allowed her clenched jaw to relax, forced her face into a composed expression, and met Susie's gaze. "I wonder if the sheriff will ask for volunteers to join the search."

"I guess but they do have the rangers." Susie shrugged and pulled a pencil from behind one ear. "Table three is ready to order. Gotta go." She hurried away.

Acting as nonchalant as possible, she returned to her table, picked up her chair, and sat down. She had to take down Bobby-Joe today and he would be her final act of revenge.

After draining the coffee cup, she dropped some bills on the table and headed for the door. She had a call to make.

By the time she slid behind the wheel of her car, sirens wailed in the distance as the sheriff department's vehicles headed toward Stanton Forest. The idea of manipulating Deputy Kane amused her. She started her car and headed for her apartment to change into hiking gear. This time, she would need the knife, her pistol, and a stun gun. The image of Bobby-Joe flashed into her mind. He was cruel and calculating but after all, he was only a man. She had proved they all had their vulnerabilities, but killing him would be special. The pain he suffered would not atone for what he had done or the lives he had taken.

I'm going to kill you slow, Bobby-Joe.
I'm going to make you scream.

CHAPTER FIFTY-THREE

Jenna decided to send Bradford and Rowley to search Macgregor's cabin the moment Kane arrived. "Lights and sirens, and call me the moment you get there. If you don't find her, get back here double time."

She glanced up from her desk, glad to see Kane ushering Stu Macgregor toward the cells. "Kane, give Rowley the keys to Macgregor's house."

"Yes, ma'am."

Moments later, he returned and informed her about a call he had received about the missing girl. The information put a completely different perspective on the case.

"How good is this lead?"

"The caller gave me details of her bicycle and what she was wearing." Kane raised one eyebrow. "She said she saw the girl heading down a trail toward the forestry cabin yesterday afternoon. The idea of her going willingly would fit, especially if we are talking about a pedophile ring. You know how predators work—they groom kids and he probably convinced her to meet him at the cabin."

Dammit! "So, it's possible Stu Macgregor has her at the cabin in the woods, near where this witness last saw her, and not at his home?"

"It's possible, and at least we have a place to start searching." He leaned on her desk. "That's one hell of a big forest out there and she could be anywhere. Right now, Macgregor is denying he is involved. The informant is all we have to go on for now."

Torn between checking out the cabin and waiting for her deputies to search Macgregor's house, she groaned inwardly. *If I had Wolfe and Webber here, this would not be an issue.* "We'll wait for Rowley and Bradford to check his house. It is the most logical place. He could have met her in the forest and taken her to his place like the others. If we luck out there, we'll head out to her last known location. I'll get onto the media again and organize a search party. As you know, the first forty-eight hours are crucial in missing kids' cases. I have a pair of Sandra's socks. Do you think Duke will be able to track her?"

"Yeah."

Jenna went to her cupboard and pulled out her emergency backpack. "Go and get Duke, lights and sirens, then head out the back road to Stanton Forest. I'll text you the coordinates. Walters can take over here. I'll meet you at the road leading to the cabin."

"Roger that." Kane strode out the door.

Worry for Sandra cramped her belly as she followed him out of her office. She paused briefly to ask Maggie to call Walters into the office to make the Lizzy Harper arrest as soon as the warrant came through. Her cellphone rang. "Sheriff Alton."

"We found no trace of the girl. This is a one-bedroom shack, no cellar." Bradford spoke and she could hear sirens in the background. *"We'll be back at the office in five minutes."*

Annoyed, Jenna sighed. "Okay, thanks."

She called Kane and gave him the information then walked into her office before striding to the front counter, waiting impatiently for Rowley's cruiser to arrive. The moment the door opened and Bradford walked in she pounced on the woman. "Where's Rowley?"

"Right here, ma'am." Rowley strolled through the front door on Bradford's heels.

"Grab your backpacks and follow me."

*

Moments later, she led the way to her SUV with Rowley and Bradford. Once the deputies had climbed aboard, she spun the wheel of her SUV, and sirens and lights blazing headed toward Stanton Forest at speed. "Call Wolfe and tell him I'll send them the coordinates of the track when we arrive. They can meet us. I want every available person searching for this girl."

"Yes, ma'am." Rowley made the call. "They are on their way."

As the perimeter of the forest came into view, she slid the vehicle around a sweeping bend and headed west. The lines of tall pine trees dashed past in streaks of green. The flashes of sunlight and shadows made the road look like a flickering silent movie. She slowed to search the never-ending line of dark brown trunks for the entrance to the access road. The forest with its abundance of wildflowers appeared beautiful set against an azure sky with the mountains as a backdrop, but she was aware of the potential danger lurking within its dark depths.

She missed the dirt road at first. Long grass partially hid it on each side and she reversed to peer down a track disappearing into the dim forest. After pulling the SUV to a halt, she checked the coordinates on her GPS then sent them in a text to Kane and Wolfe. "Make sure you have your receivers turned on and your earbuds in. I want to make sure we are all communicating." Jenna slipped from the car then heard a siren in the distance coming fast. "That will be Kane. We might as well wait for him to arrive."

"You might want to drive some ways down this road too, ma'am." Rowley's brow crinkled. "The map has a cabin marked about quarter mile down that road, at the end of a trail more than fifty feet into the forest."

"Okay. When Kane gets here, we will take his SUV and leave mine here. It will make a good marker for Wolfe when he arrives."

A few minutes later, sunlight flashed on a windshield roaring around the bend at high speed. The wailing siren did not muffle the sound of the powerful engine in Kane's vehicle. When he came to a stop parallel to her SUV, she walked to the passenger door and pulled it open. "We'll ride with you. The cabin is down that road." She turned to Bradford. "Grab the backpacks out of my car." She tossed her the keys. "Rowley, bring a rifle."

"Yes, ma'am." Bradford collected the backpacks and hauled them to the back of Kane's SUV. "Will these be okay in there with the dog?"

"Yeah, he won't touch them." Kane nodded in the affirmative. "Put them beside mine."

They all piled into the vehicle and Jenna gave Kane directions as he turned into the forest. She glanced at him. "This is a frightened kid. Turn off the siren but leave the lights on. A kid will approach a police vehicle if they're lost."

"I think the trail is coming up on the right." Rowley leaned forward eagerly.

"Okay." Kane pulled the SUV off the road beside a narrow trail. "Down here?"

"Yeah, I would say so." Rowley peered at the map then back at the trail. "Hey, look, there is a signpost some ways down the path."

Jenna leaped from the car. "Okay, grab your backpacks and leave the rifle. If you find anything, mark the area with a flag and call me. She pulled a plastic bag from her pocket and looked at Kane. "Get Duke."

"Yes, ma'am." Kane let the dog out of the car and attached a long leash to his collar. He hoisted on his backpack then walked the dog to her. "Give him the scent then all we can do is head toward the girl's last known position and hope for the best."

Jenna opened the plastic bag and offered it to the dog. To her surprise, he gave two short barks then dropped his nose to the ground and searched around. Moments later, he took off down the road away from the cabin. "Oh, that can't be good. We know she was at the cabin."

"But maybe she went this way after the woman saw her." Kane attempted to heave Duke back but the dog barked loudly and pulled at the leash. "He seems intent on heading this way. Do you want me to follow him?"

"Yeah, take Bradford with you." Jenna glanced at Rowley. "Come with me to check out the cabin." She turned to call after Kane. "Keep in contact, Kane."

"Roger that." Kane gave her a nod, and with Bradford at his side, they followed the dog.

Without hesitation, Jenna plunged down the track leading to the cabin but was soon glad to have Rowley at her side. She could not imagine a young girl walking down this path voluntarily. Deep in the woods, the pine trees and the dense undergrowth seemed to form an impenetrable wall closing in around them. Long shadows fell like prison bars across the track and the hairs on the back of her neck stood up as if in a warning. Apart from their soft footsteps and the creaking of the trees, an eerie silence descended on them. Every muscle tensed as she realized the usual birdsong was missing. Jenna slowed the pace and glanced around in all directions, sensing danger lurking in the shadows. She lowered her voice to a whisper. "Something isn't right. No birds."

"I see some crows up there." Rowley frowned. "They are all watching us." He shuddered. "That's creepy."

Jenna sniffed the air and shrugged. "I can't smell death but crows are a good sign something is dead around here." She waved him on. "The cabin must be around the next bend. Keep to the tree line. We have no idea what is around the next corner."

A soft buzzing sound reached her as they walked and the cabin came into view. Astonished, she gaped at the front door. The wooden panels moved like a heat mirage. She took a few steps closer then realized with a shudder that the black mass was a swarm of flies. They crowded over the log cabin and spread across the windows like blinds. "Oh my God, are those flies?"

"Yeah." Rowley wiped a hand across his mouth as if in disgust. "That can't be good."

The sound of Kane's voice in her ear startled her but she quickly regained her composure. "What have you found?"

"A girl's bicycle fitting the description of Sandra's. Its front wheel is bent out of shape. I've marked the place. It was on a trail just off the main road. Then Duke led us to the end of the road. Here it widens out, so I guess firetrucks used it as a turnaround spot. There is an SUV parked here, and the hood is cool, so it's been here for a while." Kane cleared his throat. *"I ran the plates. It belongs to Chris Jenkins, and guess what? He lives in the mountains. Problem is, Sandra's scent went cold here. I figure she got into another vehicle. We could have two guys working together, maybe a procurer and a client?"*

"Roger that." Jenna kept up a constant scan of the area and one hand on her pistol. "I think we have something significant here too."

She explained the flies and the silence. "I'll leave the mic open and go and take a look inside the cabin."

"Okay. We are heading to your position now."

Jenna slid her Glock from the holster and turned to Rowley. "We don't know if anyone is watching us or who, if anyone, is inside. We'll be vulnerable inside the cabin. I'm going to recon it alone. Get into the forest with a tree to your back and watch my six."

"Yes, ma'am." Rowley pulled out his weapon, gave her a curt nod, and backed into the shadows.

She knew the drill, stick to the tree line then move from the corner of the cabin and look through a window. The emergency cabins in this area were little more than one room and she should be able to see if anyone was inside. She reached the side of the cabin and listened for any sound of movement.

Nothing.

As she edged toward the window, a great cloud of flies rose into the air, buzzing with annoyance. They landed on her, covering her face as if she was their next meal. She waved them away and turkey-peeked inside the window. The quick glance gave her little information as blackness met her gaze. The only light came from the small windows and apart from the one she was looking through, flies blocked the other. She banged on the wall, sending the flies swarming again. "Sheriff's department, is anyone inside?"

Silence.

Shit! She holstered her weapon just long enough to pull on a pair of surgical gloves then spoke into her mic. "It looks empty. I'm going to try the door."

Heart thumping against her ribs at the thought of finding a murdered girl inside, Jenna eased along the wall to the front of the cabin and turned the doorknob with trembling fingers. As the door swung open, a cloud of flies rushed inside and the stench of death flooded her nostrils. Light from the door fell over the body of a man, lying on his back in a pool of blood. Multiple stab wounds adorned his bare chest and his eyes stared at her, set in a horrified expression that would stay with her for a very long time.

A swarm of flies joined the ants crawling over his face, and as nausea grabbed her, Jenna moved away from the door. The man was obviously dead and the fewer people disturbing the scene the better. She spoke into her mic then had the courage to look at the body again. "We have a naked body, male, late thirties. Stab wounds to chest. I can clearly see a scar on his knee; he could be one of the members of the pedophile ring. I would say he has been dead maybe twelve hours or so." She sighed. "I'll notify Wolfe and then start a perimeter search but if this is another vigilante murder, I doubt we will find anything."

She heard a dog barking and was glad to see Duke bounding toward her with Kane in tow. She pulled out her cellphone and called Wolfe. "We have another homicide."

CHAPTER FIFTY-FOUR

Nothing was going to plan. Irritated, Bobby-Joe dragged the girl from the bed. "Get back into the cage and don't make a sound, hear me?"

"I want to go home." She looked up at him, her chin stuck out at a stubborn angle. "You said you would take me home."

He grabbed her hair and twisted it in his fist, enjoying the flash of fear in her eyes. "You *are* home. You'll do anythin' I want, when I want, and how I want." He laughed when her eyes widened. "You're never goin' home, and if you try to run away, I'll hunt you down then go get that pretty little sister of yours. I'll slit your mother's throat while I'm there."

Coming out of the shower with a towel wrapped around his waist, he headed up the cellar steps and strolled through the pantry and into the kitchen whistling. The sound died on his lips at the sight of a young woman leaning against the kitchen counter aiming a pistol at him. He stared at the gun clasped combat-style in both hands. The weapon looked big in her small fists and her face seemed familiar. Who the hell was she and what did she want? Flicking his eyes around to look for a weapon, he spotted a knife on the counter. Confident he could overpower her, he lifted both hands and edged in that direction. "What's your problem?"

"You said that to me as well." The woman's hands held the gun with unnerving steadiness. "That you'd hunt me down and kill my parents, but you didn't find me, did you?"

"I don't know what you're talkin' about but I do know you're on private property. My gate is locked and signposted for a reason."

"I took care of the gate. You should have purchased a thicker chain; my bolt cutters sliced through it like butter." She smiled at him. "You didn't expect me to walk all the way back here, did you?"

"Okay. So, you've obviously been here before. What do you want? Did you come to tell me I'm a daddy?"

"No." Her expression turned to ice. "I'll give you one thing—you and your friends were always careful." A slow smile twisted her lips. "I guess you're running out of friends now, huh?"

Unease crept over him. How did she know two of his friends had died recently, and where the hell was Chris? He had expected him to arrive last night to use the cage, but after scaring his girl in the forest, maybe he'd decided to hole up in the cabin until later. He shrugged, trying to act nonchalant. "You're talkin' a load of shit, lady."

"Am I?" She lifted her chin and her cold eyes bore into him. "Let me see… Amos died, then Ely. I ran into Chris near where you picked up Sandra; he won't be bringing his girl here today."

Panic made his heart beat uncomfortably fast. *How does she know about the girl I met in the forest?* "I don't know any Sandra."

"Oh, that's right; you never ask their names, do you?" Her lip curled in obvious disgust. "Is she locked in the cage in the cellar?"

How does she know about the cage? Only one of *his* girls had ever escaped. Stu had lost one and paid the price for his stupidity. When his girl vanished, he had scanned the newspapers for months but had not seen one word mentioned about her. Looking at the woman standing before him, she could be the girl; there was a slight resemblance. "Is this a joke?"

"Do I look like I'm joking?" Her aim did not falter.

She knew too much and had the confidence of a cop with plenty of backup. He took his eyes off her for a split second to glance out the front window expecting to see deputies' cruisers outside but only the forest filled his view.

"If you're looking for the sheriff, she won't be coming to the party." The woman smiled as if she had read his mind. "I have big plans for you, Bobby-Joe. You *do* recognize me, don't you?"

The puzzle fell into place. She must have been one of their earlier girls. Luckily, she had never said a word to the cops. *She must have liked being here.* "You do look familiar now I come to look at you." He cleared his throat. "What do you want?"

Her eyes locked on his face but her mouth twitched at the corners as if holding a gun on him was funny. "I've been out visiting old acquaintances and thought I'd drop by. I just couldn't get our time together out of my mind."

Relieved, he smiled his best come-get-me smile. "Never found anyone as good as me, huh? You don't need to hold a gun on me, all you have to do is ask."

He opened his arms wide and held in his gut to make the towel puddle at his feet. He needed a distraction to grab the knife but the woman's attention had locked on his face; not even her eyes moved. "Like what you see?"

"I see evil. A person who hides behind a mask." Her mouth turned into an ugly grimace. "You are a pathetic little worm and not worthy to be called a man. You see, a real man protects children."

"So why are you here?"

"To even the score." She wet her lips as if savoring her words. "I know what you are and I was in the hospital when you murdered Jane. Now it's your turn to pay but first, I want your laptop, all the images you have of the girls you kept here, and the masks."

"No way."

A bullet whizzed past his ear in an ear-piercing boom, splintering the wall behind him and showering his bare flesh with splinters of wood. He flicked a glance over one shoulder and gaped at the hole in the wall. *Holy crap, she is using hollow points.* Fear shook his knees and sweat coated his skin. He held up his hands. "Okay, okay. They're locked in the pantry."

"Get them, all of them, and before you think you might try and cut me or maybe grab a gun, think again. I'll drop you before you can take your next breath." Her eyes fixed on him and she smiled. "I'm going to enjoy killing you."

Terror gripped him and, keeping his hands high, he moved slowly to the pantry door. "I'll need to lower my hand to open the door."

"Keep one hand on your head."

"Sure, anythin' you say." He opened the door wide and with trembling fingers slid open the false back to the pantry. Keeping one eye on the crazy woman with the gun, he opened the safe and took out his laptop. He piled a box of images and files on top then stuffed the clown masks into the box. He looked over one shoulder. "Where do you want these?"

"On the kitchen table. Open the laptop and show me what's on those thumb drives." Her dark eyes moved over him. "One move, one tiny move toward me, and your head is leaving your body."

He complied and turned the screen around for her to view the images. "Now what?"

"Now we're going for a little walk." She pulled out zip ties from her pocket and dropped them on the counter. "Turn around. Hands behind your back."

Anger tightened his throat. "No way. Are you jokin'? Shoot me, bitch, because as sure as hell, you'll have to kill me before I go anywhere with you barefoot and naked."

He lunged for the knife on the counter and white-hot pain sliced through him in a bolt of lightning. His limbs stiffened and his heart raced. He hit the floor face down and heard the unmistakable crack of bone as his nose shattered. The metallic taste of blood ran down his throat. He could not move a muscle. *Holy shit, she used a stun gun on me.*

"How does that feel, Bobby-Joe?" The woman bent and secured his hands behind his back with zip ties. She looped a few together and tied his ankles, leaving enough space to shuffle his feet. "I've picked out a nice tree close to the falls with your name on it." She grinned at him but her eyes were as cold as ice. "Unless you want the stun gun on your balls next time, I suggest you do as I say, but I promise you one thing: Before you die, I *will* make you scream."

CHAPTER FIFTY-FIVE

Kane caught the smell of decomposing flesh before he rounded the bend in the path to the cabin. Duke was pulling hard on the leash and making strange barking noises then stopping to howl. He turned to Bradford and took in her ashen face. "Have you attended a homicide crime scene before?"

"No, sir." She straightened as if trying to look efficient and fell into stride beside him. "It smells pretty bad."

"It's only going to get worse. Use one of the face masks in your backpack. If anyone asks you to enter the crime scene, you must be wearing coveralls and booties. Don't touch anything without wearing gloves." He glanced around, peering through the wall of trees. "Be alert, we have no idea if the area is secure. The killer could be right beside us and we wouldn't see him in the cover of the forest."

They walked around a hairpin bend and he could hear Jenna speaking on her cellphone. "What's your ETA?"

He gathered she was speaking to Wolfe, and he called Duke and told the dog to sit under a tree. He wandered over to Rowley and they walked to the door of the cabin. Covering his nose with one hand, he peered inside. Sticky black pools of blood surrounded the body, which appeared to be wearing a black shroud of flies and other insects. He stepped away and turned to Rowley. "No bloody footprints but I can see some smear marks on the floor as if the killer tried to hide his tracks." He took out his notepad and jotted down the information. "Did you see the body before the flies arrived?"

"Yeah, but I don't have anything to add to what the sheriff told you." Rowley scratched his head. "He looks familiar and I recall his name. That's Chris Jenkins, I gave him a ticket for a broken tail light a week or so ago."

"That will be easy enough to check." Kane turned at Jenna's voice. "Have you been inside, ma'am?"

"No, Wolfe is five minutes away, we'll wait for him. We have another problem: Walters can't locate Lizzy Harper." She removed her hat and wiped the sweat from her brow with a tissue. "Her mother said she didn't go to work today and she's not at home."

Kane scanned the area. "I doubt she'll be sticking around."

"I haven't seen any trace of her at all. We checked the immediate area but found nothing of interest apart from bicycle tracks over there." She pointed to the edge of the clearing. "The dirt is softer and it appears someone leaned their bicycle against a tree."

Kane wandered over, pulled out his cellphone, and took photographs of the tire marks. "I don't think this is Sandra's bicycle; the marks are narrow and more like a racing bicycle."

"So, it could belong to the killer?" Jenna's cellphone blasted out a heavy rock ringtone and she pulled it out of her pocket. "Yes, Walters, what is it? Just one moment, I'll put you on speaker."

"Still no trace of Lizzy Harper but I'm still looking as she don't know we're looking for her. If she is in town, I'll find her soon enough."

"Get Maggie to help you. Call some of the local stores—someone must have seen her. Anything else?"

"I have found something of interest."

"Go on." Jenna's brow wrinkled into a frown.

"I took the list of people working at the hospital and cross-referenced the names of those who live in the cabins up near Craig's Rock. I found four people. Three checked out okay but one man, Bobby-Joe Brandon, works nights at the hospital and he has taken a couple of days off with

the flu. He was supposed to be on duty the night Jane Stickler died but called in sick. Kinda convenient, don't you think?" He paused for a few seconds. *"I found his cellphone number and called him but all I got was his voicemail. I figure there's a slim chance he might be one of the four men the girls' mentioned in the pedophile ring, and if so, he could have abducted the girl. As he isn't answering his phone the vigilante might have killed him already."*

Kane's skin prickled. "Where exactly does he live?"

"Did you pass a private road with a lot of signs when you went up to Craig's Rock?"

"Yes, I remember the place." Jenna flashed Kane a look of concern.

"Well, ma'am, his cabin is about half a mile up that road. You would have to drive to the gate and go on foot. He has the property fenced, so I'm told."

"Okay, thanks. He might be in the shower or something, keep trying his number." Jenna worried her bottom lip. "Any relevant leads on the missing girl?"

"Not really. We've had quite a few calls, a few crackpots, and the others I'm checking out as they come in. Most are the same, as we know already; they last saw her heading in your direction. One person saw her riding along the road when he was coming into town. She was last seen after school in the area for sure." He paused and she could hear a tapping on a keyboard. *"Another thing: Mrs. Dempsy saw a late-model white sedan turning and heading to your position early yesterday afternoon. She didn't take much notice who was driving."* He took a deep breath. *"There are volunteers searching from the school, heading through the forest in your direction. The rangers have them well organized."*

"Okay, thanks. If anyone calls in with a positive sighting, call me, and keep looking for Lizzy Harper; someone must have seen her."

"Yes, ma'am."

After Jenna disconnected she stared up at Kane blankly as if thinking, then cleared her throat. "What if the vigilante killer set up this victim? You mentioned pedophiles groom kids online, and if she acted like a young girl, it's possible this is how she is getting her victims alone." She waved a hand around. "Look at this place: It's a mile or more from town but not too far to come by bicycle, and it's secluded."

"Yeah." Rowley blinked away the flies buzzing around his sweat-streaked face. "If the victims thought they were meeting a young girl, they wouldn't be over-cautious—in fact, more likely to do whatever the kid wanted."

"If we consider the vigilante is posing as a kid, yeah it makes perfect sense." Jenna sighed. "If Bobby-Joe Brandon is part of this, he is probably dead already."

A bolt of realization smacked Kane in the head. "We're missing something. Let's say the call I received about seeing the girl here was from the vigilante, and she didn't disguise her voice this time to make me think it was legit."

"She's never done that before. Why now?" Jenna raised one eyebrow.

"I figure she's been moving us around like pieces on a chess board. Think back. She blood-bombed my house and left the newspapers to justify her reason for murder, maybe in an effort to make us pull back the investigation. She wanted us out of town to give her time to kill Jenkins so she called and informed me about the graves at Craig's Rock."

"Then she lured Jenkins here." Jenna was well ahead of him. "It's obvious she knows the names of the men in the pedophile ring, and if Bobby-Joe Brandon is our fourth man, he would be next on her list. I figure Bobby-Joe planned to meet a girl here as well." She glanced up at him, eyes flashing with excitement. "It's possible she killed Chris then caught sight of Bobby-Joe with Sandra and followed him. We know someone else was here. Sandra's trail vanishes so it proves a second vehicle picked her up."

Kane rubbed the back of his neck. "The vigilante wouldn't have picked up Sandra or she would have been home by now."

"Yeah, she is using this murder scene as a decoy. I figure killing the fourth man is her ultimate prize." Jenna stared into space then snapped her gaze back to him. "Craig's Rock is close to Bobby-Joe's cabin, so she calls you to tell you about seeing Sandra here. She would know I would call in all my resources to search for the missing girl, and when we found the body, I would call in the ME and give her a clear path to Bobby-Joe."

"Oh shit!" Rowley's eyes rounded in horror. "You're saying she wanted us away from Craig's Rock so she could murder Bobby-Joe Brandon?"

Kane nodded in agreement. "Yeah. We need to get up there now."

CHAPTER FIFTY-SIX

When Duke barked and jumped, as wildly as possible for a hound, Jenna turned to see Wolfe and Webber coming into the clearing carrying a ton of equipment. She hurried to meet them and explained the situation. "I'm heading up to Bobby-Joe Brandon's cabin. I think we're wasting our time searching here."

"If you leave Webber with me, we can handle the crime scene alone. I've organized a huge team from Helena and surrounding counties to exhume all the bodies at Craig's Rock. They'll be here first thing in the morning." Wolfe walked over to the cabin and peered into the door. "I've already called the local mortician to bring transport for the body."

"We think this is Chris Jenkins; he fits the description as far as I can tell on his driver's license. Kane found his truck parked some ways up the main road. See if his prints are on file. I'll need you to confirm his ID and find out if he has any next of kin." She rubbed her mouth, remembering the flies and ants crawling over the victim's face. "You'll need to clean him up before you get a positive ID."

"That's given, ma'am." Wolfe looked slightly annoyed.

With her mind juggling a multitude of cases, being nice sometimes slipped into obscurity. "That was rude, I apologize, Wolfe. I'm sure I don't have to remind you about procedure." She turned to her other deputies. "We'll go in your SUV, Kane. Rowley and Bradford, with us." She tossed her keys to Webber. "Drive my car back to the office when you're finished here."

"Yes, ma'am." Webber's face was sheet-white.

With a girl in danger, Jenna did not have time to boost morale. She offered him a small smile. "I know you've had a gruesome introduction to Black Rock Falls but it's not like this all the time. You'll be back to writing tickets before you know it."

"I've seen death before, ma'am, but it's never easy."

"He's doing a fine job." Wolfe slapped Webber on the back. "Suit up, we have work to do."

Jenna spun away to face Kane. "Let's go."

Frantic for the safety of Sandra Doig, Jenna jogged along the trail to Kane's black SUV. When Kane moved to her side, she glanced up at him. "Lights and sirens. I want to get to Bobby-Joe's cabin yesterday." She yanked open the door to his car, tossed her backpack over the back, and climbed into the passenger seat. "Hurry!"

"You got it." Kane hoisted Duke in the back and slid behind the wheel then cast a glance over to Rowley and Bradford. "Strap in, it's going to be a wild ride." His gaze settled on Rowley. "My sniper rifle is under the seat in a case. Get it out for me, please."

"Roger that." Rowley gave him a curt nod then clicked in his seatbelt.

Thrown back in her chair as the powerful SUV took off then spun one-eighty degrees before tearing back to the main road, Jenna gripped the edge of the seat. She had confidence in Kane's ability to keep her safe but his look of grim determination worried her about his mood. His opinion of pedophiles was quite clear, and he would kill on her command without blinking an eye. She would need to keep a tight hold on her deputies if Bobby-Joe Brandon was alive and had the missing girl in his cabin.

"Go straight ahead at the intersection then take the first right. The road runs parallel to Stanton Road and will bypass the traffic in town." Rowley leaned forward in his seat. "It's residential but loops back around to Stanton Road near the college."

"Okay." The engine roared like an angry bull as Kane turned onto the highway.

Jenna concentrated on the road ahead, and with the siren blaring, the forest became a green blur as Kane increased speed, hardly slowing to take the bends. Behind her, she could hear Rowley checking his weapons and assembling Kane's rifle. They flashed past cars, most pulling over to allow them to pass, and hit the intersection doing sixty. "Holy shit, Kane, slow down or you'll kill someone."

"We're good. I could see a good hundred feet each way." His blue gaze landed on her for a split second. "Trust me."

As they flashed by houses, people came out open-mouthed to watch them go by. The end of the road came up fast, and with a quick glance in both directions, Kane hit the gas again and they surged down the open highway. Jenna gaped at the needle on the speedometer: eighty, ninety. She sucked in a breath and looked away when it slid over 120 miles per hour. She heard a strange whooshing sound as they passed cars, trucks, and buildings without slowing. The turnoff leading to Craig's Rock and the entrance to the falls was coming up at speed.

A shower of gravel had washed down in the last rain and coated the end of the road, spilling onto the highway and making a muddy smear on the blacktop. Jenna held her breath. The car slowed, the motor rumbled, and she squeezed her eyes shut as Kane slid the car around the hairpin bend on the gravel, then, wheels spinning, the SUV gained traction and increased speed up the mountain road. He was scaring the hell out of her now. With her heart pounding, she tried to act nonchalant. "You should compete in drifting competitions. You'd win."

"Nah, it's an idiot's game and I'd never risk my life on something so stupid."

"That's good to hear." She glanced at him. "Turn off the lights and sirens, we don't want to advertise the fact we are here."

"Yes, ma'am."

As they climbed high into the mountain range, Jenna scanned the forest for cabins. Her wholesome idea of a wonderful trek up the peak to enjoy nature had been shattered of late. With hundreds of log cabins spread throughout the forest, she wondered how many people used them for illegal activities. The road weaved in all directions and Jenna swallowed hard as the SUV came perilously close to the edge of the falls, sending pebbles tumbling down the rock face. Then, to her relief, Kane turned down a side road leading into the forest. As they drove deeper into the mass of trees, the shade from the tall pines turned the bright summer's day into dusk. A short time later, they approached the private road Walters had informed them led to Bobby-Joe's property. She stared at the open gate with signs all over prohibiting entry. "That was padlocked when we came past last time."

"This can't be good." Kane drove slowly through the opening and hung out the window, examining the gate. "Someone has cut through the chain."

"It might be Lizzy Harper. She could be on foot." A jolt of adrenaline hit Jenna, making her hand tremble. "Scan the area. Rowley, take the left; I'll take the right. Kane, proceed with caution."

"There's a white sedan parked off-road ahead." Kane slowed the car then pulled up. "Do you want to stop or continue, ma'am?"

Jenna shook her head. "No, keep going. Pull up just before the turn; we'll go in from there. Rowley, run the plate."

"Oh, mother of God." Rowley's voice came out in a rush of emotion. "He has Alison. That's her car."

CHAPTER FIFTY-SEVEN

It never ceased to amaze Jenna the way Kane could slip from his deputy persona into combat mode in the blink of an eye and move without making a sound. He changed noticeably and his expression became fixed, almost robotic, but his eyes moved constantly, scanning the area. With him in the lead, if someone was in the forest waiting to take a shot at them, they would not get past his scrutiny.

As they rounded the sweeping curve leading to the clearing surrounding the cabin with Kane in the lead, Jenna heard his voice in her earbud.

"If we cross the road, we'll be able to come up around the back of the cabin."

"Roger that." She could see him using a pair of binoculars to check out the cabin. "Can you see any movement inside?"

"Nope. There is a truck parked out front."

A strangled scream came from the forest, sending a flock of birds rising high in the air. In front of her, Kane froze and scanned the area with his binoculars. Jenna waved the other deputies into the trees and moved slowly to his side, taking cover behind a pine two feet wide. "Bobcat?"

Another scream and this time, a long wailing voice shattered the silence. "Pleeeease stop."

Torn between checking the cabin for a kidnapped girl and saving a pedophile from potential murder, Jenna glanced toward Kane.

"Check out who is screaming. If Alison is in danger, take action immediately. I'll take Rowley and Bradford and clear the cabin."

When Kane gave her a curt nod then took a well-worn trail blended into the forest without as much as a crack of twigs, she pressed her mic. "Rowley, Bradford, with me. We'll cross the road here one at a time then go around the back of the cabin. Kane is heading toward the person in trouble."

Without waiting, she dashed across the road and slipped into the cover of trees. Seconds later Rowley then Bradford sans dog were beside her. "Where's Duke?"

"I told him to lie down; he is in the bushes." Bradford gave her a worried look. "I thought he might get in the way."

"Okay, follow me."

Jenna approached the back door of the cabin with caution; no sound came from within and the screaming had obviously not disturbed the inhabitants. The back door hung open and she could clearly see the kitchen inside. "Sheriff's department. Mr. Brandon, are you there?"

She turkey-peeked around the door and then drawing her weapon took a few cautious steps inside. The strong odor of unwashed man and beer accosted her nostrils. The kitchen was empty but her attention went straight to a gaping hole in the wall and the splintered wood fragments littering the floor. Only a gun could make that much damage. She hit her mic. "Kane, there is a hole as big as Texas in the wall in here."

"Blood?"

"Not that I can see and it's quiet." She took a deep breath and moved into the kitchen. "The back door was open. It looks like one shot and a maybe a chase."

"I can't see anyone from my position. The screaming is coming from closer to the falls. I figure you're good to go."

"Okay." She could see through to the small living room. Another open door was on her right. "Mr. Brandon?"

With Rowley hot on her heels, she edged along the wall and peered into the bedroom. She could smell the filthy bed linen from the doorway and, heart pounding, moved inside to check the small bathroom. "Clear."

No one appeared to be home and yet a truck sat in the driveway and Alison's car was on the road. Worry knotted her stomach. *Where are they?* She led the way to the kitchen, opening cupboards to search for the concealed entrance to a cellar. She turned to Rowley. "Search for a cellar door. It might be under a mat."

"Yes, ma'am."

"Kane, the place is empty. I'm still searching for Alison and the girl." Jenna waved Bradford inside.

"The screaming has stopped. It wasn't a kid's voice; it sounded like a man. I figure the killer wouldn't hurt a kid. Sandra and Alison must still be in the house. I'm climbing to a higher position."

Glad she had Kane on the outside watching their backs, Jenna holstered her weapon. "Roger that."

In the kitchen, Bradford stood with one hand pressed to her mouth and stared at a laptop on the table. Concerned by the deputy's ashen face, Jenna walked to her side. "What is it?"

"Take a look." Bradford grimaced then turned away, shaking her head.

Disgust and anger slammed into Jenna at the lurid images on the screen, and using her elbow, she closed the lid. She dragged out latex gloves from her pocket and pulled them on then peered into a carton sitting on the table. Inside were clown masks, twenty or more thumb drives, and piles of photographs. She forced her mind to cut out the depravity and concentrate on the victims' faces. "Oh my God, I recognize some of these girls from the newspaper articles."

"Do you think he's killed the girl?" Bradford's hands were shaking.

"No, men like him prefer to keep them alive for as long as possible. She has to be here; he probably has her and Alison stashed close by."

Frantic to find them, she glanced around, then Kane's voice came into her ear.

"I've continued up the trail but I still can't see anyone. I can see a ledge higher up; I'll get up there and scan the area with my scope. Any luck finding Sandra and Alison?"

She pressed her mic. "No. The cabin is empty and we are searching for a cellar. They have to be here somewhere. I know Brandon is one of the pedophiles. He left a laptop open with porn files on the kitchen table. There's a box containing clown masks, thumb drives, and photographs. I recognize some of them from the missing girls in the newspapers."

"Roger that. Just a minute. I see movement up the top of the mountain and the sound of water is getting louder. I'm close to the falls and I can make out a few shapes ahead."

"Okay, hold your position. We'll check out the cellar then meet you on the trail."

"Ma'am." Rowley caught her attention. "I've found a safe with the door open. It looks empty." He walked into the pantry and pointed to a door set into the back wall. "That might be the cellar door. I'll check it out."

"Wait!" Jenna moved to his side and pushed him against the wall. "Always assume someone may be down there with a weapon. Keep your back to the wall and ease open the door."

The door opened without a sound but it was pitch-black at the bottom of the stairs. "This is Sheriff Alton. Come to the bottom of the stairs where I can see you."

"I can't."

Jenna's heart missed a beat at the small glimmer of hope. The voice was young. "Is that you, Sandra?"

"Yes."

She flicked a glance at Rowley, and his eyes flashed with a rage she had not seen before. She took a breath. "Is Alison with you?"

"No. I don't know Alison."

Jenna flicked a look at Rowley's concerned face then called out again. "Are you alone?"

"Yes."

It took every ounce of willpower not to charge down the stairs. She edged back into the pantry and unclipped her flashlight from her belt. "I can't see a thing down there. Can you see a light switch anywhere?"

"Nope, it must be inside." Rowley turned on his flashlight.

She turned to Bradford. "Watch the door. Rowley, with me."

With Rowley close behind and holding their flashlights flush to their Glocks, they flooded the cellar with light. She sighed with relief at finding the girl seemingly alone. Still unsure if Bobby-Joe was hiding under the bed or in the shadows, she edged down the creaky old stairs step by step. "I can see you, Sandra. If anyone else is hiding in here, we are armed. Come out with your hands up."

"I'm alone. No one else is here." Sandra's small voice sounded weak and shaky.

She holstered her weapon and ran to the girl locked in a cage. "It's okay, we're going to get you out." She opened her mic. "Kane, we have Sandra and she is fine. No sign of Alison or Bobby-Joe."

"Roger that."

"Get right over to the back of the cage, Sandra." Rowley appeared at her side with an ax and smashed the door with a couple of blows.

Jenna peered at the huddled, wide-eyed, trembling figure and her heart shattered into a thousand pieces. *What kind of animal does this to a young girl?* "You're safe now." With delicate care, she eased her from the cage and, shielding her from Rowley's line of sight, glanced around for something to cover her. "Grab me those clean bath towels then go back upstairs."

After taking the folded towels from Rowley, she turned back to the girl. With effort, she kept her emotion in check. "I'm going to catch the man who did this to you. I want you to stay upstairs with Deputy Bradford, ah, Paula, for a few minutes. She will look after you, okay?"

"I want to go home."

Jenna wrapped her in the towels. "Very soon."

In the kitchen, she instructed Bradford to find Sandra something to eat, locked the front door, then left with Rowley by the back, glad to hear the bolt sliding into position. She jogged back to collect Duke, confident the dog would lead them straight to Kane. As they headed up the mountain trail at a run, she opened her mic to speak to Bradford. "Sandra will need to be examined. Don't allow her to wash no matter what, okay? Stay alert—we don't know where Bobby-Joe is at the moment and Alison is still missing."

"Yes, ma'am."

"Kane, what's happening?"

"I've moved into position behind a boulder high up on the west side of the trail. I have a visual of a man tied to a tree. His condition is unknown but he is bloody. It looks like someone cut his throat. Hang on, I'll set up my rifle and take a look through the scope." Silence hung heavy between them for a few long seconds. *"Oh, shit!"* Kane paused and Jenna could hear him take a deep breath. *"Alison is the killer, repeat, Alison Saunders is the killer."*

Realization hit Jenna like a cannonball. She swallowed the lump in her throat as the missing links in the case dropped into place.

"Alison wouldn't hurt anyone." Rowley flashed her a look of concern. "There must be some mistake."

Jenna glanced at him but kept up the pace. "We'll find out soon enough. Did you hear that, Kane?"

"Yeah, sorry, man, it's her. She is covered in blood and pacing up and down in front of a mutilated body. She has a pistol and is scanning the trail as if waiting for someone to arrive."

"Okay, we'll keep out of range." Jenna stopped walking and surveyed the area. "We're going in left of the main trail. Can you cover us from your position?"

"Yeah, I have a clear line to the target."

"Oh, Jesus, don't kill her, Kane." Rowley's voice raised in panic as he spoke into his mic. "It has to be a mistake." His eyes pleaded with Jenna.

Panic drove Jenna faster along the trail. On her order, Kane would take out Alison without a second thought. The idea made bile rush into her mouth. She bit out the words. "Stand down unless she is a threat. We have no idea of the situation right now. If she is the vigilante, remember I want her alive to answer questions."

"Yes, ma'am." Kane's clipped reply grated on her shattered nerves. *"Standing down, awaiting orders."*

CHAPTER FIFTY-EIGHT

Hidden in shadows, Kane lay flat on his stomach and rested the sniper rifle on a convenient rock. Through the high-powered scope, he followed the movements of Alison Saunders. Her normally neat hair was tangled and her white skirt and pink blouse spattered with blood. Deranged was a good word to describe her appearance, and Jenna and Rowley would walk right into her line of fire if they continued up the trail to the top of the falls. He moved his attention to Bobby-Joe Brandon's blood-soaked naked body. He had stab wounds to his upper torso, a knife protruded from his chest, and his head hung down.

Jenna spoke in his ear. *"I can hear the falls, where are you? Duke is pulling to the right."*

Kane rolled on his side and scanned the forest until he found Jenna. "I see you. I am on the right up high in the shadows. Alison is still staring at the trail as if she is waiting for someone."

"So, if we continue on the left we'll be walking into a trap?"

"Roger that. Suggest you circle round and use the trees for cover until you are closer to her position." He sucked in a deep breath. "I won't allow her to shoot you, Jenna."

"Dammit, Kane, we don't know for sure if she is the vigilante."

He shook his head slowly in despair. "By the state of Bobby-Joe, this is her best work yet, and for the record, I don't have to kill her."

"I'll be able to talk her down."

Kane peered through the scope at the wild-eyed woman pacing the top of the falls. Talking her down would not be an option. "From what I'm seeing now, she is way past negotiation."

Rowley's voice came through his earpiece.

"I'll talk to her. She'll listen to me."

Kane shook his head. "It's not a good idea."

To his horror, Rowley burst through the trees and into the open. He could hear the conversation through his earbud.

"What do you want, Jake?" Alison placed the pistol on a rock. *"Don't worry, I'm not planning on killing you."*

"I would like to know what you are doing up here with Bobby-Joe Brandon." Rowley's voice sounded in complete control.

"You don't have to worry about him anymore. I guess you're with the sheriff?" Alison gave a short laugh. *"I guessed she would figure out who I was soon enough. I didn't think I'd have to wait so long."*

"Yeah, she's here. Why didn't you call me to help you?"

"You wouldn't understand. Men never do." Alison spread her bloody hands. *"And you'd want me to give myself up. It's not going to happen, Jake."*

Jenna's voice broke into the conversation. *"I'm right here, let's talk."*

"Sure, come on up, but leave Jake behind and don't hold a gun on me either. I'm no threat to you."

"Okay, but if you pick up your weapon, Kane has orders to shoot." Jenna's voice was as steady as a rock. *"Do you understand?"*

"Yes, I understand." Alison folded her arms over her chest in a nonchalant pose.

Kane opened his mic. "Keep her out in the open."

"Roger that." As Jenna weaved her way between the trees, Kane heard a sharp intake of breath. *"I have eyes on the victim. She has cut his throat. Use reasonable force, Kane, if she goes for her weapon. I'll keep my mic open. Rowley, watch my six but keep out of sight."*

"Yes, ma'am."

Kane aimed his rifle at Alison. "I'm locked on target."

He dropped into that place where his racing heart slowed and his breath came in an even flow. The calm he needed to make the shot, to kill, disable, or protect slipped over him and he waited.

Jenna moved through the trees, the pounding of water blocking out the sounds of the forest. She kept her attention fixed on Alison, waiting for her to dive for her weapon, but Alison had backed away from the pistol and stood perilously close to the edge of the falls. When the girl spoke, she could hardly hear her. She would need to get closer and trust that if Alison had a weapon hidden behind her back and threatened her, Kane would be fast enough to protect her. "Come closer, I can't hear you."

"No can do." Alison raised her voice. "You see, I don't trust anyone in law enforcement and you have a deputy pointing a gun at me."

Jenna shouted at her over the noise. "You can trust me, and if Bobby-Joe hurt you as a child, then I guess you had good reason to get even with him." She took in the almost blank expression on Alison's face and, seeing no obvious threat, moved closer. "Let's talk but put your hands where I can see them."

"You're not going to allow Kane to shoot me." Alison held her hands out at her sides. "I'm unarmed."

"You wanted to talk, so let's cut to the chase. Why did you murder Bobby-Joe Brandon? Did he molest you as a child?"

"Molest is such a nice, clean word, isn't it. Let me spell it out for you, Sheriff. He kidnapped me eight years ago, used me, then kept me in a cage under his bed. I was there for the pleasure of him and his friends. I watched him and his friends rape and murder innocent girls." She gave Jenna a cold look. "Bobby-Joe was a vicious son of a bitch and he laughed when they screamed. They meant nothing to him." She snorted. "If the girls died, they would say they 'planted' them at Craig's Rock or under the floorboards at Old Corkey's place."

A shiver went down Jenna's spine at the memory of the bleached white bones at Craig's Rock. "Why didn't you tell the sheriff?"

"I'm sure he was involved." Alison gave a hysterical laugh. "He could have been one of the others, the ones in the masks, so I kept my mouth shut. As soon as I could, I killed him." She smiled almost prettily. "What a surprise it was to see Amos Price in town. Soon after, I found out the others had returned to Black Rock Falls. It took some time to find them in the online chat rooms but I'm a patient woman."

"Who are these men? Tell me and I'll put them away for a very long time."

"It's too late. Amos Price, I murdered with nicotine sulfate. Ely Dorsey, the one in the motel, I skewered him through the ear. And good old Chris Jenkins, I stabbed him to death." She gestured to Bobby-Joe's corpse. "You can see how I made Bobby-Joe pay." She swiped at her mouth as if rubbing away the distaste for the men. "I've left a diary in my house with every detail I can remember: names, dates, and the girls I witnessed them kill."

Unable to grasp how cool and detached Alison appeared telling how she had murdered five men, Jenna swallowed the bile in her throat. She had to keep her talking and obtain as much information as possible while Alison was prepared to speak. "Did Stu Macgregor have anything to do with the pedophile ring? We know he went to jail for kidnapping Angelique Booval and she mentioned others were involved."

"He was the procurer. When Bobby-Joe gave him an order, he picked up a girl. Macgregor didn't join in during the time I was with Bobby-Joe. I guess he stopped kidnapping girls when he came out of jail. I read they chemically castrated him and that's the only reason he's not dead." Alison opened her arms wide. "I disposed of the monsters who hurt me but the network is wider than Black Rock Falls. I made Bobby-Joe show me all his photographs and thumb drives but he will have a camera in the cellar filled with images of his latest victim. Did you find the girl? He will have her locked in his cage. I would have searched for her but I was a little preoccupied."

Jenna stared at her in disbelief but pushed on. "Yes, Sandra is safe."

"'Safe?' What a stupid word." Alison snorted. "The memory of being raped never goes away but I guess you have some idea of what it's like to have men holding you against your will, don't you, Sheriff? Can you imagine being trapped in a filthy cabin and having men lining up to use you?"

A wave of understanding hit Jenna. Yes, she had wanted to kill the men who kidnapped and tried to rape her. She held no remorse for either of them but killing in self-defense was different. She had defended herself and not hunted them down to seek revenge. Cold realization marched a path down her spine. Before her stood a cold-blooded killer and she was trying to manipulate her. On the edge of falling into a debilitating flashback, her vision blurred then Kane's reassuring voice came in her ear.

"Jenna, she is playing for sympathy, using your experiences against you. Don't let her get in your head."

The flashback receded and she tapped her mic twice to signal she was okay. The next moment, Rowley moved in her periphery. *What the hell is he doing?*

"Ma'am." Rowley's voice was pleading. *"Let me speak to her again."*

Jenna whispered her reply, hoping her mic would pick up her voice. "Stand down, she has made it clear she doesn't want to talk to you and you will only complicate things."

She took a few slow steps closer to Alison. If she gained her confidence, she might be able to persuade her to give herself up. In the meantime, she would use her negotiating skills and keep her talking. "Do you know the names of any other men involved in the pedophile ring or any other victims you haven't recorded in your diary?"

"No, but you are aware of Lizzy Harper, Angelique Booval, Pattie McCarthy. Jane Stickler must have come after me but I mentioned her as well. You see, I was in the hospital the night Bobby-Joe killed her and I took a beating for my trouble. I escaped that night but she died in front of me just like the others. Did you know he used a dead man's card to get into the hospital that night? He was smart, but then psychopaths are intelligent." She barked out a sarcastic laugh. "I wanted vengeance for all the girls they killed, all the lives they destroyed." She rubbed her mouth. "You can tell the others they're safe now. I've killed all the clowns."

Beads of sweat turned to rivulets and ran down Jenna's cheeks. Worried she might be losing control of the situation she swallowed hard and forced her voice to remain steady. "I'll tell them but come with me now and I'll make sure you get to tell your story."

"Yes, tell my story." Alison's young gaze moved over her and her black hair moved almost in slow motion in the breeze. Behind her, a rainbow arched over the edge of the falls. Her lips lifted in a small smile then she opened her arms and fell backward over the edge, disappearing into the mist.

Jenna rushed to the top of the falls but all she could see was the pounding water rushing down the mountainside. She pressed a hand to her mouth in disbelief. Footsteps sounded behind her but she could not drag her eyes away from the tumbling water.

"God, no." Rowley dashed past her, his hat falling from his head. "*Alison.* Oh, Jesus. No!"

Jenna reached out and grabbed his arm. "She's gone."

CHAPTER FIFTY-NINE

On her return to the office, Jenna released a very disgruntled Stu Macgregor from the cells, and after the stern warning Kane had given him, she doubted they would see him in town anytime soon. After handing over copies of the information collected from Bobby-Joe's cabin to the FBI, she discovered the pedophile ring had spread throughout the country. The men Alison had murdered were the tip of the iceberg. When she read Alison's diary, the details made her sick to her stomach. The woman had suffered mental anguish after escaping Bobby-Joe's cabin years previously. With no one she could trust, she had waited patiently until she found the men who abused her then taken the law into her own hands.

Thursday, week two

The following day, Jenna regarded the deputies seated before her desk. "The information from Brandon's cabin included missing girls from throughout the state and I've turned all our information over to the FBI. We will still be involved to some extent but this is way over our heads. I believe Bobby-Joe used many of the images as security or even blackmail. I've identified a number of prominent men in the photographs." She glanced at Wolfe. "What did you discover?"

"Everything Alison told you checks out: the poison used, the meat skewer, and she left the knife used on Chris Jenkins sticking out of Bobby-Joe. Forensics teams are working on exhuming the remains of the other girls." Wolfe cleared his throat. "The only thing we don't have is information on how she killed the last sheriff. His death was recorded as natural causes."

"He was cremated as well, so we have nothing to go on. I suggest we let that one go."

Jenna rubbed her temples, it had been a long day and it wasn't even lunch yet. "So many things fell into place when I read her diary. When we checked the missing girls on file from all over the state, I read an old case file about a local girl who ran away from home then turned up with a few scratches and bruises five months later. The report said she'd suffered memory loss likely caused by a head injury but not how she survived alone up here in the mountains. I did wonder why there was no medical report to exclude sexual abuse on file. The sheriff at the time filed the report as a returned runaway and closed the case. He blacked out the names, I guess to protect her. I figure that was Alison."

"The evidence was right under our noses." Kane's gaze met hers over the desk. "She owned a late-model white Ford and it has small blotches on the paintwork. If you recall on the night Ely Dorsey was murdered, Rosa, the cleaner at the motel, noticed a white sedan parked under trees prone to drop berries." He sighed. "She was in town at the time of the murders and had access to the property where Amos Price died. Her car was seen heading to where we found Chris Jenkins." He frowned. "What we didn't have was motive so she slipped under our radar."

"I had no idea she had history here. I thought she was new in town." Jenna leaned back in her chair and avoided Rowley's pained expression. "Didn't she come from Blackwater?"

"Yeah, she did, but she used to live in Black Rock Falls as a kid. She never mentioned she'd been abused." Rowley rubbed his chin, clearly still distressed. "She returned when she heard the Rockfords were selling their properties. She had a real estate license and contacted Davis when he advertised an opening."

"When was that?" Jenna looked at him. "You seemed to know her pretty well the day we found Amos Price's body."

"A couple of weeks before then, I guess." Rowley's cheeks pinked. "We'd been out to dinner is all."

So, a nice show of affection and tears as well. Alison had "found" the body because no one had been by and she wanted the world to know he was dead. She cleared her throat. "I'm afraid no one has spotted Alison's body. I've notified everyone living in the vicinity of the river, and the team of volunteers have been searching without luck."

"She couldn't have survived." Kane's expression was solemn. "It's probably for the best."

"You all think she was an unfeeling killer but I know better." Rowley lifted his chin in a stubborn manner. "I know she had to pay for what she did, but after what she went through, I wonder what a jury would have made of what happened."

Kane flicked a sympathetic look at Rowley. "It's obvious she took her own life so none of the women involved in this case would be dragged into court to relive the abuse."

"I guess." Rowley ran a hand down his face. "She obviously thought they had suffered enough."

Jenna pushed to her feet. Getting everyone motivated again after such horrific crimes would be difficult. "Okay, Webber and Bradford, head out on patrol. Kane, check up with our FBI contact and make sure he has all the necessary files."

"And me, ma'am?" Rowley lifted his brown gaze to her.

She offered him a sympathetic smile. "You can take an early lunch."

Jenna held up a hand to halt Kane and waited for them to leave. "I hope life settles down in Black Rock Falls for a while. I sure need a break."

EPILOGUE

When Alison Saunders' body washed up on the edge of the river on the following Sunday, Jenna arranged for burial in unconsecrated ground. As Rowley had been so upset at the loss of his girlfriend, she had insisted Alison's plot lay under the only tree in the small cemetery and well away from a line of killers stretching back over one hundred years.

Driving by the cemetery with Kane two weeks later, she spotted Lizzy Harper, Angelique Booval, and Pattie McCarthy bending over Alison's grave then walking quickly out the gate. "What are they doing in there?"

"I haven't perfected the art of reading minds yet, ma'am, but I would imagine they are visiting a grave." Kane smiled at her. "Do you want me to stop and ask them?"

She ignored his dry sense of humor and nodded. "Yes, but I don't want to speak to them. One of them was placing something on Alison's grave. I want to see what it is."

Jenna was aware Rowley had erected a gravestone and laid flowers on Alison's grave, but seeing the three other victims of child abuse there spiked her curiosity. All had been suspects in the brutal murders before Alison's confession and she had wondered if they knew each other.

"Jenna. I *know* what you're thinking." Kane touched her arm. "It's not a conspiracy. Those women were not involved in the murders. We cleared them all. Alison acted alone."

"I thought you couldn't read minds." She slid from the car and walked beside Kane to the gravesite. Her gaze drifted over the white marble stone, with Alison's name carved in simple script. Jake Rowley's flowers had wilted in the sun but on the dry earth, a small bunch of flowers sat in a pretty, pink vase.

Attached to it was a card with just two words: *Thank you.*

A LETTER FROM D.K. HOOD

Dear Reader,

Thank so much for choosing my novel and coming with me on another thrilling adventure with Kane and Alton in *Follow Me Home*. If you enjoyed it, and would like to find out about all of my latest releases, you can sign up at the following link. Your email address will never be shared and you can unsubscribe at any time.

www.bookouture.com/dk-hood

Writing this story has been chilling for me but I hope it sheds light on the dangers children face inside seemingly innocent online chatrooms.

If you enjoyed my story, I would be very grateful if you could leave a review and recommend my book to your friends and family. I really enjoy hearing from readers so feel free to ask me questions at any time. You can get in touch on my Facebook page or Twitter or through my blog.

Thank you so much for your support.
D.K. Hood

: DKHood_Author

: dkhoodauthor

: www.dkhood.com

: dkhood-author.blogspot.com.au

ACKNOWLEDGEMENTS

Many thanks to all the wonderful readers who took the time to post great reviews of my books and to those amazing people who hosted me on their blogs.

I must give a shout out to Daniel and Gary for being incredible sounding boards for my story ideas, and to Veronica and Wes for their love and support.